Countdown Murder

Countdown Murder

June Drummond

ROBERT HALE · LONDON

ISBN 978-0-7090-8604-8

Robert Hale Limited
Clerkenwell House
Clerkenwell Green
London EC1R 0HT

www.halebooks.com

2 4 6 8 10 9 7 5 3 1

My thanks go to my agent Frances Bond, my editor Eileen Molver,
my publishers and all those colleagues and friends who have helped in
the production of this book

Typeset in 10½/13½pt Sabon
Printed and bound in Great Britain by
Biddles Limited, King's Lynn

I

WHAT KILLED Jock Robins?

'Greed,' said his doctor. 'I warned him time and again that the stuff he ate and drank was life-threatening. He had only one kidney and a heart like a football. He weighed over two hundred pounds and took no exercise. I told him to change his ways, and his response was to buy an apartment in the same building as the Mayfair Bonbouche, and arrange for them to send up all his meals.'

On Friday, 17th November, Jock ordered and consumed a pot of Beluga caviare, several grilled shrimps, a dish of mushrooms, a green salad, some brie on crispbread, and a selection of crystallized fruits. He drank half a bottle of sauterne.

The Bonbouche chef served the food and a waiter poured the wine. Jock being an honoured patron, both men remained while he ate. Asked if he wished for coffee, Jock declined the offer.

'No time,' he said. 'I'm spending the weekend with my sister Helen, in Abinger Hammer. She'll be here to collect me in thirty minutes.'

At 8.27 he left the building in his sister's company.

Soon after midnight he was seized with violent stomach cramps, vomiting and diarrhoea. His sister's doctor diagnosed food poisoning and prescribed remedies that seemed to beat the bug.

On Sunday night, accompanying a weak and miserable Jock to his home, Helen warned him sternly that he would not be eating any gourmet fare.

'You're your own worst enemy,' she said.

But there, as it turned out, she was mistaken.

On Saturday morning of that same weekend, Dr John Thorneycroft went Christmas shopping and found it hugely enjoyable, because he was buying presents for his wife Claudia and his ten-month-old son Luke.

At Liberty's in Regent Street he bought Claudia a suede jacket, a flagon of her favourite perfume, and a CD of carols sung by the choir of St Alban's Cathedral. Moving to Hamley's he bought Luke a teddy bear in an Arsenal jersey, a wooden trolley with building blocks, and a pedal car which would remain hidden until Luke was old enough to handle it.

The loot stored in the trunk of his car, he started home to Wimbledon. Driving through Chelsea he passed the elegant gold-striped awnings of a Bonbouche delicatessen, and remembering that Claudia's parents would be with them for Christmas, decided to splash out on wine, a cake, and some frozen dishes. He left his car in the store's parking lot and walked into gourmet paradise.

Light bathed ranks of exotic foodstuffs and delicacies, a feast for the palate and the eye. At each counter hovered an attendant in Bonbouche livery, ready to give advice, service, or merely polite chatter, a policy that paid handsome dividends.

Thorneycroft, shopping in the style to which he was not accustomed, headed for the cakes, dessert, and confectionery department. The cake counter being three-deep in American tourists, he crossed to the shelves of chocolates and sweets. Might as well be hanged for a hog as a piglet.

He found himself standing next to a pale young woman in designer jeans and a purple afghan. She looked, he thought, distinctly twitchy, her face screwed up in an anxious grimace, her gaze riveted on a boy of about six, who was contemplating a display of chocolate dogs. He reached to touch a white poodle, but the woman snatched at his hand.

'Not chocolate, Ben.'

The boy raised pleading eyes. 'I'd never eat him, Mum. I'd just keep him.'

She drew him away from the display. 'No, darling. Try the sugar toys. They have sherbet in them. You like sherbet.'

The boy moved drag-footed along the aisle, to a range of plastic boxes that contained toys fashioned from coloured sugar. Ships, railway engines, steam-rollers, each had a miniature smoke-stack made of liquorice.

The boy chose a Puffing Billy. The woman paid for it at the counter, the boy opened the box, lifted out the little model, and began sucking at the liquorice chimney.

The woman turned to Thorneycroft. 'You must think me very dictatorial,' she said, 'but I have to be. Ben's allergic to so many things. The sherbets are made by Sweeney, and they cost the earth, but they're something that Ben can enjoy.' She smiled tiredly. 'Why can't kids be allergic to tapioca and broccoli, instead of the things they crave?'

'There's no justice,' Thorneycroft agreed. He studied the boy's raised shoulders and taut neck muscles. 'Is Ben asthmatic?'

'Yes. It's dreadful. There are so many things he can't eat or drink or even touch. We can't have animals in the house, and he does so long for a dog. Last August he had an attack that landed him in hospital. The specialist put him on a programme that seems to be helping, but we have to watch him all the time.'

She turned to talk to her son, and Thorneycroft, noticing that the crowd round the cakes had dwindled, chose one decked with sugar angels and had it packed in a Bonbouche box. The woman was buying a Christmas pudding. Thorneycroft wondered if the child could tolerate highly spiced food, but supposed his mother knew best. Ben had slid to a sitting position with his back against the counter, and was still sucking sherbet.

Thorneycroft loaded his cake on a trolley and set out on the primrose path to gluttony. He bought half a dozen frozen dishes, a basket of imported fruits, and was making a leisurely tour of the wine department when he heard a woman scream.

The sound came from the front of the shop. The man serving Thorneycroft raced towards it and he followed, pushing his trolley.

The woman was kneeling near the main entrance, bent over the boy, who lay on his back, dragging in wheezing breaths. His face was glazed with sweat, and pinkish foam streaked his lips and chin. His eyes bulged, panic-stricken. The woman was trying to push a ventilator into his mouth, but she was making a poor job of it. Thorneycroft knelt beside her.

'I'm a doctor. Let me help.'

She made way for him. He felt the boy's flickering pulse, touched the ominous swelling of his neck. Putting a hand on the woman's shoulder, he made her look at him.

'What's Ben eaten in the past hour?'

'Nothing! Just the sherbet. He didn't even finish it. He said he felt sick, and then he collapsed.' Her voice soared. 'That stuff coming out of his mouth, he's bleeding, he's getting worse ... I can't ...' She was shaking violently, near to collapse herself.

Thorneycroft lifted the boy, got to his feet and drew the woman after him. 'We'll get him to hospital. Brompton Chest is just round the corner. Did you come by car?'

'No. By taxi.'

'I'll drive you. Is there any of that sherbet left?'

She blinked, then nodded. 'Yes. In the box.' She began to rummage in her carry-bag, but Thorneycroft said, 'not here. Bring it with you.' He turned to the assistants, three of them now, two holding back a growing crowd of shoppers, the third standing guard over Thorneycroft's trolley.

'Never mind that stuff.' Thorneycroft fished out a business card and handed it to the assistant. 'I'll be back later. In the meantime you should clear all those sherbet boxes off your shelves and lock them away safely. They may have to be tested for contamination. And tell your manager what's happened.'

The man took the card. 'Yes, sir.' He turned to the woman. 'And if I could know madam's name?'

'Tifflin,' she said, 'Linda Tifflin.' She tugged at Thorneycroft's arm. 'Hurry, please hurry.'

He saw her settled with her son in the back seat of his car, and drove as fast as the traffic allowed to the hospital. Ben was whisked away to an emergency ward, but when Linda Tifflin sought to accompany him, Thorneycroft restrained her.

'Better you wait here and help the admission clerk fill in all the details of Ben's illness, and what medicine he's on. She'll send it through to Dr Mason who's in charge of that department. I know him, he's a top man in his field. I'm sure that as soon as Ben's stabilized, you'll be called in to him.'

She did as he suggested. Talking to the clerk seemed to calm her a little, though the anxious expression persisted. Thorneycroft reflected that Ben might have learned his tensions from his mother.

The formalities completed, he persuaded her to move to a waiting area. Sinking into a chair, she said distractedly, 'you've been so kind and I've never thanked you. These attacks terrify me, I can't think straight.'

He smiled at her. 'Don't worry, Ben's in good hands. Should you perhaps phone home? Tell your husband what's happened?'

She gave him that rapid, blinking glance. 'Paul's in an important meeting ... the Tate gallery ... he hates to be disturbed. He'll be so angry....'

'Not with you, surely?'

'No, but with Bonbouche and the rest.' She made a helpless movement of the hands. 'But you're right, I must call him.' She began once more to fumble in her handbag. The plastic box containing the remains of the Puffing Billy fell to the ground and Thorneycroft picked it up. Linda Tifflin found her mobile phone and moved away to make her call. Thorneycroft examined the plastic box. No time to worry about fingerprints, the priority was to find out what had brought on the boy's asthma attack.

The lid of the box was missing, and the sugar shell of the toy engine lay in two pieces. In each section was a drift of pink powder, the sherbet that Ben had been sucking, and that had stuck to his lips and chin. Thorneycroft touched a sample to his tongue. The powder was sweet and fizzy, and there was an added sharpness that was all too familiar. He saw that among the pink sherbet granules lay flakes of a white substance. Painstakingly he separated pink from white, and tasted again.

As he did so, Linda Tifflin rejoined him. She was smiling.

'Paul's on his way,' she said. 'He told me to leave everything to him. He's so strong. He always knows what to do.' She drew the shuddering breath of a child recovering from a bout of tears.

Thorneycroft met her gaze. 'Mrs Tifflin, it's likely that Ben's asthma attack was brought on by his swallowing aspirin.'

'Aspirin!' She stared at him in outraged disbelief. 'That's impossible! I'd never allow him to touch the stuff, it's a total no-no. It makes his throat swell up so he can't breathe.'

'There are traces of aspirin in the remains of the sherbet.'

'That's impossible,' she said again. 'The box was hermetically sealed.'

'It could have been contaminated in the factory, perhaps an error in the supply of their ingredients. We must send this box to Dr

Mason. He can have the contents analyzed, and treat Ben accordingly.'

She said uncertainly, 'when Paul arrives ...'

'Now, at once,' Thorneycroft said. 'I'll take it myself.' He carried the box to the door of the ward where Ben was being treated, and saw it delivered to Dr Mason.

When he returned, he found that Paul Tifflin had arrived and was haranguing the admissions clerk. He was a small man, with pendulous cheeks and bright, angry eyes; the sort, Thorneycroft thought, who never missed the chance of a fight.

Linda Tifflin laid a hand on her husband's arm, and he shook it off angrily.

'What?' he said.

'This is Dr Thorneycroft, who helped me.'

Tifflin turned to glare at Thorneycroft. 'My wife says you believe Ben was poisoned.'

'Yes. The sherbet he swallowed was contaminated by aspirin.'

Tifflin's eyes bulged. 'Aspirin is poison to Ben.'

'It can be harmful to asthmatics, yes ... and also to people who have stomach ulcers, or who bleed easily.'

'To allow it to contaminate sweets is criminal. I shall take the matter up with the Bonbouche management, immediately.'

At this point a nurse approached the Tifflins. Ben was out of danger, she said. He was sleeping, but his parents could sit with him if they wished. Linda Tifflin hurried away with the nurse, but Paul Tifflin lingered to offer a pudgy hand to Thorneycroft.

'I'm extremely grateful to you, Doctor, for your help.'

Thorneycroft murmured politely. Tifflin leaned towards him, his voice conspiratorial.

'If this outrage comes to litigation, I take it you will be ready to testify in my behalf.'

'If I'm called upon to testify,' said Thorneycroft mildly, 'I'll do so in the interests of truth, not as anyone's partisan.' He had no intention of sitting in this petty despot's pocket.

'Of course.' Tifflin seemed unmoved by the snub. He made a note of Thorneycroft's address and phone numbers, and walked away along the corridor.

Thorneycroft glanced at his watch. It was now after three o'clock.

He called Claudia to say he'd be home late, and was on his way out of the hospital when Dr Mason caught up with him.

'John, thanks for sending me that sherbet. It's loaded with double-strength aspirin. Lucky you were in Bonbouche today. That woman may be a devoted mum, but she can't cope with the boy's problem, and she's terrified of her husband, he's a mean-tempered bugger. He's set to take Bonbouche to court, with some justification, I admit. Someone's been guilty of gross negligence.'

'Let's hope it was just negligence.'

Mason looked shocked. 'You think it was deliberate?'

Thorneycroft shrugged. 'There are perverts who get their kicks out of planting contaminated goods on supermarket shelves. As for Tifflin, I think there'll be a lot of forensic foreplay and legal double-speak before a case can be brought. Tifflin'd do better to settle out of court.'

'Umh, well, we've got the sherbet safely locked away, and for our own protection we'll run tests on it. The fact is, whether it was in the sweet by accident or malice, it could have killed young Ben.'

Thorneycroft nodded. 'I've asked the store to clear it off their shelves and keep it for testing. I'm going back there now to see that it's been done.'

Mason cocked his head. 'Still working with cops, are you?'

'I'm retained as a consultant on forensic psychiatry, but I'm also in private practice.'

'In today's world, that sounds like a winning combination. Keep me up to speed on developments, will you? And regards to Claudia.'

Mason hurried off to his ward and Thorneycroft walked slowly to his car. As he reached it, his mobile phone jingled.

'Dr John Thorneycroft?' The voice was soft and precise. 'Rolf Lenard speaking. I am senior chairman of Bonbouche et Cie. At the moment I am at the Chelsea branch, where you were, earlier today, and I'd count it a very great kindness if you would join me here, to discuss the events involving Ben Tifflin.'

Thorneycroft hesitated. Rolf Lenard was head of a world-famous company, and he was obviously moving fast to protect its interests. Though his approach was more diplomatic than Paul Tifflin's, his aim was no doubt the same – to enlist Thorneycroft's support in the event of litigation. Which was precisely what Thorneycroft wished to avoid. He planned to spend the festive season with Claudia and Luke. Getting involved in a messy legal battle formed no part of the plan.

Lenard spoke again. 'Dr Thorneycroft, I have many responsibilities, but I assure you that the foremost of them is to ensure that no other person, adult or child, buys contaminated food from a Bonbouche store. I have to know the facts of what happened today. In that, I need your help.'

Thorneycroft sighed. 'Of course. I'll be with you in fifteen minutes.'

II

THE UPPER FLOOR of the Chelsea Bonbouche store was very different from the lower. Here there was no strip lighting, no modern tiling. The style was a mix of Edwardian solid and clubman's cosy. The air was warm and redolent of pot pourri.

Stepping out of the lift, Thorneycroft found himself facing an enormous oil-painting of the firm's founders, Victor and Eva Lenard. They were a striking couple: Victor, debonair, with the sleeked-back hair of the 1940s; Eva, voluptuous, her blonde locks piled high on her head, red mouth smiling, eyes bright with a kind of glittering impatience.

The portrait, Thorneycroft observed, was not hung, but set into the plaster of the wall. It struck him as an odd arrangement.

As the lift doors closed, Rolf Lenard appeared in a doorway further down the corridor, and beckoned Thorneycroft forward. The personal touch, Thorneycroft wondered, or a desire for secrecy?

Lenard didn't resemble either of his parents. There was nothing flamboyant about him. A conservative grey suit clothed a stocky, compact body. His face was narrow, the nose long and sharp-tipped, the eyes a little slanted. His mouse-brown hair was cut short round the ears, but left full on top, a young man's style that didn't suit him. His handshake was cool and dry, qualities that Thorneycroft guessed might match his view of the world. The room in which he welcomed Thorneycroft was not an office but a sitting-room. Waving his guest to a wingback chair, he smiled.

'Normally I'd offer you a drink and something from our snack bar, but in the circumstances I prefer to seem inhospitable. We have already started checking the goods on our shelves, and I hope we will soon be ready to welcome customers again.'

He settled in a chair facing Thorneycroft's. 'I can't thank you enough for all you've done today. Your swift and generous response to the Tifflin boy's dilemma may well have saved his life, not to mention the reputation of Bonbouche. I spoke to Dr Mason a few minutes ago, and he told me Ben is out of danger. That doesn't lessen my distress, though, nor the responsibility I feel in the matter.

'My first task is to discover how the aspirin found its way into my stock. I've been in touch with Ted Sweeney, whose factory makes the sherbet toys. He is adamant that the contamination couldn't have occurred on their premises. Their production line is state of the art. It's monitored electronically, and they run constant tests during the manufacturing and packing processes.

'We for our part check every item of stock as it reaches us, for any leakage, damage or improper packing.

'I have questioned my staff about what happened today, and examined the video surveillance tapes covering the time of the incident. You were an eyewitness. Tell me, how did the child seem before he consumed the sweet? Did anything about his behaviour strike you? Did his mother give him anything other than the sherbet?'

Thorneycroft gave as full a report as he could of his brief meeting with Linda Tifflin and her son, and Lenard listened attentively. At the end, he lifted a plastic box from the floor beside his chair, and handed it to Thorneycroft. It contained a replica of the Puffing Billy given to Ben Tifflin. Thorneycroft examined the box. It was well made, the lid tightly sealed and the cardboard base securely glued. He gave it back to Lenard.

'It would be hard to break into it without leaving telltale marks,' he said.

'Hard, but not impossible, particularly for someone who regularly handles such merchandise.' Lenard tilted the box. 'I think the base of Ben's box was removed. The toy was lifted out and the liquorice funnel removed.' Lenard suited the actions to the words. 'The aspirin was then poured into the toy, the funnel replaced, the toy put back in the box and the base glued back in place.'

'You're assuming that this was a deliberate act? Isn't it possible it found its way into the ingredients of the sweet, before manufacture. Into the sugar, for instance. An accidental pollution?'

'No. Sweeney's would have detected it. They run constant tests on their materials. My view is that the aspirin was inserted after the box left the factory and before it was put on our sales shelves. It was done with deliberate intent by a criminal who showed total disregard for the lives of innocent people. We have to deal with a pervert who poisons goods for some crazy reason of his own. As a forensic psychiatrist, you must know that such monsters exist.'

'They exist, yes; but we can't be sure that the intention was murder. That sherbet would not have killed a healthy adult. It's mere chance that the consumer was an asthmatic child.'

'Sherbet is more likely to attract a child than an adult. Adults go for liqueur chocolates, or French nougat. I'm treating this as a crime, Doctor. I have informed the police, and Detective Chief Inspector Connor is here, taking statements from my staff. I imagine he would be glad of a chance to speak to you.'

Thorneycroft smiled. 'Liam Connor? Bright red hair and a scar on his chin? I know him. Tell him I'm here if wanted.'

Lenard got to his feet and held out his hand. 'Once again, Doctor Thorneycroft, my thanks for all you have done.' He gave a tired smile. 'I shall do my best to come to a just and sensible agreement with Mr Tifflin, but if that proves to be impossible, no doubt we'll meet again.'

He lifted a hand in a half-salute, and walked briskly from the room.

Liam Connor came into the room a few minutes later, followed by a slender black man whom he introduced as Detective Sergeant Gregory Abbot.

Liam the fox, thought Thorneycroft, a red Irishman with a broken nose, hard hazel eyes, and a soft, flat voice. Having served with him twice, Thorneycroft regarded him with mixed feelings.

Now Connor gave him a sidelong grin. 'So John. Seems you just don't know how to stay out of trouble. I'm told you witnessed young Master Tifflin swallowing an overdose of aspirin.'

'That's right.'

'Tell me about it.'

Thorneycroft repeated his account of the afternoon's happenings. At the conclusion, Connor said, 'So the balance of the sherbet is at Brompton Hospital?'

'Yes. Dr Mason has it in safekeeping.'

'We'll relieve him of that responsibility.' Connor reached for the sherbet box on the table at his side, and turned it in his hands. 'Something a kid would go for, eh? So we have a perp who knows how to put poison in a kid's sweeties ... and get them on to the shelves of a class shop like Bonbouche. Why would he do such a thing, can you tell me?'

'Lots of reasons,' Thorneycroft said. 'Could be he's mentally unhinged and likes poisoning innocent people. Perhaps his aim is to damage Bonbouche, or the confectioners who made the sweets. Perhaps he wants to publicize some cause ... if that's his object we'll get a message from him, a charge that Bonbouche exploits defence-less oysters, or the oil of endangered olives.'

'However you look at it, this perp's crazy.'

'Yes. Random poisoning isn't the act of a sane person.'

Connor made a wry face. 'God help us, there'll be other hits.'

Thorneycroft shared that fear. Serial murders committed by the criminally insane were a policeman's worst nightmare. He said, 'let's hope your investigation proves the aspirin got into the sherbet by mischance. That way the thing can become a civil case, and the injured parties can solve their problems by due process.'

'Small hope of that. Look at it any way, it's ugly. Somehow poison got in a sweet and a kid could have died. That's what the public already knows. The press will be baying for blood. You'll see your name in print. We'll be needing your testimony.'

That makes three of them, Thorneycroft thought. Lenard, Tifflin, and H.M.'s Finest are all panting to get me into this shit. Aloud he said, 'I'll help if I have to. You know where to find me.'

The interview over, the three men rode down in the lift to the ground floor. The scene there was transformed. Goods had been cleared from many of the shelves and the empty counters were draped in white sheeting. An assistant was affixing CLOSED UNTIL FURTHER NOTICE signs to the doors and display windows.

As Thorneycroft drove out of the parking lot, the music shop across the road was belting out 'Have Yourself a Merry Little Christmas'.

He arrived home as it was growing dark. Claudia was bathing Luke, and he joined in the routine of supper and bedtime cuddle, unwilling to spoil that treasured hour of the day. Only after their own dinner dishes were washed and stacked did he tell Claudia how he'd spent his afternoon.

She heard him out in horrified silence, and at the end said, 'He must be a monster. Only a sadist would do such a wicked thing,'

'It might be a woman,' Thorneycroft said, 'though the odds are it's a man.'

'I was in the local Bonbouche just last week.' Claudia was quite white. 'I thought of buying a Christmas pudding, but I decided they were too expensive. John, Bonbouche has branches all over the UK, hundreds of people could have bought poisoned goods, they could be eating lethal stuff right now. They could be sending it out as Christmas presents. It could even be going abroad.'

Remembering the American tourists clustered round the cake counter, Thorneycroft felt cold. He took Claudia's hand.

'There's a good chance today's happening was the work of a nutcase working in a small area. The police are already on the case and Bonbouche is doing everything possible to quarantine their stock. They'll certainly publish warnings to the public.'

'It must be a disaster for them. They'll lose their Christmas sales, and public confidence.'

Thorneycroft repeated what he'd said to Connor. 'We must hope this is a case of accidental contamination ... a one-off thing.'

Claudia met his eyes. 'Do you believe that?'

'I want to believe it.'

'What if it's not accidental? What if there's another victim? There'll be a huge panic and you're a key witness, you're bound to be dragged in. Our Christmas, John, all our lovely plans....'

He tightened his grip on her hand. 'We'll worry about that if we come to it, not before.'

III

ON MONDAY, NOVEMBER 27th, DCI Connor was about to leave his office when he found his way blocked by DS Abbot.

'There's a lady to see you, sir,' Abbot said. 'She says it concerns the Bonbouche case. She claims her brother's been poisoned by their goods.'

Connor showed his teeth. 'That makes twenty-nine. I don't have time to talk to all these nutters.' He made as if to brush past Abbot, who stood his ground.

'This one's got an autopsy report. She says if you won't see her, she'll take it to the press.'

Connor stopped in his tracks. 'Who called for an autopsy?'

'She did. On her twin brother.'

Connor made a sour mouth. Requesting and getting an autopsy on a close relation took unusual resolve and not a little clout.

'What's her name?' he demanded.

'Miss Helen Robins.'

'Shit!' Connor muttered. Crusading spinsters were his least favourite complainants. 'Bring her in,' he said.

Abbot returned some minutes later with a short rotund woman in tow. She had a round red face and her greying hair was drawn back and secured by two outsize Kirbigrips. Her eyes were grey, red-rimmed, with long pale lashes. She wore a brown trouser suit, a cream silk shirt, knitted stockings and brogues. She exuded the calm confidence of a woman who knows important people and won't hesitate to use them.

Abbot retired to a side table. Connor saw the visitor seated opposite him at his desk. She placed her large leather handbag on her knees and said brusquely, 'thank you for seeing me, Inspector. Mr French-Holly assured me you were the man to talk to.'

Connor's fears were confirmed. French-Holly was the Home Secretary's right-hand man, and he was not free with his favours. If he'd agreed that a post-mortem was desirable, he must have good reasons.

'I understand you lost your brother, ma'am,' he said. 'Please accept my sympathy.'

Her pale eyes surveyed him. 'Thank you, but I'm not here for sympathy. I want justice, Inspector, I want action. When I realized that Jock died in suspicious circumstances, I went at once to James French-Holly. Hard as it was for me to contemplate a post-mortem, I knew that was the only way I could establish that Jock did not die of natural causes.'

'What suspicious circumstances do you refer to?'

She drew a long breath, linking her hands together. 'Jock had a very strong stomach. He never suffered from stomach upsets. When his fool of a doctor tried to tell me he died of gluttony, I was furious. Jock was a gourmet, not a glutton. He never ate large quantities of food. He took small helpings of the best quality. That's why Bonbouche supplied all his meals.'

'What is the name of your brother's doctor?'

'Dr Hubert Filmer. He works in Harley Street and believes that gives him the right to insult people. He said, "it was greed that killed your brother, but as he had a weak heart and only one kidney, a bad attack of enteritis could well have proved fatal. I'm prepared to sign the death certificate". He spoke as if he were doing me a favour. Not only was it a gross slander, it was unforgivable at such a time. He's a disgrace to the profession, he should be struck off.'

Connor held up a calming hand. 'If you'll just give me your brother's full name and address....'

She supplied the information. Jock Robins had been 57 years old, and, by insurance standards, a poor risk. Connor thought that a bad go of food poisoning might well have tipped the balance. But the woman must be carefully handled.

'I see that Mr Robins was a widower,' he said. 'His wife died six years ago and there were no children of the marriage. Did he have any other relations, besides yourself?'

'None. Our parents were both only children.'

'I have to ask you, Miss Robins, do you know of anyone who might have wanted to harm your brother?'

'No!' She shook her head violently. 'Jock was very well loved. He was kind and generous, he gave to charities and to individuals, he had a great many friends. No enemies. Not one in the world.' Tears filled her eyes and she brushed them away with her fingertips. 'He was my twin brother. We were very close. I knew everyone he knew.'

'You were with him throughout his last illness?'

'Yes. He was taken ill on Friday night, at my home. I took him back to his apartment on Sunday night. I'm a trained nurse, Inspector, I couldn't leave him alone in that weakened state. I was with him constantly. He took only liquids, which I prepared for him. I assure you that his last full meal was the Bonbouche meal, taken the Friday before he died. After that he touched nothing but what I had prepared.'

'The Friday meal was provided by the Mayfair Bonbouche, right?'

'Yes. Jock had an apartment in the same block. I picked him up at about 8.30 on Friday night … November 17th … and drove him to my home in Abinger Hammer. He was taken ill at midnight, and I called in my doctor, Dr Hamish McIlroy. He diagnosed food poisoning … Jock had eaten shellfish … and he prescribed medicine that appeared to help. On Sunday evening Jock said he wanted to be in his own home. I drove him back to his flat. He refused to go to hospital, or call in a nurse, so I stayed with him. Dr Filmer came, and said he wouldn't change the treatment.

'In the early hours of Tuesday morning, Jock collapsed. He experienced an irregular heartbeat, difficulty in breathing and back pain. I got him to the London Clinic by ambulance. He was unconscious when he was admitted, and running a high fever: it was total renal failure. He never regained consciousness. He died on Wednesday morning.'

Connor said placatingly, 'Miss Robins, both Dr Filmer and your own doctor, McIlroy was it? They both diagnosed food poisoning. Don't you think, perhaps …'

Helen Robins banged a fist on Connor's desk. 'My brother was poisoned. I'm not hysterical. It's true Jock had only one kidney. He lost the other in a car accident and would never consider a transplant. His heart was also faulty. I would have agreed to Dr Filmer's signing the death certificate, despite his appalling behaviour, but the morning after Jock died, I saw the story on the front page of the Independent, about the little boy who was poisoned by a sweet loaded with aspirin. It happened in a Bonbouche store. I couldn't dismiss the possibility that Jock ate something planted by the same madman.

'I made my decision, Inspector. I went to see James French–Holly. He was Jock's closest friend. At first he thought I was just ... distraught ... but I warned him that there could be other victims, children perhaps, if this lunatic isn't stopped. I convinced him. He arranged the ... the autopsy. It was done by a Mr Duncan Brews. Perhaps you know him?'

Connor nodded wordlessly. Duncan Brews was a pathologist of the modern school, dedicated, ascerbic, armed with miraculous technology. Coroners hung on his words.

Helen Robins was delving into her handbag. She produced the autopsy report and handed it to Connor. He read it twice. Its concluding paragraphs, translated into basic English, stated that Jock Robins died at 7.15 a.m. on Wednesday November 22nd in the London Clinic. The cause of death was given as heart and kidney failure, brought on by the subject's consumption of a poisonous substance. The probable toxin was given as Gyromitra esculenta, traces of it having been found in the subject's blood.

Connor shook his head. 'I thought I knew poisons, but I don't recognize this one.'

'It's a toadstool,' Helen Robins said. 'It's highly poisonous. Mr Brews told me that in either cooked or raw, it's a danger even to an adult in good health. It killed Jock.'

As soon as Miss Robins had left, Connor reached for the telephone, and spoke to Dr Brews, then to Superintendent Hogarth.

'Mushrooms,' he said, when at last he reached Thorneycroft. 'Brews told me he believes Jock Robins died of mushroom poisoning. He said people all round Europe die of eating this Gyromitra thing. Someone in Poland did research: of 138 known cases, 100 had to be hospitalized, and 6 died.'

'What makes it so lethal?'

'According to Brews, the kidneys remove the toxin from the bloodstream and for a short while it seems the victim's getting on OK; but then, instead of getting rid of the toxin via the urine, the kidneys return it to the bloodstream. In severe cases there's liver damage, high fever, convulsions, coma and death. The patient dies two to four days after the stuff's consumed. Robins lasted a few hours longer.'

'And the mushrooms came from Bonbouche?'

'Yep. Mayfair Branch. I checked. Robins lived over the shop, got his graze from there. On Friday, 17th he ate caviare, shrimps, a plateful of raw mushrooms, Greek dressing, brie on crispbread and crystallized fruits. Drank half a bottle of sauterne.'

'The symptoms you described ... did he display them?'

'All but the convulsions. As is typical of this poison, he suffered an initial, violent attack, seemed to recover briefly then collapsed and died, fast.'

'Assuming the mushrooms came from Bonbouche shelves, how did they get there?'

'God knows. Bonbouche grows its own mushrooms in nurseries around the country. They're vacuum-packed in polystyrene boxes with see-through lids, then they're labelled, bar-coded, and delivered to Bonbouche sales points.'

'Delivered how?'

'The nurseries put the boxes in polystyrene cartons, so many boxes to a carton. The cartons travel in refrigerator cars, owned by the company and driven by their own employees. When they reach the sales points, some packs are used by the chefs, others are displayed on the fresh-food counters, and a few are stored for a while, then trashed.'

'Obviously the nurseries don't grow Gyromitra esculenta. So who does?'

'It grows wild in cold areas, in woods where conifers thrive.'

'In the UK?'

'I'm checking on that.'

'The poisoner must have access to a source, here or abroad.'

'Yeah, and having access, could buy a harmless pack of mushrooms from any Bonbouche store, substitute chopped-up puff-balls for the kosher goods, and return the pack to a Bonbouche counter. It would be possible.'

'Possible, but bloody risky. They have trained staff in every area of their stores, and video cameras on all the aisles.'

'We have the video tapes. We need to establish how the Bonbouche systems work. My thinking is, the perp could be an employee of the company. There are thousands of those, across Europe.' Connor sighed. 'It's going to be hard to nail this sod. He has a plan, and he doesn't care who he kills.'

'Maybe he doesn't mean to kill anyone,' Thorneycroft said. 'The Tifflin kid and Jock Robins both had physical weaknesses that made them more vulnerable than healthy folk.'

'Ben Tifflin was lucky. If you hadn't been on the spot, and a hospital right round the corner, he could have died. We are dealing with a poisoner. The public's in a panic, and the press is all over us.'

'Umh. I can see how they got the Tifflin story, the store was crowded and newspapers pay well for good leads. But Jock Robins's death? There's no way Miss Robins would have made it public, nor would anyone in French-Holly's department, or on Brews's mortuary staff.'

'I'll lay odds the perp leaked it himself,' said Connor grimly. 'However it happened, it's on the front pages, and the case is now a top priority. Hogarth's setting up a regional crime unit, personnel handpicked from the London divisions.' Connor paused. 'He wants you in, John, to cover the forensic psychiatry angles. He's convinced there'll be other victims. Kids maybe.'

Thorneycroft was silent. He'd met Detective Chief Superintendent Hogarth. A wily one, who knew which buttons to press. Claudia shopped at Bonbouche on occasion. She might have bought poisoned sherbet. Luke might have eaten it.

'Where will you work from?' he said.

'Our new nick, 73 Concorde Street,' Connor answered. 'Half a mile from the Chelsea Bonbouche, great facilities, computerized incident room, the forensic labs are a class act and Kevin Prout's in charge of them. You've worked with him, haven't you?'

'Yuh. OK. Tell the Super he can fix the paperwork.'

'That'll take a couple of days. I thought we might have a chat right away, off the cuff. Consider the angles.'

'I'll have to clear my diary. How about The Fat Lady, four o'clock?'

'That'll be good. See you there.'

Which was the closest Connor ever came to saying thank you. Thorneycroft checked his diary, already thinned down for the hoped-for Christmas break. He made the necessary phone calls, then picked up a pen and wrote 'Bonbouche Investigation' across the diary's pages.

IV

THE FAT LADY was the haunt of jazz musicians and their *aficionados*. Most nights it was packed and swinging, but by day during the week it was possible to hold a quiet conversation.

Before his marriage Thorneycroft had been a regular, and the barman greeted him warmly and gave him a window table in the private bar. Thorneycroft ordered lager and a pork pie for himself and stout for Connor, who refused food.

'No time,' he said, 'too much pressure from the press, the public, the top brass. That's par for the course. What isn't, is the Super's heard from the Home Secretary.'

'The Robins connection?'

'Yeah, and Rolf Lenard is pulling strings. He's big money, City clout, links all over the effing world. Hogarth's heading the investigation, but I'm the man on the ground, the fall guy. You know how it is. Make or break. The big one.'

Thorneycroft did know. Success in a major case meant promotion and public recognition. Connor had to handle things right. He needed a good team and expert advice.

'Let's start with the basics,' he said. 'Could Helen Robins have poisoned her brother? Does she inherit?'

'She does, but I don't think she did for him. She doted on him, and she's filthy rich in her own right. She could have accepted the doctor's readiness to sign the death certificate, but directly she read about the Tifflin episode, she called for an autopsy.'

'Maybe a move to divert suspicion?'

Connor frowned. 'Why would she use poisonous mushrooms? She's a trained nurse, she could have found something lethal that wouldn't leave traces. We'll follow up on her, but I don't think this case is going to be that straightforward.'

'Second question,' Thorneycroft said, 'have there been reports of other poisonings?'

'Dozens.' Connor pulled a sour mouth. 'Everyone with a runny tummy thinks he's going to die, but not one of them has, and not one of them bought food from a Bonbouche outlet. Lenard says there were 48 of the sherbet toys in that delivery, and they've all been tested in our laboratory. The only one that contained aspirin was the one Ben Tifflin sampled. Sweeney, the confectioner, has recalled all other deliveries, and none of them contain aspirin.'

'So the perp fixed just one toy in one batch. Doesn't look like a mass murderer.'

'Rolf Lenard is convinced it's a serial killer.'

'Two cases, with just one death, doesn't amount to serial killing,' Thorneycroft pushed aside his empty tankard and leaned back in his chair. 'But we do know that two people have been seriously affected by eating food bought in a Bonbouche store ... two branches of a single company.'

Connor nodded and Thorneycroft continued. 'Why would the perpetrator target a single company? London's full of supermarkets. Is Bonbouche the specific target? There could be several motives for such an attack; the perp has a hatred of rich gluttons, or he hates Bonbouche's business methods, or he bears a grudge against the Lenard family.'

'The first thing I asked Lenard,' said Connor, 'was did anyone hold a grudge against him, and he said "yes, every delicatessen owner in the world". He said he'd check if any of the firm's employees had been dismissed, or involved in union or legal disputes with Bonbouche; but according to him the workers love their jobs, and stay till they're pensioned off.'

'Next time you question him, I'd like to be present.'

Thorneycroft knew that Connor was a good policeman, trained in the law and in the mechanics of detection; but to him, forensic psychiatry was akin to witchcraft. He saw it as guesswork where there should be hard proof, fingerprints, trace elements and the where and when and how of scientific investigation. Also, no senior police officer likes intervention by an outsider on his manor.

'I'll fix it,' Connor said. He changed the subject. 'What's the difference between a mass murderer and a serial killer? They're both crazy, right?'

'Yes, but their motivation can be very different. Jack the Ripper, and the men who committed 9/11, were impelled by very different motives, and had very different behaviour patterns.'

'So if I'm chasing a serial killer, what do I look out for? In the cases I've been on before, the killer wasn't obviously insane: I mean, the Lincoln bus-stop murderer, for example, was married with two kids, a pillar of the church. A good neighbour, people thought.'

Thorneycroft shook his head. 'There's no one-size-fits-all description, but there are characteristics you'll find in most serial killers. They tend to be white males, heterosexual, aged under forty. Sexually dysfunctional. There's a sexual impulse in almost all of their crimes. Most of them grow up in violent homes, often they've suffered abuse of some sort.

'There's a childhood history of bed-wetting, brutality to animals, fire-setting. They're misfits, don't succeed socially. They create fantasies that build up until they explode in a spate of murders.

'Having killed, the killer may lie low for a period. But he'll kill again, using the same m.o. Very often, he will torture his victim. Sadism is typical, and so is the use of some mark or emblem left on the body, or in its vicinity. The Boston strangler left a bow tied in a specific way. This "signing" of the crime is done to satisfy the killer's ego ... and to jeer at the police.

'Some killers visit the burial sites of their victims. Some even try to invade the investigations, they write letters to the police or to their victim's relations. A few even leave evidence for the police to find.'

Connor nodded agreement. 'That I've seen. Almost like they want to be caught. But I don't see that with this perp.'

'Not so far. This m.o. doesn't exactly fit the profile of a serial killer. They don't go for random killings. They select their victims ... women and children of their own race ... hookers, hitch-hikers, vagrants, people who don't have a safe environment.'

'And so far we have as victims a kid and an older man, both from safe environments. Another thing, don't serial killers want to watch their victims suffer? Isn't it the blood and screams that turn them on?'

'In general, yes.' Thorneycroft hesitated. 'But in this case it may be that the Bonbouche company is the perp's target. He chooses his victims for their link with Bonbouche. He gets his kicks from watching Bonbouche bleed.'

'Which means that Bonbouche is not a safe environment. Anyone who buys their goods is a potential victim. How many million does that involve, for God's sake?'

Before Thorneycroft could answer, Connor's mobile rang. He answered it, listened attentively, his eyes fixed on Thorneycroft. Eventually he said. 'Right. Will do.' Sliding the mobile into his pocket, he got to his feet.

'The Super says that Rolf Lenard has the list of employees who might harbour grievances against the company. Lenard wants to hand it over. I'm going to see him, now. You want to come?'

'I'm not officially on the case, yet.'

Connor's teeth showed in a wolfish grin. 'Yes you are. The papers are ready at Concorde Street. We can get you signed on before we visit Lenard.'

The new police building in Concorde Street was twenty-first century in design and intention. Thorneycroft followed Connor past doors that promised computers, chromatography and mass spectrometry equipment, a fingerprint bureau, DNA co-ordination, as well as the more mundane laboratories, staffrooms and storerooms of police work. In Connor's office Thorneycroft read and signed the papers that appointed him forensic psychiatry consultant in the Bonbouche investigation.

Handing the papers back to Connor, he said, 'Before we see Lenard, there are a few points I'd like to clear. First the question of the Bonbouche staff. The sherbet could have been planted by a Chelsea-branch worker, the mushrooms by someone at the Mayfair branch ... the chef or waiter who served Jock Robins's last meal, for instance. That angle's being covered, isn't it?'

'Yes. The staff at both branches have been questioned. The Robins dinner was prepared by a chef who's been with Bonbouche for twenty-seven years. He and the waiter went up to Robins's flat together, saw the meal served and the wine opened and poured. Robins was a star customer, and they liked him. They're both still in shock at his death. Neither of them stood to gain by it, on the contrary it's bad for their reputations.'

'Second point,' Thorneycroft said, 'have you questioned the people who handled the sherbet toys, and the nurseries that supply Bonbouche with mushrooms?'

'That's ongoing,' said Connor impatiently. 'The Sweeney factory is mechanized and supervised, the workers have been screened exhaustively, and we're working on the packers and delivery men.' He paused, staring into space. 'I think this perp, whether he's an insider or an outsider, is very smart. He hasn't left anything that could identify him; no prints, no trace material, nothing. He allows other people to convey his poisons to his victims. He's clever with his hands, he knows his way around at least two of the Bonbouche outlets. I reckon he's studied the Bonbouche systems; admin, supplies, transport, sales. We have to match him, there. We have to know what he knows. We have to outwit him to nail him. And we'll nail the sod. These fancy fellows always get too clever.'

He gave Thorneycroft a measuring look. 'Rolf Lenard's been co-operative, but he thinks he's running things. He plays his cards close to his chest. Maybe he'll talk more freely to a doctor than to an ignorant flatfoot like me.'

V

DS ABBOT DROVE them to the Chelsea Bonbouche, and accompanied them to the boardroom on the top floor of the building. It was like walking through a morgue. The store was closed to the public and its counters were shrouded in dust sheets. Guards paced the aisles, and a cold silence hung over all.

Rolf Lenard greeted them at the boardroom door, and saw them seated at the long table. Taking his place at its head, he handed Connor a file.

'I've prepared a dossier for you,' he said. 'The list of staff members who might harbour grievances against my company is on top ... only five of them, you'll notice, and all very minor matters. I simply cannot imagine any one of them as a poisoner. Frankly, Inspector, I don't believe this was what you'd term an inside job. In my view, Bonbouche is the target of a deranged outsider. A serial killer. Do you agree, Dr Thorneycroft?'

Thorneycroft met Lenard's intent gaze. 'It's a possibility, but not the only one. The attacks could have been made by a jealous competitor.'

'Oh yes, success produces its share of enemies. Bonbouche caters for prestigious events ... royal weddings, charity fund raisers, ambassadorial visits. The file contains brochures and clippings that describe that part of our work, and it may be that some rival hopes to destroy our supremacy in the field; such a person is clearly insane, clearly homicidal. We are dealing with an insane murderer, never mind the semantics.'

Thorneycroft saw that Lenard's face was dewed with sweat and that his hands trembled. The strain was getting to him, and small wonder, with his business at a standstill and his staff enduring police grilling. Lenard seemed protective of his employees. Had he supplied a full list of possible troublemakers?

Connor was lifting a photograph from the file. 'Is this your warehouse, sir?'

Lenard smiled. 'One of them. We have others, in all the major ports and cities of Europe. The same applies to our offices. Our head office is in the City, where our financial and legal arms are centred, but we decentralize powers to our branches, of course. My father started that policy, and we retain it. It has stood the test of time.'

There was pride in Lenard's eyes as he spoke of his father, and Connor took his cue.

'It was your dad who founded the firm, wasn't it, sir? I saw the picture of your parents downstairs. A fine looking couple.'

'Ah yes, the Anigoni. It's a superficial likeness, but it doesn't convey their energy, their fire. My father supplied the business acumen that planned and established our interntional chain of delicatessens. My mother provided capital ... she was a member of the Brompton family of merchant bankers. She was also an excellent judge of food and wine, and a popular socialite. Her friends became Bonbouche's brilliant clientele.'

'So it's a real family firm, eh, sir?'

'Yes, and will remain so.'

'Are your parents still alive?'

Lenard frowned slightly. 'My father died in 1973, of cancer of the throat. My mother is still alive.'

'Is she still active in Bonbouche affairs?'

'No.' Lenard's frown intensified. 'She is 72 years old and in poor health. As a matter of fact, after my father died, she went into semi-retirement. My father had foreseen that she wasn't up to running the company. He left that to me and my brother Silas. My son Jason and my daughter Fenella inherited substantial blocks of shares. My mother is handsomely provided for, by a trust administered by our lawyers, and she also retains shares in the company.'

'So you, your mother, your brother, your son and your daughter are all major shareholders in the company; a majority holding, would that be?'

Lenard made an impatient movement. 'My brother Silas was never interested in the catering trade. We bought him out and he is now a practising doctor. I am Chairman of the company, my son Jason is in charge of British supplies, a very senior post. Fenella takes no part in running Bonbouche. You will find lists of all our main operatives, and their shareholdings, in the file.'

Lenard seemed ready to end the interview, and Thorneycroft intervened.

'I understand you're divorced from your first wife. Is it possible that she might harbour some resentment—'

Lenard cut him short. 'Zoe has been out of my life ... out of my family's life ... for 26 years. She left me in 1981, ran off with the architect who'd designed Coventry Hall, our family home. In time she married him. She has her second family. The idea that after all this time she would resort to poisoning our customers is utterly ludicrous.'

Thorneycroft raised a temporizing hand. 'I'm sorry to ask questions that must seem both stupid and impertinent, but we need to identify any person who might have reason to attack your company, or through it your family. You have all suffered a great deal of mental distress, and of course substantial financial loss.'

Lenard drew a long breath. 'Yes. That's true. But I can't see my ex-wife as the source of that. Zoe is so far removed from us, now. The break was complete. She cut us out of her life. I was faced with raising two young children. If it hadn't been for my mother's help, I could not have coped. But we managed. Zoe is past and forgotten by us, as we are by her.'

Connor said flatly, 'that may be so, sir, but we'll need to speak to her ... to all the members of your family.'

Lenard swung to face him. 'Why is that necessary? I can see that you must question Jason, he's part of the top management, but the others aren't remotely concerned. As Dr Thorneycroft said they've suffered enough distress. Why put them through more?'

Connor leaned forward. 'Mr Lenard, there've been two attacks on Bonbouche customers. One of them died and the other could have died. Their families have suffered a good deal more than yours has. There's a madman out there, what if he stops focussing on strangers and goes for your own flesh and blood? There's only one way we can protect your family, and that's by identifying the poisoner and putting him behind bars. So please, let us get on with our job.'

For a moment it seemed that Lenard would protest, then he said slowly, 'you're right. I'll have my secretary fax you their names, addresses and contact numbers. You'd better begin with Minette, my second wife.' Lenard fiddled with the top button of his jacket. 'I must ask you to be careful how you speak to her about recent events. She's nervy at the best of times, and these attacks ... the death of Mr Robins ... well, she's deeply distressed. I'm packing her off to her sister in Weybridge, tomorrow morning. She wants to be away by 11 a.m. Can you come to my home before that, say at 10 o'clock? My town residence is 12 Ennisdale Square.'

'We'll be there, sir.' Connor folded his hands on the file before him. 'Tell me about your son Mr Jason Lenard. I hear he's abroad at the moment. Is he up to speed on all that's happened?'

'Of course.' Lenard's eyebrows rose. 'I've discussed the events with him, our lawyers, and the members of the national board. Jason will be back from France shortly, and will remain in London until this terrible situation is resolved. I suggest you phone him at our Paris office, and fix an appointment with him on Wednesday.'

'I'll do that. You mentioned that he's in charge of British Supplies for your company.

'Yes, it means he travels a great deal, to all parts of the world. He has a flat in central London, but he prefers his out-of-town pad, on the premises of our Goldmead warehouse. He'll meet you wherever suits you best.'

Connor smiled. 'I want to have a look at your warehouse. Whoever planted poisoned food on your shelves, knows a lot about how your merchandize is handled. I know you have your own trucks and refrigerator cars, I've seen them driving about, but how do you handle small items, like, say, a package of mushrooms?'

'As little as possible,' Lenard said. 'Hygiene is very important. Our kitchens are scrupulously clean. The packers and the men who transfer goods from warehouse to branch, or from storeroom to counter, wear white coats, caps and gloves. Those who enter the cold or freezer-rooms have padded uniforms with hoods. Temperatures that freeze food can also freeze people.'

'My prime concern, sir, is how did the poisoned goods reach your salesrooms? I'd like two of my team ... DS Justin Malherbe and DC Ayusha Ramiah ... to conduct dummy runs at your Chelsea and Mayfair branches. Can you arrange that?'

Lenard looked surprised, but he said, 'Certainly. I'll supply them with the gear my handlers use, and with identity passes. They're welcome to access any part of the stores, except the administration areas. My staff will co-operate fully with them.'

'Thank you.' Connor lifted a handsome brochure from the file and flicked over its pages, scanning photographs and blocks of typescript.

'Some big names on your Board,' he commented. 'Old hands and young faces, too.'

Lenard hunched his shoulders. 'The times demand new skills; modern methods of moving and marketing goods, people who can speak foreign languages, go-getters and streetwise executives. We meet those demands. But the essential Bonbouche, the firm that supplies superb food and wines to people of taste and discernment, that will not change.'

Connor laid the brochure aside. 'You are the head of the entire company, here and in the USA?'

'Yes. I am Chairman of all the Bonbouche operations. I inherited the job from my father, and when I'm gone, Jason will take over. He is growing into the position, as I did.'

'Could you, or your son be challenged?'

Lenard smiled. 'Of course. That is the nature of commerce. But we hold the high ground. We are not just the major shareholders, we have the ability and experience to maintain and increase the efficiency of the company. We intend to retain control of it.'

Though Lenard spoke quietly, there was a fire in his eyes that Thorneycroft had seen before in men determined to command. Rolf Lenard was at the pinnacle of the Bonbouche structures, and any challenger would find him a formidable opponent.

Now he was getting to his feet. 'Gentlemen, if you have no further questions, I have an appointment with my insurers ... rather a pressing concern at this time.'

Connor rose, picking up the file. 'Nothing more for the moment, sir. Thank you for your assistance.'

Lenard walked with them to the lift and bade them a polite farewell; every inch the old-style city magnate, urbane, smiling, conceding with reluctance that this time around, he would not be calling the shots.

*

As they drove back to Concorde Street, Connor said, 'Well, what did you make of him? Cagey, I thought. Told us only what he wanted us to know. Didn't like being asked about his private life.'

'Who does?' Thorneycroft said. 'I agree though. We only saw the outer skin of the onion.'

'We'll keep peeling,' said Connor grimly, ''till we reach the juicy layers.'

'And the tears,' murmured Thorneycroft.

Arriving home at six o'clock, Thorneycroft found that Luke was already in bed and asleep.

'We went to Kew,' Claudia said. 'He ran and jumped and rolled down hills for three solid hours. When we got back here I gave him an early supper but he keeled over into the custard. He's out like a light.'

Thorneycroft poured white wine for her and Scotch on the rocks for himself. As he handed her the glass, she smiled. 'Don't look so hangdog. You had to take the case. We'll make other plans for Christmas. Do you have any idea who's behind the attacks?'

Thorneycroft swirled the ice in his glass. 'Connor thinks it's a serial killer. Rolf Lenard agrees with him.'

'But you don't?'

'At this point I have no theories. There are some things that don't fit the profile of serial killing. There are no sexual overtones, none of the signs that serial killers leave. Jock Robins's death doesn't fit the picture.'

'Do you think there'll be other attacks?'

'If it *is* a serial killer, of course. Time will tell.'

Claudia shuddered. 'That's horrible. Waiting for someone to be killed.' She hesitated. 'You'll be working full-time, won't you?'

'Yes. I've cleared my diary. I can't make other commitments.' Thorneycroft tried to sound unconcerned. 'What's for supper?'

'Lamb stew, new potatoes and courgettes. Apple pie and cream. We'll kill the bottle of wine.'

During the meal they spoke of normal things, turning their thoughts away from Bonbouche. They were drinking coffee when the telephone rang. Thorneycroft answered it. It was Connor on the line.

'There's been a development,' he said. 'Mr Tifflin was here with something he got in the post.'

'A letter?'

'No. A plain buff envelope with nothing inside but a cardboard number, the kind you can buy in novelty shops. The number 4. Tifflin had the sense not to handle it, he brought me the card and the envelope. Forensics are testing for prints or trace material. I doubt they'll find anything. I called Helen Robins. She got card number 5 this afternoon. You see the sequence?'

'Yes, Robins ate the mushrooms on November 17th, Ben Tifflin ate the sherbet on the 18th. It's ... like a countdown.'

'Exactly. I thought at first it could be some hoaxer who'd read about the poisonings in the press, but a hoaxer would have sent number 5 to the Tifflins and 4 to Miss Robins, because that was the way the stories broke. The poisoner sent the cards. He's on a countdown. If ... when ... he makes another attack, there'll be card number 3.'

'Do the press have the story?'

'Not yet, but it's just a matter of time. The perp will see to that. I'll see you tomorrow, matey. Ten o'clock at Lenard's place.'

VI

ENNISDALE SQUARE MUST have been a country meadow when the gentry drove their carriages from London to Knightsbridge. Number 12 was a Georgian villa with a view of Kensington Gardens and the Round Pond … a fitting choice, Thorneycroft felt, for a man who valued elegance and disliked change.

A muscular young man in an Armani suit and gold ornaments escorted him and Connor past a pile of luggage stacked in the hall, to a formal drawing-room.

'Mrs Lenard will be down directly,' he promised, and strolled away to the rear regions of the house.

'King of bling,' muttered Connor, gazing about him with a jaundiced eye. 'This place is a bloody museum.'

Thorneycroft was inclined to agree. The room's furniture, pictures and ornaments perfectly matched the period of the building … antiques lovingly maintained, paintings cleaned to their original brightness, china and silver that would move an auctioneer to tears of joy, but the whole was curiously impersonal.

The woman who appeared moments later did not live up to her surroundings. There was nothing of the full-bosomed Regency beauty about her. She was small, frail-boned and nondescript. Her thin pointed nose and large brown eyes, the brown hair cut close to her head, were undeniably mousy. Expensive clothes merely created the impression of a mouse in fancy dress.

She stood uncertainly at the door, then came forward to shake hands with Connor, saying in a high little-girl's voice, 'I'm sorry, I've kept you waiting. I lost the keys of my car. Arnold found them for me.' She turned to Thorneycroft. 'Rolf says you're a doctor?'

A strange greeting, Thorneycroft thought. He smiled. 'Yes, I am.'

She blinked rapidly. 'I wish you'd persuade him to leave London.'

'I don't think I could, do you?'

'No.' She shook her head sadly and her eyes shone with tears. 'I'm afraid for him.'

'I'm sure he'll be very careful.'

She drew a long breath. 'He says he will, but he only thinks of the company. He says I'm just being silly.'

'It's a nasty situation,' Thorneycroft said, 'but I expect he feels his place is here. You'll help him by going to stay with your sister. He'll have one less worry on his mind.'

'I suppose so. He's made his decision. He won't change it. Please sit down, both of you.'

She settled in a straight-backed chair, left foot tucked behind right heel, hands clasped in her lap; royalty giving an audience. Staring at Connor, she said, 'What is it you want of me?'

Connor adopted an avuncular mode. 'Just a few questions, Mrs Lenard. We're looking for information, anything that might cast light on the events of the past two weeks. Two people, apparently chosen at random, have been poisoned by Bonbouche food....'

She waved impatient fingers. 'I know all that. Rolf told me. I don't have anything to do with the business, or the stuff in the shops. My job is to help Rolf socially. I go to formal dinners and gatherings with him. I entertain all the time. I'm good at that. I enjoy it. But I don't interfere in Rolf's work.'

'It must be heavy going, entertaining on that scale,' Connor said. She gave him a half-contemptuous smile.

'Not at all. I was trained for it. That's how I met Rolf. I ran a cookery school. And I can spend what I like. That makes it easy to host a dinner for a hundred people. Jason helps me with the catering, especially the wines.'

Thorneycroft said casually, 'do you entertain the family as well as outsiders?'

Her face seemed to contract, her eyes narrowing, her mouth tightening to a button.

'Sometimes,' she said. 'Not often. Rolf's mother is old, she doesn't like dining out. Jason and Fenella have their own lives.' Minette hesitated, smoothing the folds of her skirt, twisting the rings on her thin fingers. She said flatly, 'Eva, Rolf's mother, doesn't like me much. I don't mind. Rolf and I don't need her approval. We travel.

We go to the States at least once a year, and in winter we follow the sun ... to Egypt or the Far East or wherever. And I go to the Grand Prix venues. I don't race, but I like to watch the experts. I have a Ferrari.'

A mouse in a Ferrari. Curiouser and curiouser.

'And when you and your husband are out of England,' said Connor smoothly, 'who heads the firm?'

'Jason, of course, or one of the other seniors. Rolf keeps in touch, wherever we are. It's easy, these days, with all the machines.'

Connor questioned her about the poison attacks, seeking to learn how she felt about the invasion of the Bonbouche kingdom. She answered in a matter of fact tone. Rolf would see to everything. She had read in the papers about the man who died, and the poor little boy, she was sorry for them. Rolf didn't talk about horrible things, she didn't like to hear about them. 'It's caused us all a lot of trouble,' she concluded. 'I had to throw out all the Bonbouche dishes in our fridges and freezers, such a waste.'

'How about the wine? Did you throw that out?'

'No. The wines are sealed. Rolf says they're safe.'

'Tell me, Mrs Lenard, have you any idea who might be responsible for doing these horrible things?'

She pouted. 'No. None. It's your job to find who's guilty, not mine.'

Connor ignored the snub. 'We're appealing to everyone to help us. If you remember anything unusual that happened in Bonbouche circles around the beginning of November, or since, please let me know.'

'I told you,' she said loudly, 'I don't have anything to do with all that. I run Rolf's home and I entertain for him, I play my bridge and tennis, I travel. I don't have time for anything else.'

Her face was set in cold determination, and there was a spark of malice in her eyes. She got to her feet. 'I'm sorry, I must leave. I want to reach Weybridge by noon.'

They accompanied her through the hall and out to the columned portico. A Ferrari sedan was parked there, and the muscle-man was loading the last of her suitcases into the boot. Thorneycroft held the door of the car for her. She thanked him with a nod, and drove smoothly through the gate into the westbound traffic.

Connor beckoned to the young man. 'What's your surname, Arnold? Not Schwarzeneger, is it?'

The young man grinned. 'No. Arnold's the surname. Mrs Lenard thinks it's classier to call me Arnold. First name's Terry.'

'How long you been working here, Terry?'

'Three years, seven months.'

'Cushy job, is it?'

Terry's bronzed face flushed, but he held Connor's gaze. 'If you're up to it,' he said, 'and mind your manners.'

Connor waved him away, and he and Thorneycroft moved to their car.

'Waste of time,' Connor said. 'That woman told us nothing. Close as a clam. She must know something about Bonbouche, she throws all those parties, hob-nobs with the top brass, she'd pick up some gossip, wouldn't she? Unless she's too stupid to remember.'

'I don't think she's stupid,' Thorneycroft said.

'Why won't she talk to us?'

'Self-preservation.'

'You think she could be a target for the perp? Who'd want to poison that poor little bunny-rabbit?'

'She's not scared of being poisoned,' Thorneycroft said. 'It's her way of life she's protecting. Think about it, Liam. She's a woman without any great attributes ... not beautiful, not rich or amusing. But she has everything she wants. She lives in the lap of luxury, drives a Ferrari, travels to exotic places, shops for designer clothes, entertains the beautiful people. All that depends on her doing nothing to upset the Lenards. They're the source of all delights.

'People like Minette know what happens to folk who step out of line. She's developed a safe formula. She helps her husband as wife and hostess, but she steers clear of his workplace, and his rich, powerful family. Like a small animal in the presence of a predator, she keeps still and makes no sound. She survives by not attracting attention to herself. And she doesn't talk to strangers like us.'

'That's a crook's trick,' Connor said. 'Crooks say "I dunno, I forget, I take the fifth amendment". When they try that crap, I know they're hiding something.'

'Minette Lenard won't talk unless she sees a predator moving in for the kill.'

'Which could happen,' Connor said. He cast a backward glance at the house. 'I'll put Abbot on to Mr Prettyboy Arnold, see what he has to tell us.'

Thorneycroft forbore to point out that Arnold was just as cosily placed as his employer's wife, and therefore no more likely than her to risk indulging in careless talk.

Reaching the car, Connor handed Thorneycroft the keys. 'You drive. I want to bounce some thoughts off you.' He settled himself in the passenger seat.

'Like I told Lenard,' he said, 'our priority is to find out how poisoned food packages reached the sales floors of Chelsea and Mayfair Bonbouche. We've questioned the staff who work in both stores, the nurseries, and the Goldmead warehouse, about their systems. So far we haven't identified any suspects.

'We've established that the staff on the sales floor of a Bonbouche outlet don't go into the areas where the food is stored, or into the kitchens and delivery zone. To my mind it's those areas we need to concentrate on, because the perp probably planted his poisoned goods there.

'The employees who handle the food … collect it from the warehouse or nursery, deliver it to a store, convey it from the storage rooms or kitchens to a sales counter … all wear white uniforms, and an identity tag with a photograph. They sign on in the morning, and sign off when the stores close, but in between those times they move around a lot.

'The employees who drive the delivery vans or motorbikes don't go beyond the delivery port at the back of the store.

'The sweets in the display cabinets are freshly stocked every week. The cabinet at the Chelsea store, where Ben Tifflin got his confectionery, was restocked on the morning of Friday 17th. The video tape shows a handler unlocking the cabinet, clearing out some of the old stock, and arranging the new items on the shelves. The handler concerned was easily identified. He's been with the firm for twenty years, clean record. I don't think he placed a poisoned sweet there, knowing the camera was full on his face.

'What does emerge is that whoever is planting the poisoned goods has access to the handling areas, and probably wears the Bonbouche uniform and follows the Bonbouche routines.'

Connor paused, and Thorneycroft said, 'Who has keys to the cabinets?'

'That,' Connor answered, 'is where Bonbouche security breaks down. It's a lot too easy for handlers to get hold of a key to a cabinet or to the storage areas. Until these attacks, as long as a person was wearing Bonbouche kit, and had an identity tag, nobody questioned his actions. Now of course the stable door's been closed. If the perp makes another hit, he'll have to be a lot sharper how he makes it.'

'He could already have planted poisoned packs. They could already have been sold.'

'In which case,' Connor said, 'all we can do is issue warnings and pray. We're doing all we can. We're examining the video tapes, going back two months, enhancing the pics to look at people in the background. Malherbe and Ayusha will try to establish how the poisoned goods reached the sales shelves.' He rubbed a hand over his face. 'This sod's clever, and he has cool nerves, to walk on to Bonbouche premises and switch poisoned packs for kosher ones.'

'He's insane,' Thorneycroft said. 'He thinks he's invincible. What puzzles me is that he poisons at random. If he has a grudge against Bonbouche, why doesn't he go for one of the top men?'

'I don't know why,' said Connor savagely, 'and right now my worry is, where will he make his next hit? There's no guarantee he'll stick to London.'

'If he's on a countdown, the chances are he's picked his launch pad. It's here, in London. Is Jason Lenard back from France yet?'

'No.' Connor seemed glad of the change of subject. 'I put a call through to him in Paris. He told me he's been detained at some big wine show he has to attend. He'll be back tonight. He'll phone me and fix a time for us to visit the warehouse.'

Connor knew the rules of police questioning. Testimony could not be obtained by physical coercion, witnesses must not be unfairly harassed, police officers should work in tandem to ensure that statements could be confirmed.

He was also aware that much useful information was obtained by men and women far from the public eye. And he knew that a few policemen and women had the ability to listen, without seeming to ask questions, and to learn a good deal about the characters and actions of their companions on the right and wrong side of the law.

Detective Sergeant Abbot had that gift of listening. He also had a strong sense of what could and could not be done, and when Connor instructed him to 'have a word with Rolf Lenard's houseboy', he enquired mildly how that was to be achieved at six o'clock on Friday evening?

'Arnold will either be serving whisky to his boss, or he'll be down the pub with the lads,' he said.

'If he's pubbing, find him,' Connor said. 'He's muscle-bound and suntanned, start with the Warwick Arms. That's where the body-builders hang out.'

The advice was good. The barman at the Warwick Arms pointed out Arnold as the bloke in the corner, watching the telly.

Abbot purchased a pint, elbowed his way across the room, and sat down on the bench facing the television set. The programme was not body-building but swimming, and Terry Arnold was watching it intently. His right hand grasped the handle of a tall beer stein, and the slackness of his mouth suggested it wasn't his first or even his second drink. The race in progress ended, and he threw up his hands in disgust.

'Tha' Keenan,' he said, 'bloody amateur. Loses a yard on the turn, ev'y fuckin' time.'

Abbot, who knew nothing about water-sports, said sagely, 'too right.'

Arnold took a pull at his drink. 'I was a life-saver. Not that piddlin' pool-stuff. S'okay when you're young, but there's no money in it.'

Abbot looked admiringly at Arnold's cashmere pullover, designer jeans, and thin gold wristwatch.

'You made a good switch, I'd say.'

'Butler.' Arnold giggled as if at some private joke. He turned to stare at Abbot. 'Wha's your line?'

Abbot considered his options. Tell someone you're a policeman, and he'll either run for the door, or try to get free advice about his speeding-fines, or his daughter's nasty boyfriend.

'I'm a copper,' he said.

Arnold blinked, but stayed in his seat.

'Wha' sort?' he demanded.

It was then that Abbot saw in Arnold's face the tremor of fear, not fear of the law, but something more fundamental, the animal fear of impending danger.

'I'm a detective sergeant,' he said quietly. 'I'm working on the Bonbouche poisoning case.'

For a long moment, Arnold neither moved nor spoke. He seemed to be forcing himself to concentrate. He pushed his drink away and pointed a shaking finger at Abbot. 'You lot were at the house this morning. Mr Lenard's res'dence. Mrs Lenard tol' them she doesn't know anything about that stuff. Poisons. They sh'd leave her 'lone. She's scared enough already.'

'Nobody wants to scare anyone,' Abbot said. 'We need help. We need people to tell us anything that will help us track down a poisoner.'

''At's nothin' to do with me,' Arnold muttered.

'You work for the family.'

'I'm a servant. Servant, a's all. Nobody confi's in me.'

Thinking of the young man's swift defence of Minette Lenard, Abbot wondered if that was true. A good-looking hunk, a wife whose husband was totally absorbed in his work, that was a formula for a bit on the side, which led to pillow talk. But Arnold was not going to speak of that. He was shaking his head violently.

'Arnold,' Abbot said gently, 'what is it you're afraid of?'

The effect was startling. Arnold's face contorted, his eyes bulged, searching the crowded bar-room.

'I don't know,' he muttered. 'Something, someone out there, waiting.'

Abbot believed him. Arnold was telling the truth. He didn't know who or what he feared, and there was no point in questioning him about it.

He drained his own glass, set it down, and smiled at the young man. 'Well,' he said, 'if you want to talk, any time of the night or day, call me.' He pushed across a card with the numbers of the Concorde Street station, and his own mobile number scrawled across the bottom.

Arnold picked it up uncertainly. Abbot left the bar, but on reaching the street, he did not go directly to his car. Instead he waited in the shadow of the alley.

Within minutes, Arnold emerged, and set off towards Ennisdale Square as if the Devil were after him.

Perhaps, reflected Abbot, the Devil was.

VII

CONNOR'S INVESTIGATING TEAM met on Wednesday morning. Thorneycroft arrived early to inspect the incident room that would be the team's headquarters.

It was large, air-conditioned, and equipped with all the high-tech machinery the investigators could possibly need. Through a connecting door was a theatre for the screening of films and videos, and an office for secretarial staff.

On the same corridor were the forensic laboratories, safe-storage vaults, and a communications centre that could link Concorde Street with the investigative networks of the world.

The walls of the room already bore a series of maps showing the location of all the Bonbouche stores, nurseries and warehouses in the UK. Pegboards displayed photos of the Tifflin family, and Jock and Helen Robins, as well as ground plans of the Chelsea and Mayfair stores which had provided them with poisoned delicacies.

Thorneycroft knew that as the investigation advanced the displays would feature every name and address, every picture, news report or scrap of material evidence so far discovered.

He paused to study photographs of the sherbet toy that Ben Tifflin had eaten; of the innocent-looking mushrooms that had killed Jock Robins; and of the cardboard numbers that had been sent to the victim's families. The numbers filled him with cold rage.

The cards were not the work of some moronic prankster. They were a malign declaration of intent, sent by a madman who rated the life of a human being no higher than a cardboard number.

Connor and Abbot were talking together and he joined them. Abbot was describing his meeting with Terence Arnold.

'I drank a beer with him,' he said. 'He was over the limit, but still not chatty. He's shit-scared, but says he doesn't know what of.'

'If I lived in a Lenard house,' Connor said, 'I'd be scared. Ducky ducky ducky, come and be killed.'

'That could be it,' Abbot agreed. 'The thing is, if we hammer him, he'll panic, and bolt. He's that sort.'

'Bolt alone?' Connor's eyebrows rose. 'Or with a significant other? I thought Ms Lenard had eyes for Arnold. Living where he does, he might know something useful. All right. Keep a watch on him, and if he tries to run, bring him in for questioning.'

Footsteps and voices in the corridor announced the approach of the rest of the team. First to enter was Detective Superintendent Edgar Hogarth, the man in overall charge of the investigation. A burly, balding man with tombstone teeth, he looked more like a coal-heaver than a senior policeman. He had risen to his present rank by honing his skills, and never allowing an opportunity to pass him by. His bland and cheery manner masked a prodigious memory and ruthless determination.

He greeted Thorneycroft with a smile and a handshake, and introduced his companions.

'This is Dr Gavin Prout,' he said, indicating a lean and swarthy man in a white lab coat. 'He's the little tin god around here, head of the Forensic Department. DCI Liam Connor and DS Greg Abbot you've already met.

'Behind Connor is DC Ayusha Ramiah. Step forward, Ayusha.'

A young Indian woman moved past Connor. She wore a black skirt and a white blouse, and her hair was cut in a trendy style, but the red dot in the middle of her forehead said she was married in the Hindu tradition.

'Ayusha knows how to call up fingerprint systems, trace records, and DNA analyses,' Hogarth said. 'And in the back row are DS Sam Koch, financial systems and records; DS Harry Davidson, computernik; and DS Justin Malherbe, legal angles.'

He turned to face Thorneycroft. 'This is Dr John Thorneycroft who is the team's consultant on forensic psychiatry. He'll say his piece later. Now if you'll get seated, I'll give you my take on the case.'

They took their places in a half-circle of chairs. Hogarth sat at a table facing them.

'This team,' he began, 'has been picked on merit, to identify, arrest and charge the Bonbouche poisoner. You are all from the

Metropolitan area, and you all have special experience and skills. You've been selected because this case is already big, and it's going to get bigger.

'I have several reasons for saying that. First, the victims make it big. Ben Tifflin's dad is a City businessman, and his mum is the daughter of the editor of Business Indicators. Jock Robins was a millionaire who gave very generously to sports and charities, his sister is a rich lady who chats up half the Cabinet. Finally, Bonbouche is a company with international status, run by a billionaire hierarchy, and its clientèle is like Napoleon Pig, "more equal than others".

'The result is, these two attacks have started fires all over the effing world. The press has got the case between its teeth and won't let go. The public is scared and panicky. Although both the attacks took place in London, our stations all round the country are being flooded with enquiries, reports, and demands for a quick arrest.

'On Sunday night, as you know, Rolf Lenard went on TV to announce that Bonbouche is doing all it can to ensure there are no more victims. A good many branches have been closed down, and those still operative are selling only canned and bottled goods that we hope can't be tampered with. Which is all very nice, but the fact is that closing branches and limiting sales is no guarantee of safety. Goods already sold could be out there in fridges and freezers, waiting to kill someone.

'According to Koch, Bonbouche has lost millions because of just two attacks. Its sales are down, and its share values are dropping. The company's holdings in Europe and the USA are feeling the effects.

'So ... Ben Tifflin and Jock Robins were the primary victims, but the lousy creep who's putting poison into Bonbouche products is victimizing not just individuals, not just members of the Lenard family, not just the Bonbouche stores, but a whole network of customers, employees, provisioners, dealers, and shareholders.

'That's the big picture, and it's going to put us under a lot of pressure from a lot of people. However, that's not our worry. It's not our job to settle the financial problems of the world. Our job is to find the pervert who's poisoning innocent folk and put him inside.

'Liam and the rest of you have worked your butts off, these past few days, but so far no suspect has been identified. All our stations are on the alert, and we'll have their backing in conducting the investigation, but the coalface is here in London, and the point of the drill is this team.'

Hogarth hunched his heavy shoulders. 'There're some who think I'm overreacting about the urgency of this case. I'll just say this. My gut tells me there'll be other victims. We're here to assess where we are now, and where we need to go. I want Dr Prout to kick off by reporting on the forensic evidence that's already on hand.'

Dr Prout rose to his feet, hands in the pockets of his lab coat. 'I'll give you the basics,' he said. 'I'll take questions after.' He began by describing the Puffing Billy bought by Ben Tifflin.

'We have what remains of the box, the sugar engine, and the engine's contents,' he said. 'The sherbet was pink in colour, and crystalline. We examined it by GCMs ... that is by gas chromatography with mass spectrometry. I won't bore you with the scientific details, but it's a process that allows us to identify by computerized detector, the separate elements in a material, and to quantify their individual molecular weights, down to the smallest trace.

'Once we had that analysis, we ascertained from the maker of the sweet, Messrs Sweeney and Co, what was the amount of sherbet that was originally in the toy. Obviously when the sugar container was breached, and the aspirin added, the weight of the contents altered; but allowing for that, I estimate that the poisoner added enough double-strength aspirin to constitute plus/minus 9% of the original contents. The aspirin used is readily soluble. The sherbet would have to a large extent masked its taste.

'The dose I've indicated would not necessarily be lethal, but it would make a normal adult feel sick, and might endanger a young child who, like Ben Tifflin, is allergic to aspirin. If Dr Thorneycroft had not been on hand to rush the boy to hospital, we could be looking at two murders, not one.

'Coming to the rest of the toys on the shelf when Ben chose his Puffing Billy. We examined them all. They were clean. They contained nothing but sherbet.

'Our tests indicate that the box containing the toy was opened from the base, the toy was lifted out and the liquorice funnel removed. The aspirin was poured in through the resulting hole, the funnel replaced, the toy returned to the box, and the base replaced.

'An interesting point is that the resealing glue was not that used by Sweeney's manufacturers. That is made in Birmingham, and contains nothing that could harm a child. The glue used to reseal Ben Tifflin's box is Harrington's Stickfast, which can be purchased anywhere. The poisoner has deft hands, and he's sharp. He left no trace material on or in the sherbet toy.'

Dr Prout glanced at Thorneycroft. 'I'll see you get copies of all our reports,' he said, 'and I'd be happy for you to attend any further tests.'

Thorneycroft nodded his thanks, and Prout continued. 'With regard to the murder of Jock Robins, we were not able to examine the remains of the meal he ate on the night of Friday 17th. These were cleared away directly he finished eating, as he was leaving for Abinger Hammer, with his sister. Robins died on the following Wednesday, by which time all salad material from that date had been dumped in the rubbish bins of Mayfair Bonbouche, and removed.

'I have discussed with Dr Duncan Brews the mushroom species that he has identified as the cause of Mr Robins's death. It is a mushroom named Gyromitra esculenta. It grows wild in cold climates, in coniferous forests or cold woodlands. It is highly toxic. Though it's not your run-of-the-mill field mushroom, people do find it, and eat it and some of them die from doing so.'

Connor raised a hand. 'Does it grow in the UK?'

'Yes,' Prout said, 'though it's not abundant. Which raises the question, how did the poisoner find it and gather enough of it to fill a Bonbouche pack?'

'Could it have found its way into a pack by accident?'

Prout shook his head. 'That's very unlikely. Bonbouche sells only mushrooms grown in their own nurseries. And as in the Tifflin poisoning, only one pack was poisoned, as far as we know. It seems to me that someone planted a single pack of the poisonous mushrooms. Jock Robins was the unlucky man who found them on his dinner plate.'

Prout looked at Thorneycroft. 'The question in my mind,' he said, 'is why did the poisoner choose such a bizarre poison? There are plenty of mundane, lethal substances that can be bought in a supermarket or a hardware store. Why choose mushrooms?'

'I think,' answered Thorneycroft slowly, 'the poisoner aims to attract attention. He needs publicity. His first attempt with the mushrooms was deliberately bizarre. He knew it would be widely featured in the media. Poisoned sherbet would very likely be swallowed by a child ... again, there'd be wide publicity and shock.'

'And the profile of this man? Is he a serial killer?'

Thorneycroft hesitated. 'So far, his actions have shown disregard of the suffering of others typical of such killers. He's totally callous. He's deft with his hands. Ready to take risks. He makes plans and carries them out. The numbered cards show he's working to a plan.

'It's likely he lives in or close to London. Both attacks have taken place in London, and the cards sent to the victims' families were posted in London. The fact that Robins was fed poisoned mushrooms, which are highly perishable, shows that they must have been placed in the Mayfair branch of Bonbouche close to the day he ate them. That also suggests the killer's proximity to London.'

Connor leaned forward in his chair. 'So he's probably in Town, watching the results of his work, planning his next job.'

'Probably, but as I told you, there are points that bother me. In general, serial killers shed a lot of blood. Blood turns them on. But poisoners don't get their orgasms from blood-letting. They tend to be cold, secretive, mean-spirited, avaricious. They move in the shadows, avoid publicity. So how do we reconcile this poisoner with a deliberate intention to publicize his actions?'

'He's mad, isn't he?' demanded Connor. 'Capable of anything?'

'There are various forms of insanity; they have differing profiles.'

Connor's teeth glinted. 'I'm looking for a sod who's killed one man, and put a kid in hospital. I want to know, will he make other hits?'

'My guess is that he will make attacks on random victims. If he's planning a countdown, we can expect victims number three, two, one and possibly zero ... the lift-off number. The fact that he's sent the cards suggests he needs to boast of what he sees as success. He wants to taunt us, and the general public.

'I think he is psychotic, clever, cruel and very dangerous. He may experience the drives felt by sane people ... greed, lust, anger ... but his response to those drives is not normal. He has a compulsive need to exercise power, to prove his superiority over ordinary folk.

'All that fits the profile of a serial killer, but there are things that don't fit. This man seems to commit his crimes to destroy not human beings but the Bonbouche empire. Perhaps watching that crumble gives him a perverted pleasure.

'We need to ask, why would anyone want to destroy Bonbouche? Does he have a hatred for gourmets, for all rich people? Is he nursing a grievance, does he want revenge on the Lenard family, or some other major shareholder? It's possible that he sees Bonbouche as a business rival, and wants to wipe it off the face of the earth.'

Connor shrugged. 'That could be. DS Koch, here, watches the markets. Big blocks of Bonbouche shares have been sold, these past few days, and they've been snapped up fast. I'd like to know who's buying – the Lenards, other Bonbouche associates, people outside the company? We need to learn more about Bonbouche as an organization, and about the people who run it.

'Rolf Lenard has given me the names of a few employees who may have a bone to pick with the firm. We've questioned them, but found no likely suspects. I'm wondering, whether there could have been something in the past; a deal that went wrong, or a fiddle that could land Bonbouche in court? Would Lenard hand us that sort of information? The perp could be nursing a major grudge that we don't know about.'

'The grudge doesn't have to be major,' Thorneycroft said. 'A psycho can build a trivial slight into a massive injury.'

'So we have to check the Bonbouche records for individuals with grudges great or small?'

'Yes.'

Connor sighed heavily. 'That takes time, mate, and to my mind this perp's in a hurry. The attacks occurred within a few days of each other. If he's working to a countdown plan, he'll be looking for quick results. In both the attacks, the poison was in food that was likely to be eaten within a few days. Those sherbet sweets move quickly, Sweeney distributes fresh supplies every week, and mushrooms have a short shelf-life.'

Thorneycroft nodded. 'If the poisoner is working to a countdown, certain things follow. He's tied to a schedule. He has to make good his threats. I believe—'

He was interrupted by the burr of the red telephone at Hogarth's elbow, an unlisted line reserved for communication with senior police officials and persons of rank in the affairs of state. Its ring was an imperative summons.

VIII

HOGARTH LIFTED THE receiver, listened briefly, then barked, 'How the hell did you get this number?'

The phone emitted quacking noises. Hogarth pressed the button that made the voice audible to everyone in the room.

'Cut the crap, Edgar,' it complained, 'your secretary put me through to you. We've had a call from the poisoner.'

Next to Thorneycroft, Sam Koch swore softly. 'Tertius Bloom,' he said, 'editor of *The Challenger*. Sex, sin and murder, massive circulation of other people's blood.'

The disembodied voice soared higher. 'It was the poisoner, I'm telling you, not a hoaxer. If you ask me ...'

Hogarth cut him short. 'What did he say, Tertius?'

'He said "with reference to the Bonbouche case, keep space on your front page for number three in my series. You'll get a story that's hot and spicy."'

'Did you record the message?'

'Couldn't. He had himself put through to the typists' pool and spoke to a teenage temp, Lisa Stokely. Smart kid, she got the text of the message and asked the caller to identify himself. He laughed and hung up on her. There wasn't time to set up a phone trace.'

'How does she describe the voice? Was it male or female?'

'Muffled, she said. Could have been a man, or a woman faking a man's voice. She brought the message straight to me, and I called your office at once.'

'We'll get someone over to you right away.' Hogarth signed to Abbot and Davidson, who hurried from the room. 'Where's Ms Stokely now?'

'In my office.'

'Good. Keep her there. Give her sweet tea and don't question her, understand? Leave that to people who know how to do it. And thanks for your cooperation, Tertius. Much appreciated.'

Broom was not to be sidelined.

'It's my duty to publish,' he said. 'The public must be warned.'

'I agree, but stick to the facts, keep it cool, don't start a panic.'

'You'll hold a press conference?'

'Yes. You'll be informed.'

Hogarth dropped the receiver back on its cradle, and pressed the replay button on the instrument. He allowed the whole conversation to run.

'If it's a hoax, and we follow it up,' he said, 'we'll slow down the whole investigation.' He looked at Thorneycroft. 'What's your take on it, John?'

Thorneycroft shrugged. 'We have to treat it as genuine. Hoax or not, it has the mark of a psychopath. He's malicious and self-serving. He's hungry for publicity. He's chosen to alert *The Challenger*, a scum-sheet that'll make sure that by tonight he'll be headlines across the country.

'He's also clever. He made his call to the typists' pool, which is unlikely to have message-recorders on every phone. He disguised his voice and kept the call short, so it couldn't be traced.'

Connor spoke. 'A hoaxer could have done all those things.'

'True, but there are other things that suggest it was the killer speaking. He gave notice of another attack, "number three in my series"; and he said the story would be "hot and spicy". That could be a pointer to his next victim. Psychopaths like to drop clues. It gives them an adrenalin rush to play games with the authorities.'

'Are you saying the poison will be in hot and spicy food?'

'It's possible.'

'So who eats stuff like that? Pakistanis, Indians ...'

'Mexicans,' Thorneycroft said, 'Spaniards and Italians, Arabs, Thais, Europeans, anyone who likes that kind of food. Millions of Londoners eat it. He's taunting us, not helping us.'

'Or he could be sticking to his plan. So far he's poisoned a little kid and a public benefactor, both attacks have got him headlines. What if he wants to play the race card, go for a minority racial community ... immigrants, victims whose deaths will get his message to other countries. Muslims maybe?'

Hogarth was getting to his feet. 'I have to talk to Rolf Lenard about the call. I'll ask him if any of the Bonbouche branches specialize in that kind of food. And I'll ask the Home Office for the demographics of immigrant groups.'

He moved away, heading for his own office. Connor beckoned to Ayusha Ramiah, who crossed the room to his side.

'Where in London,' Connor said, 'are there groups of people whose staple diet is hot and spicy, and who can afford to buy it from Bonbouche?'

'There are thousands of people, scattered all over London, who fit that description,' Ayusha answered. 'It would be easier to start with the Bonbouche outlets, and try to pinpoint the immigrant communities round them.'

Connor nodded. 'Start there.' He turned to DS Malherbe. 'I want a press conference, here, at 1.30. Be sure to include the foreign language media, press, radio and TV.' He caught Thorneycroft's sceptical glance, and said, 'we have to go public on this. *The Challenger*'s presses are already rolling.'

'Oh yes, I agree,' Thorneycroft said, 'but I'm not sure how we define "hot and spicy". Claudia was shopping in the Wimbledon Bonbouche a few days ago. She nearly bought a Christmas pudding. That's hot and spicy, isn't it?'

'Only on Christmas Day,' Connor said. 'I don't think the perp will wait that long. He's started his countdown. I'm putting out a general alert to all stations to expect hit number three within the next few days.'

Thorneycroft had shared in enough police investigations to know when he should, like Brer Fox, lie low and say nothing.

He sat quietly while Connor's team alerted the police network of the country to the possibility of another poison attack. The divisions would try to identify potential victims. They would issue warnings, reach out to vulnerable individuals and communities, appeal to clubs, societies and religious bodies to spread the message. They would attempt what was clearly impossible, because that was their only option.

A secretary from Hogarth's office brought Connor a sheaf of faxes. He glanced through them and grunted.

'From Rolf Lenard,' he said. 'Lists of the take-away dishes stocked by Bonbouche. He's starred the branches that have the highest sales of curry, biryani et cetera. He's also pointed out that a lot of customers buy dishes in bulk, and freeze them. How do we deal with that ticking time bomb?'

Despite the shortness of notice, the press conference was packed. Connor addressed it in his shirtsleeves, prowling to and fro as he spoke.

'The odds are against us getting to this man before he kills again,' he said, 'because he's a psycho. He doesn't follow normal patterns, he can't be reached by appeals to conscience or pity or even self-preservation. He's a loner. He is single-mindedly vicious, way beyond the limits of what you and I can understand.

'Our investigation is going well. We're reaching targets, following leads, preserving the chain of evidence. That's the minimum required of us. We have a good team working on the case. We have forensic experts on hand, we have the backing of law-enforcement agencies here and abroad. All that put together isn't enough.

'To nail a crazy criminal who poisons innocent people, we have to have the co-operation not only of state authorities, but of ordinary citizens. This has to be an open campaign. The media has a key role to play. The killer has shown, in his message to *The Challenger*, that he's a glutton for publicity. He thinks he can make the media his tool. You can turn that weapon against him. You can tempt him into making mistakes. You can help us put him away.

'I'll see to it that communications between you and my team are open 24/7. We'll give you as much information as we can, without prejudicing the course of our enquiries. Are there any questions?'

There were plenty, and Connor fielded them smoothly. Watching him, Thorneycroft saw that the press liked him. He had a cynicism to match their own. The few promises he made, he kept. And he had flair, his cases made news, and he achieved a high degree of success.

The conference over, Connor came to sit beside Thorneycroft. His face shone with sweat and he scrubbed it with his handkerchief.

He said abruptly, 'you really think we should be looking for a perp with a personal grudge against the Lenards?'

'Well,' Thorneycroft answered, 'you've drawn a blank looking for people with grudges against the Bonbouche Company. Maybe one or other of the Lenards has made an enemy. The only way we can test that theory is by talking to the Lenards themselves.'

Connor muttered, unconvinced. At last he said, 'I spoke to Jason Lenard last night. He can see us at the warehouse at 3.30 this afternoon. We can grab a bite in the canteen, before we leave.'

IX

THE POLICE CAR that whisked Connor and Thorneycroft to their appointment with Jason Lenard was driven by a silent man with close-cropped hair and the pallor of a sun-starved plant. Connor sat in the rear seat with Thorneycroft. 'The Bonbouche warehouse is at Goldmead Park,' he said. 'It's a commercial enterprise, trendy and very expensive, developed by a consortium of eleven specialist firms. They deal in up-market clothing, exotic plants, jewellery and perfumery, personal computers and other electronic gimmicks. Bonbouche is a member of the consortium.

'Davidson's done some research on the members. They're all in the luxury class, and can afford to pay for top-grade storage facilities, in an area that's tailor-made to their needs ... dockyards right on the doorstep, a commercial airport licensed to handle small aircraft just a couple of miles away. The park has its own helipad, a railway siding, and first-class security.

'According to Rolf Lenard, the Bonbouche warehouse is fully mechanized and computerized. A lot of the stuff that Bonbouche sells, is imported. It's stored in warehouses around the country. The London warehouse is controlled by Jason Lenard.'

'I imagine that most of that stuff is sitting on ice at the moment,' Thorneycroft said, and Connor nodded.

'Yeah. Rolf says their trade is practically at a standstill. They're selling canned goods and sealed bottles, but there's not much demand. Sales are better in Europe and the USA, but they're way below normal. As you say, the perp could be getting his kicks from bringing Bonbouche down.'

They circled the City and headed east. The weather was dismal. Soggy clouds hung low in the sky, and occasional glimpses of the river showed a sluggish tide capped with yellow foam.

Soon after 3.00 o'clock, they reached the boundary of Goldmead Park, a high electrified fence punctuated by watchtowers and ranks of floodlights.

They followed the fence for some two miles, passing hoardings that bore the names and logos of famous enterprises. At the main gate a uniformed guard checked their identity, spoke briefly on a mobile phone, and waved them through. They entered what looked like the embodiment of a town-planner's dream.

The Goldmead site stretched southwards towards dockland. On its western boundary, fat-bellied choppers were lined up on a large heliport. To the east lay an automated parking lot, a coach-house, filling stations, utility shops, and a clinic.

They followed signposts along a broad road that led them to the Bonbouche warehouse. The brick buildings formed three sides of a square. The central and largest part appeared to be the storage area. In the wing on the left was a garage housing rows of trucks, vans, and refrigerator cars. A small crane and several forklifts were ranged along the outside of the building, and a small group of workmen were unloading crates from a container on to a moving belt that rolled away through high metal doors. Some work was being done, Thorneycroft thought, but not much.

A carguard directed them to a covered bay next to the right-hand wing. This was apparently the administrative sector of the complex. Its façade bore the Bonbouche name in curling gold script, and over the entrance was the hallmark pink and gold striped awning. A blonde in a pink trouser suit emerged and ushered them into the main foyer.

Here the Chocolate Soldier image vanished. There were no pictures or flowers, just plain steel counters, and an even plainer receptionist who told them that Mr Lenard was ready for them, and directed them to a private lift in a corner of the foyer.

Arriving at the third floor, they stepped into a wide hall with a single doorway, at which stood a man in jeans, white sweater, and trainers. He came towards them, hand outstretched.

'Detective Chief Inspector Connor ... Dr Thorneycroft ... welcome.' He smiled, shook hands, made eye contact, charm personified.

Connor mistrusted charm. 'It's good of you to make time for us, Mr Lenard.'

Jason Lenard smiled less broadly. 'At the moment I have more free time than I care for.'

Studying him, Thorneycroft thought that he didn't take after his father. He was more like the portrait of his grandmother, at the Chelsea branch. Same large, slightly protuberant blue eyes, same thick fair hair with gold highlights, (real or artificial he wondered). There was a fullness under the jaw that spoke of sybaritic living. The mouth was small and tucked in at the corners: a taker, not a giver? Lenard had a good physique, clearly a man who trained regularly. The waterproof Rolex on the left wrist suggested that the deep tan had been acquired in the surf, not the beauty parlour.

Jason tilted his head at Connor. 'So what's it to be, walk or talk?'

'Walk and talk,' Connor answered. 'I want to know as much as possible about your systems here ... what products you deal with, where they come from, who's involved in the transactions, how goods are handled, stored, or passed on to your outlets.'

Jason leaned forward to summon the elevator and stood aside to let them enter. 'I'll do my best,' he said. He sounded confident, and a little bored. Thorneycroft decided to rattle his cage.

'The mushrooms that killed Jock Robins,' he said. 'The Gyromitra esculenta. Did they pass through your hands?'

'No,' said Jason flatly. 'Neither the toadstools nor the Puffing Billy came through Goldmead. Sweeney deliver their sweets straight to our branches, and all our salad material comes from our own nurseries and goes directly to our outlets.'

They rode down to the ground floor and Jason led them across the foyer and along a short corridor to a steel door. It gave access to the warehouse, a vast space divided into sectors by counters, conveyor-belts and unfamiliar machines. There were no goods in evidence, and the men posted at intervals seemed to be guards rather than ware-house hands.

Thorneycroft spoke again. 'So, Mr Lenard, how do you think the poisonous mushrooms arrived at your Mayfair branch?'

Jason halted and turned to face him. 'Obviously, the poisoner delivered them there. The real question is, how did he lay hands on them? Not that that'd be too difficult. Toadstools grow everywhere in this country.'

'Do you think the poisoner went out into the fields and collected them? How would he know what species they were?'

'I've no idea.' Jason seemed to give the matter some thought. 'It's possible he bought them.'

'From whom?'

Jason surveyed him almost pityingly. 'If you have enough money and nerve, you can buy whatever you like. Stolen art or jewels, weapons, drugs, newborn babies, a government or so. A few toadstools would be easy. I'm in the business of buying and selling. I hear things. I get some weird offers, but Bonbouche doesn't touch the quirky stuff.'

Connor looked curiously at the young man. 'Why do you think he chose such an outlandish poison? He could have bought drugs over the counter that are just as lethal, and a lot less chancy in effect.'

Jason spread his hands. 'Learning why is your job, Inspector, not mine. My job is to show you how this warehouse functions. I'll take you round and explain the systems. Ask whatever questions you like. Our records department will supply documentation, and if you have a tame computernik, you're welcome to send him to talk to our resident nerds. So, if you'll follow me....'

It had to be admitted that Jason Lenard made a good guide. He explained how the goods were imported, delivered and stored in various areas, at optimum temperatures. He spoke with the authority not just of a boss, but of a man who has learned the job from the ground up.

'We can keep meat in cold storage for some time,' he said, 'but we don't like storing fruit and vegetables, or dairy products. They don't improve in cold rooms, and we promise quality fare to our customers. Our sell-by times are extremely short.' His bulbous gaze fixed on Connor. 'Which is why we hope to God you'll arrest this bastard fast. Every day costs us millions in lost sales.'

'We appreciate that, sir,' Connor said. 'Your loss is a loss to the national economy. Catching the guilty person is a matter of national concern.' He hesitated. 'I understand you're still selling wines. I'd like to see that department, if you please.'

'Certainly.' Jason led them to the back of the building, to a vast cavern lined with wine racks. In the centre of the floor was a system of machines and conveyor belts, idle now.

Jason turned to the wine racks and lifted out a bottle. 'This is an Australian Shiraz,' he said. 'Very good and a lot cheaper than the French. There's a big market out there for a nice wine that a family man can afford. I'd like to see wine drunk in every home, the way it is in France and Italy. Normally I'd offer you a couple of bottles, but I suppose at the moment that would not be a welcome gift.' He replaced the Shiraz in its rack.

'This is the worst loss for me,' he said. 'Our wines are the heart of our business. We import from producers all over the world, not only the standards such as champagne, port and sherry, and our range doesn't only cover the vintage wines.

'We're developing a new practice. We bring in wine in bulk, from the smaller producers, and we transfer it to our own bottles, under our own label. The producers avoid the bottling costs, we're happy, the consumers are happy ...' The warmth died from his voice. 'On those machines over there, we can bottle and cork and label wine, without laying a finger on anything. The machine does it all, and a computer records the whole process, type and origin of wine, amount, price, date. We can't do any of it, not as long as there's the risk of a poisoner invading the system.' He turned a cold gaze on Connor. 'Our work's being destroyed by a maniac. All I'm good for is damage control.'

'That's right.' Connor's voice was harsh. 'You have to prevent damage to your business. I have to prevent damage to the public. I take it your father has told you about the approach made to *The Challenger*?'

Jason's face puckered. 'Yes, I heard. The hot and spicy story. I'm afraid you're closing the stable door too late.'

'Why do you say that?' demanded Connor.

'Our sales of far-eastern dishes peak in October, round the time of Ramadan and Deepavali. Our Muslim and Hindu customers buy large supplies and freeze them. We can't recall those sales, because we can't identify the buyers.'

Connor held Jason's gaze. 'You're anxious for an early arrest, Mr Lenard. To achieve that, we'll need your full co-operation.'

'Of course I'm ready to help in any way I can.' Jason looked at his watch. 'I suggest we adjourn to my apartment and continue our discussion in comfort.'

X

THE LONG ROOM on the third floor contained, at the near end, a desk, a maplewood table with matching chairs, a personal computer, fax and copier, and a rank of red-enamelled filing cabinets. At the far end, couches and easy chairs were grouped round a bar-counter with a fridge and microwave oven. An enormous flat-screen television was set in the farthest wall.

Floor to roof windows provided a fine view of docks and river. Near the entrance door, a video screen was showing a picture of a van unloading crates at the west wing of the building; passing it, Jason pressed a switch and the screen went blank.

Connor joined Jason at the central table, but Thorneycroft paused to study a spread of photographs fixed to the inner wall of the room – some of them were black-and-white shots of machines, vehicles, and the warehouse storerooms. There was also a selection of snapshots of women, some clothed, some naked, all strikingly beautiful. A few pictures showed Jason in sporting mode, climbing a rock-face, soaring in a microlite, standing at the wheel of a racing yacht. There were no group photographs, nothing that spoke of a family gathering.

Thorneycroft took his place at the table. Connor was leafing through one of the brochures given him by Rolf Lenard. Laying it aside, he said, 'you have quite a c.v., sir. Degrees from Oxford and Harvard, management experience in England, France, the USA ...'

'... and Japan,' Jason said. 'The Japs have the best work ethic, and they're artists at presenting food. Their sushi is amazing.'

'I prefer my fish deep fried,' Connor said. 'Tell me, what do you think is the motive for these attacks?'

Jason blinked. 'Obviously, the destruction of Bonbouche.'

'Why poison innocent people, to destroy Bonbouche?'

'The man hopes to erode our share values and wreck public confidence in us. He's trying to create a take-over climate. He's crazy, of course. We've beaten raptors far more dangerous than this oaf. But I repeat, we want to finish him fast.'

Connor folded his hands on the table. 'Your father is very worried about the goods already sold, that may contain poison.'

'Worrying doesn't solve anything,' said Jason impatiently. 'We've taken what action we can. We've stopped selling goods that could be contaminated, we've issued warnings. I don't see what else we can do, but if you have suggestions, Inspector, do say.'

Connor looked as if he might explode, but he said calmly, 'you say this is an attempt at a business *coup*. Do you know of a competitor who might make such an attempt?'

Jason's mouth tightened. 'There are several possibilities, and we have people watching them, but frankly, I don't think this is coming from any of our recognized rivals. Sooner or later, we'll know what we're up against, and we'll deal with it.' He caught Connor's frosty look, and smiled. 'Lawfully, of course.'

Thorneycroft intervened. 'It's possible that the poisoner is driven not by business aspirations, but by a personal grudge against Bonbouche. DCI Connor asked your father if there'd been any incidents in the past that could create such a grudge, and he gave us a list, a very short one. None of the people on it seem likely suspects. Perhaps you can think of someone who harbours a grievance against the company?'

'No, I cannot. I can't recall a single acrimonious dismissal in all the time I've known the firm. We pay exceptionally well, there are a great many perks for Bonbouche workers. And frankly, I can't think of anyone, past or present, who'd do what this slimeball has done.'

For the first time during the interview, Jason's calm seemed to have deserted him. He sat with his chin tucked in to his throat, and his fingers drummed on the smooth surface of the table.

'Your father said the same thing. Let me raise another possibility. Perhaps the poisoner feels animosity not towards Bonbouche, but towards some member of your family and by damaging Bonbouche, he strikes at the Lenards. Can you think of such a person?'

'No.' Jason drew a deep breath. 'That's insane.'

'The perpetrator is insane, Mr Lenard. We have to stop him, and to do that we need to know what's driving him to commit these crimes. We need to know if you or any other member of your family has become the target of a murderer.'

Jason's mouth tightened even further. He said abruptly, 'my family is a close one. We value privacy, we don't fraternize with the world at large and we don't seek popularity. But we respect the law. We pay our dues. We don't deserve this ... this abomination.'

'No-one does,' Thorneycroft said. 'Not the Lenards, nor the Tifflins, nor Miss Robins.'

Jason made no answer, and Connor spoke. 'We'll be talking to all your family, sir. We've already consulted Mr Rolf Lenard and he's agreed this is a necessary step. You can help by telling us a bit about your relations, so we'll know how best to approach them. Let's start with the most senior member. That'd be your grandmother, Mrs Eva Lenard. She lives in Richmond, so your father said.'

Jason scowled. 'She does, but I doubt if she'll talk to you. She's frail. She doesn't like visitors.'

'If I can confirm the address. Coventry Hall, 27 Allenby Close. That's near the river, isn't it? You say she's frail. Does she have someone to look after her?'

'She has a cook, two housemaids and two gardeners,' said Jason tartly. He paused. 'And she has a companion, Miss Hester Plum, who is a trained nurse and a friend of long-standing.'

'Your grandmother helped to invent the Bonbouche stores. Is she still active in the business?'

'No. She's a shareholder, but her health doesn't allow her to take an active part in things.' Again Jason hesitated. 'She suffers from depressions. We try to protect her from bad news. From what's going on now.'

'You mean she doesn't know about the attacks?'

'I didn't say that. She watches television and reads the papers. She's as sharp as a tack, but she knows she doesn't have to deal with any problems. She knows we'll see to that.'

'Your father and you will deal with all the problems?'

'And the Board of Directors and our structures around the world.' Jason's face was flushed. 'Understand, Inspector, I don't want her troubled in any way.'

'I understand. Does the companion ... Miss Plum ... live-in?'

'Yes. She has her own apartment in the house.'

'Your father mentioned that he and your mother divorced when you and your sister were very young. Do you count your mother as a member of your family circle?'

'I do not. She ran off with the man who designed Coventry Hall for my grandparents. She married him. They have four children. They live their own lives, as we live ours.'

'I see. And your sister? Are you in touch with her?'

'Occasionally. Fenella's a singer. She's with a group that does baroque music, madrigals, folksongs, that sort of thing. She's a mezzo-soprano.'

'Is she married?'

'Yes, to the group's principal baritone. They travel a good deal. Their permanent home is in Rome. When she's in England, we meet.'

'What's the name of the group, sir?'

'The Saffron Singers, God knows why. They're pretty good, they're just back from an American tour. They're staying at the Hotel Cornwallis. Fenella and David, not the rest of the group.'

Connor laid his notebook aside. 'That's everyone, then? Quite a small family.'

Connor the Fox, Thorneycroft thought, playing the bumbling flat-foot, encouraging people to underestimate him.

Jason said impatiently, 'there's Silas, my father's brother. He lives in Russell Square.' He gave the address and telephone numbers, then added, 'you won't get him now, he's at a medical convention in Berlin.'

'Does he know about the attacks?'

'Yes. I phoned him. He didn't offer to come back. He's not interested in Bonbouche. My grandfather left the business to my father and him, but he sold out. He's a paediatrician. His practice is in Portland Place.' Jason's small mouth curled. 'He's like my father, believes in tradition, wants to keep things the way they are. He makes an exception for plastic surgery.'

Thorneycroft leaned forward. 'Your father implied that Bonbouche would not be changed, that it would remain a family firm catering for an élite clientele. Do you support that view?'

Jason's eyelashes flickered. 'We're the majority shareholders. I think we must preserve what's good in Bonbouche, but some things have to change. The world's changed. People want fast foods. They want big showy launches for new products, exotic menus and loud music. We have to go with the flow, but within those new parameters, we have to serve the best on the market.'

'Are you currently providing that kind of service? Big launches, loud music?'

'Not yet, but it's only a matter of time.' Jason got to his feet. 'Now, gentlemen, if you'll excuse me, I have an appointment to keep. If there's anything else I can do to help the investigation, let me know.'

He accompanied them down to the car, pausing at the reception desk to collect a large buff envelope, which he handed to Connor.

'Facts and figures relating to my work,' he said. 'If you need more, you know where to reach me.'

As Thorneycroft took his place in the car, Jason leaned to the open window.

'Watch your step with my grandmother,' he said. 'If she takes against you, you'll get nothing from the rest of the family.'

Once clear of the Goldmead gates, Connor gave vent to his feelings.

'I hate these bloody tycoons,' he said. 'That one back there, all he can think of is profit and loss. His fucking business. There's a man dead, and a kid could have died, and not one word did he say about them or their families. He's dead cold, and he thinks he's God. "We'll deal with it" he says. He thinks money buys anything. Said so, didn't he, drugs or hot goods or poison. Half of what he told us'll turn out to be lies, it's a habit with his sort. They lie on principle.'

'I think he's too smart to tell a direct lie to a cop,' Thorneycroft said, 'but I suspect he's an expert at half-truths. When I asked him if he knew of anyone with a grievance against Bonbouche, he answered that he couldn't recall a single acrimonious dismissal. He didn't mention dissatisfied customers, or angry litigants. He didn't lie, but he didn't tell the whole truth.'

'Yeah, and I'd say he enjoys taking risks; wouldn't deal in drugs, but he might snort coke at a party, or go for kinky sex. He was right about one thing. If you have the cash you can buy anything. There are dealers here in London who'll procure girls, boys, snuff movies, prohibited substances, nasty weapons.

'I've spoken to DS McGivern in Vice. He's covering the weirdo shops to see if anyone's been looking for Gyromitra esculenta. If we can find a vendor, we can maybe trace the buyer.'

'You have to admit that Jason Lenard is good at his job,' Thorneycroft said. 'The warehouse is amazing, and he's also done all he can to see that Bonbouche doesn't market poisoned goods.'

'Self-interest. Every time there's an attack, their shares tumble. Rolf Lenard ordered the sales shutdown directly after Ben Tifflin got his dose of aspirin. One thing's clear, Rolf and Jason don't get on. Dad's for the old ways and sonny's after changing them.' Connor sighed. 'Mind you, I can sympathize with the old man. My son wears silver pants and a ring in his nose. He wants to be a chef on telly.'

Thorneycroft laughed. 'Don't fight it, he may make you famous. As for Rolf and Jason, they do have one thing in common, neither of them is prepared to name their enemies.'

The car left the riverside traffic and slid on to a ring road. A thought occurred to Connor. 'What did the Warehouse Wonder say to you as we were leaving?'

'He said we should be careful how we handle Granny Lenard, because if she's doesn't like us, she'll muzzle the rest of the clan.'

Connor smiled grimly. 'I'll set up a meeting with her for tomorrow. Explain to her what happens to old ladies who try to defeat the ends of justice.'

That plan was destined to come to nothing, for in a snug townhouse in Islington, Vabashnee Murugan, aged 72, was busy defrosting one of Bonbouche's hot and spicy mutton curries.

Back at Concorde Street, they listened to reports from the team members.

Abbot and Davidson had questioned Tertius Bloom and the staff of *The Challenger* about the telephone call. 'The Stokeley lass is sensible and truthful,' Abbot said. 'The call only lasted two minutes, but it scared her. She believes it was the perp. I checked the text of the story the paper's putting out. It's sensational, but not over the line.'

Ayusha Ramiah produced lists of immigrant communities that might be Bonbouche customers. 'I phoned the Bonbouche branches in those areas. They've already returned whatever hot and spicy dishes they had in storage. Forensics are testing them, but so far, they've found no poisons. It's the dishes already sold that we have to worry about.'

Justin Malherbe reported that there was good co-operation from the media. 'They've faxed us copies of their stories, and the TV circuits are putting out warnings in Hindi, Tamil and Urdu, as well as Arabic and European languages. Our divisions are contacting community leaders, clubs and religious bodies.'

Sam Koch then took over to present the financial information. 'The Bonbouche shares are still dropping. Members of the board say frankly that they're buying to defend the firm's interests.'

'Is that legal?' Connor asked. Koch looked surprised.

'Sure, why not? It's not a question of insider trading. It's obvious that Bonbouche is under criminal attack, that they'll fight back, and if they come right, the shares will be back to full value. There's no shortage of buyers.'

'Do you think that someone is hoping for a power shift, a situation where there could be a take-over of the company?'

Koch's dark face puckered. 'Someone's out to damage the company,' he said, 'but I don't buy the idea of a take-over attempt. Take-overs don't happen overnight, there have to be negotiations, consultations with shareholders, bids and counter-bids. What we have here is a killer working to a short-term countdown, not a rival group looking to wrest control.'

'Umh. Well, the Super's got Commercial Division on the job. We have to leave it to them to cover the broader field.'

It was at 6.30, as the discussions came to a close, that Superintendent Hogarth's secretary brought in the sheet of photocopy paper. The message on it was hand-printed in rough capitals.

YOU TOP COPS BETTER WATCH OUT. BEN TIFFLIN WAS LUCKY. YOUR KIDS HAVE RUN OUT OF LUCK.

Connor read it stony-faced, then passed the page to Thorneycroft. 'Have forensics checked it?' he asked, and the secretary nodded.

'Yes. It's covered in prints. We're looking for comparisons with known hoaxers, but I don't think the Bonbouche perp would have left prints.'

'No more do I, but if he used a public copier, the page could carry prints of other users, or the person who loaded the sheets into the machine. If you do find a match with a known hoaxer, charge the silly prick.' He looked at the message. 'Waste of good felt tip pen, but run all the tests on the crap, just in case.'

Thorneycroft asked Connor, 'have there been a lot of hoax letters?'

'Dozens,' Connor answered.

'I'd like to see all of them.'

'Sure, I'll have them brought up for you.'

Driving home, Thorneycroft thought of Ben Tifflin, struggling to breathe, and of Luke, who was at the age when he put everything in his mouth. He reached the house at seven o'clock. Claudia was in the kitchen, grilling sausages, and Luke was sitting under the kitchen table. Thorneycroft scooped him up in his arms and kissed the top of his head.

After supper, with Luke asleep, Thorneycroft and Claudia talked about Christmas.

'I think,' Claudia said, 'that we should make new plans. I don't want Mum and Dad to come to London. It'll be distracting for you, and no fun for them. We can ask them to come later. You can take leave in the New Year.'

'What I'd like,' said Thorneycroft slowly, 'is for you and Luke to go down to them for a spell. Have a proper Christmas. It's Luke's first, he should be able to enjoy it with you.'

'And with you.' Claudia watched him frowning. 'There's something you're not telling me.'

'It's a dangerous situation, Clo. He's planning another attack, and we don't know where.'

'Have you been threatened?'

'There was a message this evening. Probably from a hoaxer, but we can't take chances.'

'What was the message?'

'It said, "you top cops better watch out. Ben Tifflin was lucky. Your kids have run out of luck".'

Claudia swallowed. 'I see.'

'You'll be safe in Appledore. You dad and the local cops will see to it.' As she still hesitated, he said, 'for my sake as well, love. If I know you and Luke are safe, I can do a better job.'

'All right. I'll phone Mum in the morning, and explain.' She attempted a smile. 'There's no Bonbouche outlet within miles of Appledore.' She got to her feet, holding out a hand. 'Come to bed, we'd better make up for time about to be lost.'

XI

THE TELEPHONE WOKE them at 1.30. It was Connor speaking rapidly. Thorneycroft rolled to his feet. 'Who and where,' he asked, and listened to Connor's instructions.

Claudia was already out of bed and pulling on a dressing-gown. As Thorneycroft ended the call, she said, 'another attack?'

'Yes, a Mrs Murugan, aged 72, an Indian immigrant, lives in Islington. She's alive but unconscious.'

In the nursery next door, Luke woke and began to make a niggling sound. Claudia went to fetch him.

'I'll make you some sandwiches,' she said, and went off, carrying Luke.

Thorneycroft pulled on warm clothes. Rain was drumming on the windowpane. He found his raincoat and car keys and started for the door. Before he reached it, the phone rang again.

He half-expected to hear a muffled voice, spilling malice, but it was the Northumberland burr of Mike Nicolson, of the Wimbledon precinct.

'Hey John. On DCI Connor's orders, I'm sending Policewoman Lynn Rudge over, to be with Claudia. They know each other from church, Lynn says. The patrol car will drop her off at your place right away.'

'Thanks Mike,' Thorneycroft said, 'that takes a load off my mind.' But as he turned from the phone, anxiety was replaced by a surge of rage, that a pervert could invade his life and threaten what was most precious to him. He made a rapid tour of the house, checking that windows and doors were secure, and the alarm system switched on.

Claudia had packed ham sandwiches, a banana, and a bar of chocolate. Thorneycroft took the package and kissed her.

'Lynn Rudge is coming over to keep you company,' he said. 'Do

what she tells you, don't leave the house and don't admit anyone
Lynn doesn't know. Phone your folks as early as is decent and make
a plan to stay with them. I'll be back as soon as I can.'

The patrol car arrived and Lynn Rudge walked into the house, a
large woman, smiling and blessedly matter-of-fact. Thorneycroft left
them brewing coffee, and drove through rain-slick streets to the
Whiteriggs Estate in Islington.

It was a new upmarket development, its security gates flanked by
powerful lights. A uniformed constable greeted Thorneycroft and
told him to follow the left-hand road past the tennis courts.

The street lamps showed him free-standing bungalows with lush
gardens and double garages. Outside number 127 a second constable
was holding back a crowd of onlookers. There were several cars
drawn up on the verge, and a silver BMW and an ambulance were
parked in the driveway. Thorneycroft left his Volvo next to Connor's
Toyota, and spoke to the man on duty.

'It's the Murugan house,' the man said. 'Owned by Mr Ronnie
Murugan, he lives here with his mother and daughter. He's been away
in Birmingham, on business. His daughter and Mrs Murugan had
their supper and went to bed. At midnight the girl heard the sound of
a heavy fall, and went and found her gran lying on the bathroom
floor, out cold. The girl phoned the doctor right away, and then her
dad, got him on his mobile, on his way home. Soon as he got here,
he phoned DCI Connor.'

They were interrupted by a high keening that came from inside
the house. The onlookers, scenting drama, surged forward.
Thorneycroft dodged round them and made his way up the drive. As
he reached the front door it opened, and he was confronted by three
women. The two older ones wore saris, the younger one wore jeans
and an Arran jersey. She sagged between her companions, wailing
dolefully.

Thorneycroft let the trio pass and went into the house. Connor,
Abbot, and a man Thorneycroft guessed was a local police officer
stood round a tall portly man in a sleek grey suit and Gucci loafers.
The man was declaiming in a high, shrill voice, his hands flailing.
Connor saw Thorneycroft and crossed to meet him.

'That's Mr Ronnie Murugan,' he said. 'It's his mother that's ill.
She's in the next room with the family doctor, a Doctor Sastri who

seems to know what he's doing. Murugan says his ma's been poisoned. He found a Bonbouche curry carton in the kitchen. There was a little curry left in it. I've sent it to Prout. He'll give us a quick analysis.'

'Shouldn't she be in hospital?' Thorneycroft said, and Connor sniffed.

'You tell that to Dr Sastri. He says she's stabilizing, and when she's stable he'll move her to hospital. You're a doctor, why don't you go and talk to him?'

Thorneycroft complied. The next room proved to be a bedroom and on the bed lay a very fat old woman who breathed heavily, purple mouth wide open. Thorneycroft joined the man standing at the bedside.

'I'm a doctor,' he said. 'How's your patient?'

Sastri frowned, but decided to answer the question.

'She's coming round. She's diabetic and a naughty old woman. She eats and drinks substances with a high sugar content, and relies on the insulin to mend the damage. Her granddaughter Queenie says that tonight she ate a half-litre bucket of ice-cream.'

'Did she have her insulin shot?'

'Queenie says she did, but that fool Murugan won't believe it. He's yelling murder.'

'The curry came from Bonbouche. You've read the papers?'

'Yes. The remains of the curry is being tested. Mrs Murugan has had the proper medication, she's alive and will live to pig out another day. Go and tell Murugan to stop shouting, I'm going to convey his mother to hospital.'

The woman on the bed was making fluttering movements of the hands. Her eyelids flickered, she opened her eyes and stared at Dr Sastri. He took her hand and patted it, saying something soothing in a language Thorneycroft didn't recognize. She answered haltingly, tears running down her cheeks.

Thorneycroft returned to the living-room. Mr Murugan was still shouting. 'That Queenie,' he cried, 'that stupid, wicked girl, I told her over and over, watch Granny, Granny doesn't speak English, she can't read the papers, she can't understand what they say on TV. I warned Queenie, no Bonbouche stuff. Look in the fridge, I said, make sure there's none of that stuff!'

'And did she?' Connor asked. 'Did your daughter look in the fridge?'

'Yes, yes, yes, but she forget about the freezer in the storeroom. My mother is always putting things away. No use to tell her "stick to your diet", she likes to eat rich curries, fig jam, ice-cream. I told my daughter, watch what she eats, but young people today, they don't know what is it to be obedient. I told her, if Granny dies, you are responsible. You are to blame.'

'Hence the wailing,' Thorneycroft thought. At that moment Murugan clapped his hands to his face and burst into tears. 'I didn't mean it,' he sobbed. 'I'm upset. I saw the carton in the kitchen, I thought "my mother is dying". I just shouted at Queenie, you know? It was the shock.'

Thorneycroft put a hand on Murugan's arm. 'Your mother is conscious, Mr Murugan. We'll get her to hospital and she'll be all right.'

Murugan moaned, hands still clamped to his cheeks. Dr Sastri leaned round the door of the inner room.

'Inspector Connor, if you please, ask the ambulance men to bring the stretcher. And you, Ronnie Murugan, stop acting the monkey and go and phone your daughter. She's with the neighbours. Tell her her Granny's going to be all right, and tell her you love her, chop chop.'

Connor and Dr Sastri made the journey to hospital in the ambulance with Mrs Murugan. Ronnie Murugan insisted on driving with Abbot in Connor's car, and Thorneycroft travelled alone in his Volvo.

The local police remained to disperse the crowd, and give assurances that the old lady was out of danger.

Easing the car past groups of chattering people, Thorneycroft wondered how long it would be before Mrs Murugan hit the headlines. People could smell bad news from a mile off, and they loved to spread it.

He wondered, too, what the killer would make of it. Sastri could be right in thinking that tonight's drama was nothing more than a case of gluttony: a silly old woman who had eaten things that are poison to a diabetic and survived because her doctor was at hand with the right antidote.

He did not believe that that was the way it happened. Mrs

Murugan had eaten a Bonbouche take-away, kept for days in her deep-freeze. She had just missed going into a diabetic coma, and it happened only a couple of days after the poisoner had promised *The Challenger* a 'hot and spicy' story.

The matron of the hospital was against police interviewing her patients, but she reckoned without Granny Murugan. By dawn the old lady was fully conscious and demanding to speak to her son and the police. In the presence of Connor and Thorneycroft, she harangued Ronnie Murugan at length, in what was evidently pungent Gujarati.

Murugan translated. 'My mother says she did eat the curry and also the ice-cream, but then she gave herself the insulin shot. I know she's telling the truth. She doesn't lie about insulin, only about food.'

'Which means,' said Connor when he and Thorneycroft left the room, 'that she shouldn't have gone unconscious, doesn't it?'

'I'd expect the insulin to work,' Thorneycroft said, 'unless it was stale. Drugs deteriorate with time, and some patients are careless about checking the use-by date of their medication. The hospital will run tests on the old lady, and Prout will test the remains of the curry. The results will give us answers.'

The test reports were delivered that morning. Blood samples taken from Mrs Murugan on her arrival at the hospital contained traces of cortisone.

'She must have absorbed a large dose,' Prout said. 'Cortisone is dispersed rapidly. There was also cortisone in the curry she ate. We can give you the amounts found in both sets of tests, as indicated after adjustments relating to the time of ingestion, and the dispersal time of the drug.'

'I thought cortisone was for athletes, or people with injuries or infections,' Connor said. 'I didn't know it was poisonous.'

'It depends who takes it, and how much,' Prout said. 'People with diabetes can't produce enough natural insulin in their own bodies. In severe cases, patients have to have regular injections of artificially-produced insulin to keep them alive. Such patients must avoid taking any drug that may inhibit the effect of the insulin. Cortisone is such a drug.'

'Can you buy it over the counter?'

'Technically, no. But there are a lot of sources that bend the rules a bit. It's not that hard to acquire.'

Prout returned to his laboratory, and Connor laid the reports aside. 'Could you kill a diabetic by feeding her cortisone?'

'There's that risk,' Thorneycroft said, 'Mrs Murugan was lucky. She was found quickly, and given expert treatment by the doctor who knew her case.'

'It's another random choice,' Connor said. 'There's no way the perp could be sure that take-away curry would be eaten by a diabetic.'

'True, though curry is the staple diet of Indian people, and they have the highest incidence of diabetes in the world.' Thorneycroft paused, frowning.

'What?' demanded Connor.

'I'm beginning to think,' Thorneycroft answered, 'that this poisoner doesn't necessarily need his victims to die, to achieve his aim. Ben Tifflin and Vabashnee Murugan ingested what was for them poison, but they didn't die. The point is that such attacks are likely to achieve massive coverage by the media. This man is telling the world he's on a countdown course. I believe that the final victim will certainly die.'

'If you're right, we have to stop giving him publicity.'

'That wouldn't defeat him. He'll go to the press himself, if need be, and the public will help him. Dozens of people witnessed the Murugan drama. You can be sure that story's already in print. The media should urge anyone who's stocked up on Bonbouche dishes to turn them in right now to their nearest police station.'

For the rest of the day, Connor was tied up in the routine of the investigation. Thorneycroft devoted himself to making a search of police files, business reports, family histories, and the gossip columns of certain newspapers, in an effort to learn more about the Lenard family. They were, he discovered, abnormally secretive. The reports of their public appearances gave no insight to their private lives.

At five o'clock, an uproar in the corridor announced the arrival of Ronnie Murugan, once more in tears. He thrust into Connor's hands an envelope and a card inscribed with the number 3. It had arrived at his home, he said, by the evening post.

'I demand action,' he shouted. 'It is only by the grace of God that my mother is alive. Now we are sent this horrible card. Why do you not protect us from this maniac? He's a mad dog, you should shoot him before he murders someone. If you can't do the job, they must find someone else. We are citizens, we demand protection.'

When Murugan at last departed, Connor came to talk to Thorneycroft.

'The old story,' he said, 'police incompetence. They want instant arrests. I don't blame them, this bastard spreads fear. I'm scared for my own wife and kids.'

'You're doing everything you can, Liam.'

'Sure, I'm following procedure, running tests, checking on known offenders, while the scumbag is counting down to the next victim. You're the profiler, John, what can we do that we're not already doing?'

Thorneycroft surveyed the mass of files, reports and press cuttings on the table before him.

'To recap,' he said, 'we've known from the outset that the poisoner is targeting Bonbouche. Bonbouche is, in a sense, the Lenard family. They created the company, they've maintained control of it world-wide. They enjoy a prestige, a business confidence, that gives them immense power.

'They are mega-rich. If they want something, they have only to drop a hint in the right ear. They have the world at their feet, but they don't appear to enjoy it. They attend charity functions, they entertain business associates, but I haven't found a single photograph of them at a family party. They seem to be isolationists.'

Thorneycroft pushed the pile of papers aside. 'I repeat, you have done everything reasonable to identify this man. You have established facts and amassed evidence. I'm going to leave the realm of reason, and go for gut-feeling. I feel that this poisoner doesn't care whether these first victims live or die. He is psychotic. He has no feeling of guilt for his actions. He does not ... cannot ... empathize with other people.

'I think that Bonbouche the company is an intermediary target. It's a way to get at the Lenards. I think that his ultimate target ... the person he means deliberately to kill ... is a member of the Lenard family.'

'Which one,' Connor said, 'and why?'

'I don't know. What I do know is that the poisoner is obsessive about Bonbouche, and about the Lenards. We need to know what caused the obsession. These past few days I've been trying to figure out what circumstance or act could make someone determined to kill a member of the Lenard family.'

Connor stared. 'Are the Lenards aware of this?'

'I think they probably are. I think they know what is the cause of the obsession, but they're not going to tell us what they know.'

'They've given us some names …'

'… of people who clearly had nothing to do with the attacks.'

'So they're lying to us?'

'Withholding the truth. They want to handle things their own way, in privacy. Or perhaps they don't dare give us a name that could lead to the poisoner, because he might expose something they see as a greater threat than their own personal danger.'

'You make them sound crazier than the perp.'

Thorneycroft said earnestly, 'we have to talk to the Lenards as a matter of urgency. We should begin with Eva Lenard. She helped to found Bonbouche. According to Rolf, she's frail and takes no part in the business. But Jason says she's tough enough to muzzle the whole family. Set up an appointment with her, Liam, so we can judge which of 'em's right.'

'You're asking me to trust your gut.'

Thorneycroft nodded. Connor sighed, reached for his mobile phone, called up a number and entered it.

'Good afternoon.' His voice was uncharacteristically deferential. 'This is Detective Chief Inspector Liam Connor. May I please speak to Mrs Eva Lenard?' A pause. 'I see. To whom am I speaking? Miss Hester Plum, ah yes, Mr Jason Lenard spoke of you. Would you please ask Mrs Lenard when it would be convenient for me to call on her? It concerns the investigation into the troubles affecting Bonbouche et Cie…. Certainly, I'll wait. Thank you, Miss Plum.'

The wait was not long. Connor lifted a thumb. 'Tomorrow morning at ten o'clock. Thank you that will be very satisfactory. My colleague Dr John Thorneycroft will accompany me. Please convey my thanks to Mrs Lenard.'

Replacing the phone in his pocket, Connor grinned at Thorneycroft. 'One thing about pounding a beat, you learn how to cope with watchdogs. We'll need to clear this with the Super. He'll be OK. He's a gut-feel man, himself.'

XII

COVENTRY HALL STOOD on high ground, facing a double bend of the river. Thorneycroft doubted if its occupants spent much time admiring the view. A thick ring of trees and a high security fence emphasized its owners' love of privacy.

Connor pressed the remote control button at the gate, which opened at once. A pencil-straight drive led them to a house that made Thorneycroft stare. It was a perfect example of art deco, with fluted columns rising from ground to roof, pot-bellied balconies, and scroll-work picked out in contrasting colours. Round it stretched intricate gardens, raked and pruned for winter. Two gardeners were clipping shrubs into elaborate shapes.

'There were live peacocks on the lawn, once,' Thorneycroft remarked. 'I saw pictures in an old magazine.'

Connor grunted. 'Noisy brutes. I wouldn't want them on my lawn.'

They left the car on a sweep of gravel and advanced to a front door that was part carved oak and part stained glass. As they reached it, it opened to reveal a stocky woman flanked by a Borzoi and an Aberdeen terrier. The Aberdeen growled and the woman silenced it with a word. She fixed Connor with a calm, measuring stare.

He smiled at her. 'Miss Plum, is it? We spoke on the phone. I'm DCI Connor, and this is Dr John Thorneycroft.'

She nodded and stepped back, waving them in. She led them along a broad corridor, the two dogs at her heels. Thorneycroft, following behind with Connor, took note of her elegant blue suit, her suede shoes, and the platinum and diamond watch on her wrist. Nothing art deco about Miss Plum, he decided, and nothing from the bazaar. No doubt a companion to a millionairess could afford the best.

Reaching the end of the corridor, she halted at a door and knocked softly. A muffled voice called 'enter' and they stepped into Eva Lenard's boudoir.

There was no other word for the room. The thick cream carpet, the walls hung with shantung silk, the rose brocade curtains, all spoke of an age before plastics and drip dry fabrics. Small tables bore jars of pot pourri, painted ostrich-shells, shagreen boxes, and photographs in malachite frames. Eva featured in all the pictures, always in the company of people of note, royals, statesmen, athletes and filmstars.

Eva herself reclined on a *chaise-longue* near the windows. She was watching a television screen, one beringed hand rummaging in a box of pralines. She made no attempt to acknowledge the arrival of the visitors, but caressed the two dogs, who ran to her side, tails wagging. It was only when Hester placed a hand on her shoulder that she turned her head to gaze first at Connor, then at Thorneycroft.

She was not the beauty depicted in Anigoni's portrait. Fat had blurred the lines of cheek and jaw, and her thin dry hair was dyed an improbable yellow. Her skin had the tautness of too many facelifts, and she affected the heavy makeup of her heyday ... dark red lipstick, white powder, eyelids plucked to a thin arch, eyelashes spiked with blue mascara.

She wore a silk caftan somewhat blotched with food stains, and her small plump feet were thrust into fur-lined slippers.

Hester Plum murmured something that the men at the door couldn't hear, and the old woman used a remote to switch off the television. She swung her feet to the ground, breathing heavily. Hester Plum extended a hand to her, but it was struck aside. Eva Lenard heaved herself upright, and walked slowly to the nearest armchair. The dogs settled at her feet.

Hester Plum beckoned the men forward and announced their names. Eva ignored Connor's outstretched hand, and scowled at Thorneycroft.

'You're a doctor. I don't like doctors. They charge the earth and cure nothing.'

Thorneycroft smiled. 'And they don't do house calls.'

Eva's face twitched. 'They do, for me.' She pointed a finger at Thorneycroft's chin. 'How did you get that scar?'

'Skiing,' he said. No need to mention it was on winter patrol in the Balkans.

'My grandson Jason is an eagle skier,' she said. She shifted her gaze to Connor. 'He told me you asked him a lot of questions, at the warehouse. Why?'

'I'm in charge of the investigation into the attacks made on Bonbouche customers,' Connor began, but she cut him short.

'I know that, but why did you question Jason?'

'Because he is in charge of the Company's supplies, their distribution and marketing,' Connor said. 'I have to understand those processes. I have to know who has control of, and access to Bonbouche goods. I have to discover how and when they became accessible to a poisoner. Your grandson has been helpful. He answered my questions willingly.'

She seemed mollified. 'He's the best of the bunch, he's clever and amusing. He'll head the business one day ... if he can stop chasing skinny gold-diggers. Did you speak to Rolf?'

'Certainly. He applied to us as soon as he learned that young Ben Tifflin had been poisoned by a Bonbouche product.'

'A Sweeney product,' she said sharply, and Connor bowed his head.

'So Mr Lenard told us.'

Her mouth twisted. 'Good for Rolf. He's such a rock. Of course a rock is stationary, it never moves, never grows, never changes. The world changes. Change is inevitable, however much one may dislike it. Why do you want to talk to me? I have no influence over the running of things, now. I've been retrenched.' She waved a beringed hand. 'Sit down, for God's sake.'

Connor took the chair nearest to her. Thorneycroft moved to the side, where he could watch her less obviously.

She's like a child, he thought, asking 'why? why? why?' But she's no fool. Her rudeness is deliberate. She's testing us, seeing how far she can go. Her apparent sloth masks a steely determination to dominate this interview. Her questions are designed to find out what we know and don't know. She's a manipulator, she's spent her life wielding power. She's capable of withholding information and she could persuade her family to do the same. But she won't rattle Connor. He's used to dealing with her sort.

Connor said blandly, 'You're a major shareholder in the company, ma'am, and I'd say your family still relies on your experience, your deep knowledge of the organization you and your husband created.'

She frowned and turned to Thorneycroft. 'And you, Doctor? What part do you play in the three ring circus?'

'I'm a consultant in forensic psychiatry,' he said.

She blew out her cheeks. 'Worse and worse. What are the police coming to? Set a shrink to catch a madman, is that it?'

'Catching him may depend on the help we get from you,' Thorneycroft answered. 'It's obvious the poisoner aims to destroy Bonbouche. I believe he harbours a grievance not just against the company, but against you and your family. Can you think of anyone who might bear such a grudge?'

Her hands, which had been moving restlessly on the arms of her chair, became perfectly still. Her tongue curled over her upper lip. She sighed heavily.

'Rolf told me you thought we might be in danger. It's true we have business rivals, some of them quite ruthless, but I can honestly say I don't see any of them as killers. What's happening is beyond belief.' She waved a hand at the photographs on the table at her side. 'I was a social butterfly, once. Now I seldom leave this house. Most of the people I partied with are dead or in their dotage. I don't have friends, or enemies. I do very well with Hester to keep me company, and servants to attend to the house and gardens. Why would anyone wish to kill me?'

Connor hitched his chair closer to hers, leaned into her space, making it clear he was in charge of the interview. 'What about your family, Mrs Lenard? Do you keep in touch with them?'

She blinked slowly, and again her tongue ran over her lip, as if she tasted the question. 'Why yes,' she said. 'They visit me, you know. Rolf and Jason come often, Fenella, my granddaughter, lives abroad but she comes to see me when she and her Wop minstrels are in England. Silas, my younger son, is a busy doctor.' She smiled. 'I said I don't like doctors, but I make an exception for him.'

She bent to caress the dogs' heads, murmuring to them, and allowing them to lick her fingers.

Hester Plum, who had been sitting quietly in the background, rose to her feet and moved towards the door, and at once Eva jerked upright and snapped, 'where do you think you're going?'

Hester Plum said evenly, 'it's time for your medicine, dear.'

'I don't want it now, I'm busy, can't you see?'

Hester said nothing, merely tilted her head and smiled.

Eva leaned back in her chair and closed her eyes. 'Oh, very well. I'm tired. Take these men away. They can have tea with you if you like.'

Clearly the meeting was closed. Connor and Thorneycroft rose, said their thank yous, and left the room. Hester Plum followed them into the corridor.

'The offer of tea is genuine,' she said. 'If you don't mind waiting in my flat? It's right here.'

She opened a door to her right and led them through. 'Sit anywhere,' she said. Crossing to a glass-fronted cabinet, she unlocked its doors, and lifted out a small box.

'I'll just give Mrs Lenard her medicine,' she said. 'I won't be long.' She went out, closing the door after her.

Connor at once began to prowl round the room. It was comfortably furnished in modern style, the fabrics and carpet of good quality, the pictures chosen to please rather than to impress. Near the window was a formica-topped table on which was a large tray divided into compartments. Each section contained beads of various colours and sizes. On a second tray were arranged needles, threads, and coils of gold and silver wire. A completed necklace of crystal and pearl beads was spread on a square of blue velvet.

'She doesn't wear jewellery, she makes it,' Connor said. 'Calms her nerves, I shouldn't wonder. Can't be a rest cure, looking after that old dragon.'

Thorneycroft didn't answer. He had moved to the medicine cabinet and was scanning the labels on an array of bottles, pots, and pill boxes. Connor came to join him.

'What's this lot?'

'Tranquilizers,' Thorneycroft said, 'anti-pyretics, vitamins, antibiotics, probiotics, laxatives, you name it.' He hesitated, bending to peer at the front row of medicines. 'Digitalis and quetiapine.'

'Poisonous?' Connor asked, and Thorneycroft shrugged.

'With drugs, it's a matter of correct choice and usage. The doctor selects the right medication and gives written instructions about how it's to be administered. Get those two things wrong, and you can be in trouble.'

They heard footsteps in the passage, and moved away from the cabinet. Hester Plum came into the room, smiling.

'Now, what shall it be? Tea, coffee, a cold drink?'

'Nothing, thank you,' Connor said. 'I'd like to ask you a few questions, in connection with the investigation.'

'Of course.' She settled in a chair, hands folded in her lap. Her face expressed polite attention and complete self-confidence.

Connor cleared his throat. 'Miss Plum, I'm sure I don't need to remind you of the seriousness of the situation. Over the past fortnight, three people have been poisoned by food obtained at a Bonbouche outlet. One of the three is dead.'

'I know, it's a very dreadful affair. Rolf and Jason have kept us fully informed, and Eva and I have been so distressed for the victims and their families ... and of course for the company. I can only hope and trust that you will find the guilty person quickly. No-one can rest easy while such a criminal is at large.'

'Exactly, and we're doing everything in our power to identify him and arrest him. Normally, in a murder investigation, the first question we ask is "who benefits from the crime?" But when a criminal is psychotic, his motive is very likely abnormal. He doesn't murder for financial gain, or because his wife's cheating on him. He kills to satisfy abnormal drives.'

Hester Plum nodded sagely. 'A serial killer, Rolf says. However do you deal with such an abnormal monster?'

'We try to discover why he's making the attacks. We're here today to talk to you and Mrs Lenard because for years you have been close to Bonbouche. You might be able to name someone who is hostile to Bonbouche, and to the Lenards.'

Hester Plum started to speak, but Connor held up a hand. 'When I asked Mrs Lenard if she knew of such a person, she said she did not. Perhaps she needs more time to consider the question. I don't want to press her too hard. I know she's in frail health.' Connor was watching Miss Plum closely. 'You are her constant companion. You care for her, right?'

'Yes. We have been friends for years.'

'Then as her friend, persuade her to think carefully about my question, and if she does come up with a name, let me know at once.'

'Yes. I understand.'

'Tell me, what is the nature of Mrs Lenard's illness?'

'I can't discuss that, it's not my position.'

'Who is her doctor?'

Hester hesitated, twisting her fingers. 'As she told you, she doesn't like doctors. We ... the family and I ... have brought in many excellent practitioners, over the years, but Eva is a bad patient. She doesn't follow instructions. She gets rid of any doctor who opposes her wishes. The present man, Dr Joliffe, has lasted longer than most.'

Thorneycroft intervened. 'Would that be Dr Serge Joliffe?'

'Yes.' Hester sighed. 'He seems to know how to handle Eva.'

'He's a psychiatrist.'

'Yes. We thought perhaps she would respond better to him than she did to the previous man, Dr Benson. Eva hated him, he was so abrupt and dictatorial.'

'Did Dr Benson prescribe quetiapine, or was that Dr Joliffe's prescription?'

'Neither. It was prescribed by the man before them. Eva tried it but it did her no good, and it had awful side effects.'

Thorneycroft nodded. 'Yes, it can have. Tell me, does Mrs Lenard suffer from depression?'

'I've told you, I can't discuss her private concerns.'

'A man's been murdered, Miss Plum. The poisoner is likely to make another attack, and the Lenard family could be his target. In such circumstances, private concerns don't count for much. Anything you choose to tell me, as a doctor, I will treat as confidential.'

Hester pressed a finger to her mouth, considering. 'Eva has periods of depression,' she said at last. 'They don't last long. Over the past two weeks she's been under great stress. She's troubled by the attacks on innocent people, she's angry about what's being done to the business she helped to build. And she's vulnerable. Her husband and her friends are gone. She's alone. She's no longer active in Bonbouche. She feels empty and useless.'

'She has her family,' Thorneycroft suggested, and Hester waved an impatient hand.

'They are adults, they have jobs, their own interests, they go their own ways.'

Connor said quietly. 'Miss Plum, you speak as if Mrs Lenard and her family are also your family. You call them by their Christian names. You must be close to them, worried for them.'

She drew a long breath. 'Yes. I am very close to them. I first came to Coventry Hall as a nurse, when Eva was suffering from post-natal depression, after the birth of her second son, Silas.'

'You're a qualified nurse?'

'Yes. Eva was slow to recover, and Victor, her husband, asked me to stay on to help care for the children, Rolf and Silas. When they were beyond needing a nanny, Victor employed me as his personal secretary. I learned a great deal about Bonbouche in those years.

'Victor died in 1973. He was only 43. His death hit Eva very hard. She needed help. I became her companion. Rolf was totally absorbed in Bonbouche affairs. It was hard for him, trying to fill Victor's shoes, but he did it. He also got married, in 1974. There were two children, Jason and Fenella. With Rolf having so little time for them, and Eva being delicate I spent a lot of time with the children. And when Rolf's wife deserted him, well, I found myself being a part-time nanny for the second time.'

'And you stayed on in Coventry Hall.'

'Yes. I took over a lot of the running of the property. Eva never liked household chores, or doing accounts. But they aren't chores to me. I love the house and gardens, and the woods.'

Connor studied her, chin on chest. 'You've been here for over forty years, in this house, with the Lenards. You must know them very well indeed.'

She regarded him levelly. 'Yes, very well.'

'So can you think of anyone who might wish to harm them?'

'No I cannot. They are good people, they work hard, they are creative, they provide things that people need and want, they give millions to charity. Who could want to harm them, who could want to ruin Bonbouche, a company that gives employment to thousands of people around the world? The poisoner must be insane, an insane murderer.'

'Exactly, and that is why you should be afraid for the people you care about.'

She lifted her chin. 'We have excellent security here, Inspector, and if we leave the property, one of the men drives us. As to poison, there's no chance of that being a danger. I know exactly what food and drink is on these premises. I know exactly what the people of the household eat and drink.'

As she spoke a buzzer sounded in the corridor, and she rose from her chair.

'I'm sorry,' she said. 'That means the gardeners have finished pruning, and want instructions. If there's anything more you wish to ask me ...'

'Nothing for the moment,' Connor said, and she smiled.

'Then I'll walk you to your car.'

Connor walked beside her. 'Is giving the gardeners their instructions one of your chores, Miss Plum?'

She nodded composedly. 'Yes, I look after all the staff. I know the routines so well, I can take that burden off Eva's shoulders. Of course, Rolf and Jason keep an eye on things. We meet at least once a fortnight, to discuss expenditure and maintenance. The house is a protected building, you know.'

'It's a fine place. Why was it called Coventry Hall?'

'That goes back centuries. It was owned by a man of that name. The original house burned down in 1900. The land was unoccupied for years, there was no piped water or electricity. Victor bought it and built the present house.'

'Are the meetings you mentioned held here?'

'Sometimes, but usually we go to Rolf's office, or his home.'

'Are you still active in the running of Bonbouche?'

'No. I used to help in organizing their charity events. I know all the best promoters and sponsors. But Minette, Rolf's second wife, is an expert in that field, so I'm not needed there any longer.'

She spoke without sign of resentment. She seemed sure of her position and her competence to retain it.

They emerged from the house to find the two gardeners waiting on the driveway. Their topiary work had produced two swans, a peacock, and an eagle with spread wings. Miss Plum beamed approval.

'Thomas and René are experts,' she said. 'They keep the garden just as Victor planned it. Thomas was a sergeant in The Blues, he runs things. René is a bit slow, not much education, but he's wonderful with his hands. He makes things grow.'

Connor gazed about him. 'So there've been no changes here, then.'

Hester Plum turned a pale blue stare on him. 'Not here. I keep things as Victor planned them ... as Eva likes them.'

Thorneycroft smiled. 'One last question, Miss Plum. Those chocolates Mrs Lenard was eating ... I trust they weren't from Bonbouche?'

She eyed him coldly. 'Neither Bonbouche nor Sweeney,' she said. 'They are handmade Belgian chocolates. Jason brought them back from his last trip. He often brings us little gifts. He's Eva's favourite.' She held out her hand to Connor. 'If you have any further queries, Chief Inspector, please let me know.' She ducked her head at Thorneycroft. 'You too, Doctor. Good day, gentlemen.'

XIII

ONLY WHEN THEY had driven through the gates did Connor speak. 'That place gives me the creeps. It's like a lizard in pickle, everything in place and nothing you want. Old Mrs L is a witch with a nasty tongue. She said ugly things about her own family. Spoiled rotten all her days, I'd say. Sits there on her fat bum, watches TV and gobbles chocolates. It's Plum that gives the orders and keeps things going.'

'She certainly seems to be devoted to her job,' Thorneycroft said.

'And why? Because it gives her money and power. You know the kind as well as I do. Starts as a servant, works her way into favour with the boss, ends up being the boss and owning the property. Something else that struck me, she's a trained nurse with a cabinet full of potential poisons. She makes regular visits to the Bonbouche offices. And she makes jewellery. I had an aunt did that, and she told me it takes steady hands, a good eye, imagination and patience. Miss Plum could open a sherbet toy, load it with aspirin, and get it on to a Bonbouche shelf without too much trouble.'

'Liam,' Thorneycroft said, 'being capable of doing something doesn't mean you'll do it. Why would she attack the Bonbouche empire? As you say, it's given her money and power. I'd like to know if she owns Bonbouche shares.'

'I'll find out,' Connor promised, 'and I'll see if there are any priors on her. I don't trust her. I don't think she was telling the truth when she said she didn't know of anyone with a grudge against the Lenards. Those two could have fixed things between them, Eva could make the plans and Plum could carry them out. They have the cash to procure poisons, and the opportunity to plant them on Bonbouche premises.'

'With what possible motive?'

Connor scowled. 'Don't know yet, but one thing I do know, Eva Lenard was lying when she said she has no enemies.'

'I agree. Her body language betrayed her. When she's relaxed, her hands move constantly, but when she lies she keeps them perfectly still, and she licks her top lip.'

'Very interesting,' Connor said, 'but body language doesn't win court cases. Face it, John, all we got this morning was the feeling that those two birds know something they won't tell.'

'They know of a person or persons who have reason to hate the Lenards.'

'Which is all guesswork, mate. I can't act on bloody guesses. If they know names, why don't they tell us? I warned them their own necks could be at risk. That should be enough to make them speak out.'

'Unless they think that by speaking out, they'll expose themselves to a worse danger.'

'What's a worse danger than being poisoned by a maniac?'

'Well, let's say that one or more members of the Lenard family have been involved in something deeply discreditable, even illegal … something that, if exposed, could threaten the Lenards' hold on Bonbouche. The Lenards certainly won't tell us about it. What we need is to talk to someone who knows the family history, but isn't of the family.'

'Such as?'

'Mrs Zoe Wolpert, formerly Zoe Lenard, Rolf's ex-wife. According to Rolf she ran out on him and their two kids, but I'd like to hear her version of the story. She left Rolf for Ian Wolpert, who designed Coventry Hall for Victor Lenard. She married him, raised a second family. She may have things to say about the Lenards.'

'John, man, I'm supposed to run this investigation by the book.'

'Which you're doing, very efficiently. Zoe Wolpert is an optional extra. Fix an appointment with her.'

'If I can swing it with the Super.'

'I'll buy you a beer.'

Connor relapsed into brooding silence. Thorneycroft leaned back in his seat and closed his eyes. He thought about Eva Lenard, subject to depressions, prone to dumping doctors, complaining of feeling empty and useless, indulging in rudeness more typical of a child than an adult; yet still sharp-witted, and still in possession of a large slice of Bonbouche shares.

He thought, too, of Hester Plum and her rise to fortune; first a nurse, then a nanny to two motherless boys, then secretary to a tycoon ... his mistress, very likely, since his wife was frail and fat and of uncertain temper. And when Victor died, Hester became companion to his widow, virtually in charge of the woman and all her possessions.

Hester Plum lived in luxurious circumstances. She wore expensive clothes, hobnobbed with Eva, Rolf and Jason, had five servants to do her bidding. But ultimately her success was conditional on Lenard approval. If that was threatened in any way, she could face dismissal, and her chances of inheriting Lenard money, or even Coventry Hall, would melt faster than snow on a barbecue.

Hester Plum, as Connor rightly said, controlled a cabinet full of dangerous substances. Morphine, digitalis, quetiapine. Quetiapine was used in the treatment of patients with serious depression; an antipsychotic drug that could reduce suicidal tendencies and the urge to self-mutilation.

What place did quetiapine have in the Coventry Hall pharmacopoeia?

That afternoon the investigatory team met to discuss progress in the case. DCS Hogarth was present and in a bad temper. 'The Assistant Commissioner's singing soprano,' he complained, 'Wants to know why we haven't made an arrest yet. I reminded him, the last serial murderer kept us busy for eighteen months before we nabbed him. How can anyone predict what a crazy pervert is going to do?'

Thorneycroft, finding a seat for himself at the back of the room, thought that Hogarth's question lay at the heart of this investigation. Hogarth, Connor had said, believed in gut-feeling, which meant he followed the promptings of his unconscious mind ... not a process approved by police chiefs, but possibly the only way to catch this murderer.

In the vast majority of crimes, the criminal had an easily identifiable motive, and stuck to a well-known modus operandi. Very often, the detectives on the case could predict what the offender would do next, and how he would do it.

It was infinitely more difficult to understand and predict the actions of a serial killer. Killing satisfied some need in him, but the catalyst that triggered his violence and made him more dangerous than a rabid dog ... that was buried deep in his distorted mind. On the surface he might appear to be a well loved father, a congenial neighbour; yet he could go out some dark night and commit a murder that was unimaginably horrible.

Experienced doctors and policemen advised that one must try to think as the criminal thought; but that was impossible when there was no sanity in his thinking.

What sane person could poison an unsuspecting stranger? The commonest motive for murder was financial gain, but in the Bonbouche case, who gained? Not the company, not its shareholders, not the Lenards.

Yet this poisoner must have a motive, albeit an insane one. He was working to achieve a desired result, following deliberate, if insane arguments. Connor and his team would carry out the routine police procedures – collect and examine the physical evidence, see to the forensic tests, question hundreds of people, study the business factors that formed the background to the attacks, establish times and numbers and places. They would set the parameters of the crime and eliminate from the list of suspects those who were clearly innocent.

All too often though the thinking of a madman eluded these sane and logical procedures. Small wonder that on occasion, policemen applied to psychics to help them locate a body, or forensic psychiatrists to point them to the sort of perpetrator they were looking for.

My job, Thorneycroft thought, is to project myself into this killer's mind, and walk the nightmare path he walks. I must follow his countdown course, focus on the Bonbouche stores and think how to plant poisoned packages in those stores.

He relaxed the brakes of reason, and allowed his mind to drift through the interviews of the past few days. They had haunted his dreams, as he lay alone in his empty house. What stayed with him was not the rational answers given to rational questions, but his sense of the turmoil lying deep beneath the surface in the lives of those questioned.

What was becoming clear to him was that the Lenards were a dysfunctional family, headed by an old woman with a sick mind; a family with a history of neglect, of rejection, and of obsession that in some cases had festered into hatred.

Someone was banging on a table.

Thorneycroft sat up straight. It was Connor, ready to make his report. Thorneycroft settled back to listen.

'I don't propose,' Connor said, 'to repeat what you already know; but to summarise:

'Exhaustive questioning has not established by whose hand poisoned sherbet, mushrooms and curry were placed on Bonbouche shelves, but Malherbe and Ramiah have conducted tests in that regard, and will report the results later this afternoon.

'No members of the Bonbouche Board, staff, or deliverymen have so far proved to have had a part in the attacks, or to possess previous criminal records. The same applies to Sweeney Confectioners.

'Our forensic laboratories have found no trace material on the sherbet box, or the carton of curry.

'The countdown cards left or posted by the poisoner could have been purchased at any of hundreds of outlets in Britain, are sold in such large numbers that no seller has so far been able to point to an individual buyer.

'The poisoner has not made any direct approach to the media since the Murugan incident. The media continue to be supportive of our efforts to warn and advise the public, but public unease is heightening daily, as are strident calls for more and better police action.'

'So what's new?' muttered Abbot.

Connor's smile became satirical. 'I have met the members of Bonbouche's London Board. They say flatly they can't think of anyone who could be responsible for the attacks. The Board, they say is united in its shock and anger, and offers deep sympathy to the victims and their families.'

Sam Koch made a derisive sound, and Connor cocked his head at him. 'What?'

'That all-for-one-and-one-for-all story, sir, it doesn't ring true. Boards are where top-level decisions are made, and there's nearly always argument, Bonbouche is no exception. I've been asking around, and what I hear is that there's been an ongoing dispute between European Bonbouche and its USA counterparts about future company policy. The European sector wants Bonbouche to remain the doyen of gourmet establishments. The USA is pressing for parallel outlets selling machine-produced fast foods, and for a racier, younger image. There's plenty of dissension, believe me.'

'Maybe there's unity in the face of adversity,' Connor said.

'Oh, sure, but it won't last.'

'Can you find out how the London members stand on the issue? Are they united, or do they split, and how?'

'I'm working on it,' Koch said, 'but I have to tread carefully. Nobody's keen to hand out information.'

Connor read aloud a report from DI McGivern, whom he'd deputed to discover where the Gyromitra esculenta might have been bought. McGivern identified three possible sources, two in dockside areas, and one in Camden Town.

'They're procurers, not shops,' McGivern wrote. 'You have first to find a person who can approach them. For money they can get you whatever you want. Their regular customers are weirdos ... perverts, Satanists, witches' covens, Voodoo worshippers.... I may identify a seller for you, Liam, but you know as well as I do that I won't be given the buyer's name. For reasons best known to themselves, such traders protect their customers' identities.'

Connor laid the report aside. 'McGivern will do his best,' he said, 'but I don't pin great hopes on the results. One important point has reached us, though, in connection with the Murugan case. Mrs Murugan has been in hospital for a couple of days. She's given the nurses a hard time, but she's a good witness. She's adamant she bought that carton of curry three weeks ago, from the Hampstead Bonbouche. Which means that the attacks were planned and prepared more than three weeks ago, possibly in mid-November. So whatever triggered them, happened several weeks ago. We'll have to refocus on time scales.'

'How's Ben Tifflin doing?' Thorneycroft said.

'He's made a good recovery, and Mr Tifflin has given up any thought of suing Bonbouche or Sweeney. He's taking his wife and the boy to France for Christmas. Helen Robins phones from time to time, as does her friend the Home Secretary's blue-eyed boy, James French-Holly. The inquest on Jock Robins will be attended by me, Thorneycroft, and Dr Prout. We'll probably get a verdict of murder by person or persons unknown.'

Connor went on to describe the visits he had made to Goldmead

Warehouse and Coventry Hall, and the discussions with Jason and Eva Lenard and Hester Plum.

'They're a cagey lot,' he said. 'We'll keep on at them. But there's another aspect of the case I want to concentrate on, and that's the question of how the poisoner managed to introduce poison into Bonbouche food at their Chelsea, Mayfair and Hampstead branches.

'We've known from the start that the security in the Bonbouche outlets varies: some good, some bad. All the attention in the three stores I've mentioned is concentrated on protecting them against attack from the outside. They have burglar-guards, armed guards, electronic surveillance, alarms to police stations. But the inner systems of the stores played right into the perp's hands.

'I arranged with Mr Rolf Lenard for DS Malherbe and DC Ramiah to conduct tests in those three stores, to try to find out how the poisoner was able to access them and plant poisoned packages on their shelves.

'Malherbe and Ramiah will report their findings to us, now.'

XIV

JUSTIN MALHERBE AND Ayusha Ramiah had donned white boiler suits, hospital boots, and white gloves. Malherbe carried a padded jacket with a hood. He slipped it on and pulled the hood over his head, but left the centre zip unfastened. The jacket sagged open and the sides of the hood hung forward, so that when he was not directly facing the watchers, they could not see his face. He took the jacket off and laid it on Hogarth's table.

'As you see, it's hard to identify the features of anyone wearing this kind of jacket,' he said. 'What Ayusha and I are wearing now is standard issue for all Bonbouche food-handlers. Every handler is given two sets which he retains himself, and which he turns in when he quits the job.

'Every Bonbouche store has three refrigeration rooms; a cool room for fruit and vegetables; a cold room for take-aways for freezing, and dairy products; and a freezer room for meats and ice-creams and long-life take-aways.

'Each store has a supply of cartons used to transfer goods from warehouse to store, nursery to store, or from one store to another. The cartons come in several sizes. The smallest can hold a dozen of the polystyrene flatpacks used for packing fresh produce like tomatoes, beans or mushrooms. Ayusha?'

Ayusha picked up a white cardboard carton in one hand, and a flatpack in the other, and held them up to be seen.

'These items,' Malherbe said, are kept in stock at all Bonbouche outlets ... shops, nurseries and warehouses. Supplies are not allowed to run out. A handler who finds that a pack or carton is damaged can apply for a replacement. It's issued to him by the person in charge of containers at any specific outlet. The controller at all the three stores tested is a woman, an employee of long standing who tends to be lenient in handing out containers.

'Every handler has an identity tag with a name and number, but without a photograph. Tags are handed in to the storeroom manager at the end of the day, and issued every morning. So if you're dressed right, and the manager knows your face, he'll give you a tag for the day.

'Ayusha took the tag she was given to an acquaintance with a print shop, and was able to go back two hours later and collect two copies of the original.'

'So the key,' Hogarth said, 'is getting hold of the right clothes. Getting the identity tag is just a formality?'

'It was, until the attacks started,' Malherbe said. 'Now the system's being changed. But there's another loophole in the system that's not so easily closed.

'The white boiler suits are produced en masse by Pembury Outfitters, who sell to scores of business houses, not just Bonbouche. The boots and gloves are also available from Pembury. Bonbouche buys large stocks, doles them out to employees, and replaces any that look stained or worn. Rejected uniforms are given to employees for a very small price.

'What are special are the jackets. They're drip-dry, fleece lined, and have the Bonbouche logo on the breast pocket. They cost an arm and a leg, and handlers who lose jackets have to cough up the replacement cash, so they're careful what they do with them.'

'It's possible a jacket has been lost or stolen, and the perp got hold of it,' Connor said.

'Yes, sir. It's also possible the perp nicked a jacket, or that some employee said he's lost his, paid up, and kept the jacket, which would be his passport to any Bonbouche store.'

'Right,' Connor said. 'So until recently, there was plenty of opportunity for an unauthorized person to put on the right clothes, and enter Bonbouche premises.'

Malherbe nodded. 'Yes. Dressed right, and with a name-and-number tag pinned to his lapel, he could move around those three stores. He wouldn't get past the gate of the Goldmead estate, or get into a warehouse, but he might well penetrate the storage areas in the stores, walk into a salesroom, and load a package on to a shelf or into a cabinet.'

'The cabinets are locked,' said Hogarth sharply, and Malherbe nodded.

'Yes, sir, but just a few keys are needed to unlock the lot, and the handlers get given them without any fuss.'

'God help us,' Hogarth muttered.

'Are you suggesting,' Connor asked, 'that the poisoner was, or is, a food-handler at Bonbouche?'

'Not necessarily,' Malherbe said, 'although it's clear that he knows his way around the stores. Most of the handlers are long-term employees, and they move around constantly in a day's work. They're skilled workers who know their jobs and the foods and wines they handle. Nobody is surprised to see a handler on the sales floor or in a storeroom. Nobody questions them. That's the trouble with Bonbouche security, there's too much trust and not enough suspicion.'

Hogarth sighed. 'How about the video tapes?'

Connor answered the question. 'They were all checked the day after Ben Tifflin was poisoned. We ran them, going back three months. They all showed handlers moving about, during the day, but not at night. The only people on the night-time tapes are the guards at the doors, and the patrol men inside the building. The tape for November 16th showed a handler clearing out a couple of the past week's sherbet toys and putting in a fresh supply, direct from a Sweeney carton.'

'Was the carton sealed?' Hogarth asked.

'Yes,' Connor answered. 'The tape shows the handler slitting the paper seal, lifting out the sweet-boxes, and arranging them on the shelves. We identified the man by his face and by the tag on his lapel. He's been with Bonbouche for years. We found no reason to suspect him. When he'd unpacked the carton, he took it back to the storage area, and returned the key of the cabinet to the woman in charge. What this all comes down to is that anyone accepted as a handler, could access a locked storeroom, remove an item, stuff it full of poison and replace it.'

'Excuse me, sir,' Malherbe said, 'but I don't see why he'd have to take it from the storeroom in the first place. He need only buy what he wanted from another Bonbouche store, miles away, and doctor it at home. He'd replace the poisoned food in the same package, and just seal it with a gadget you can buy in any hardware store. I think that's how he worked. Once the poisoned package was placed in the storage area, another handler would convey it to the sales area ... do his dirty work for him, so to speak.'

'Which means,' Connor said, 'that the poison could have been inserted a day or two before the package was taken from store to the salesroom. And the poisoner didn't need to take the mushrooms to the kitchen, or the curry to the frozen foods counter. He need only leave the packs in the storeroom, and in time they'd arrive at the table of a victim.'

A silence fell on the room. Connor broke it, turning to DC Ramiah.

'Ayusha, you did the checking at the Hampstead branch. What happened there?'

Ayusha cleared her throat. 'I interrogated the staff there, and, as reported before, they were unable to say with certainty when a particular curry take-away was sold, or to whom. They sell a lot to Indian and Pakistani families, at around Deepavali and Ramadan, quite some time before the first attack was made.

'Mrs Murugan told me she bought her curry three weeks before she ate it.' Ayusha hesitated. 'I questioned her most closely, about when and where she bought it. I thought she was not telling me the whole truth. At first she was quite stroppy with me, you know, but then she admitted she did not actually go and buy the curry from Hampstead. She ordered it by telephone. A nephew of hers works at the Hampstead Bonbouche. He came by motorbike to Mrs Murugan's home, with the curry dish and also a box of ice-cream. Mrs Murugan paid the correct amount and a nice tip.

'I questioned the nephew. He confessed that he just took a pack of curry from the shelf in the cool room, and a box of ice-cream from the freezer, had a proper account made out, and delivered the lot to his auntie. You know, with Asian people, it's a duty to do a favour for an older relative.'

'In my next life,' Connor said, 'I want to be a handler in a Bonbouche store. The perp played the same game there. Put poison in the curry pack, and left it on a shelf for a dutiful nephew to find. Lucky he didn't kill auntie.'

Hogarth heaved himself to his feet. 'Malherbe and Ayusha have done a good job. All we can do is pursue the enquiries. I suggest you all go home and get some rest.'

He made his way to the door. The younger members of the team clustered together, talking eagerly. Connor turned to Thorneycroft.

'You've been very quiet. What's your take on the perp's methods?'

'I think Malherbe and Ayusha are probably right. The poisoner planted his packs in the storage areas of the shops, and left the rest to chance.'

'Risky, going on to Tom Tiddler's ground.'

'Dressed as a handler, with a forged identity tag, and his hood well pulled up, he'd seem to be part of the landscape. It shows he's familiar with the layout and systems of the stores.'

'An employee, or past employee?'

'Perhaps. It needn't be someone so low down the scale. It could be someone in an administrative job, or a Board member ... or a member of the Lenard family.'

'Committing crimes that are destroying the family business?'

'It's not likely, I agree, but it's possible. We'll just have to keep on keeping on.'

'Yeah,' Connor said. 'After all, we've reduced the list of possible suspects from 30 million Londoners, to no more than several thousand who understand the structures and workings of Bonbouche and Company. I'm going home to catch some sleep. See you tomorrow.'

Thorneycroft's drive to Wimbledon was slowed by a clammy mist that swirled between buildings and transformed traffic lights to shifting blobs of colour.

His dark house looked secretive, he parked the car in the garage, locked it in, and made a circle checking exterior burglar-guards.

Indoors, he made sure the security system was operating, and that nothing in the house had been disturbed. He switched on the heating in the living-room and put through a call to Claudia.

It was a long call, Thorneycroft mostly listening to her account of life in Appledore. A walk this morning on a stormy beach; (Luke found a starfish skeleton and wouldn't part with it, I've added it to his cot mobile.) The vicar called; (I'm to do a solo at the carol concert.) Preparations for Christmas dinner; (please say you'll be with us, we miss you so much). Mum and Dad send love and here's

Luke to talk to you; (guggle guggle guggle, then an unmistakable 'Dada').

Warmed as much by the voices as by the oil heating, Thorneycroft made himself supper and ate it in front of the television. He hardly noticed what was on the screen: other images filled his mind. A shadowy figure in a hooded jacket. Hands pouring aspirin into a child's sweet, cortisone into an old woman's favourite dish. He saw the faces of Jason and Eva Lenard and Hester Plum, liars all, and of Rolf Lenard, watching his empire crumble.

The roundabout of thoughts lulled him to sleep in his chair. He was wakened by the jangle of the telephone. It was Connor, speaking from his home.

'Your idea about questioning all the Lenard family,' he said, 'I ran it by the Super and he likes it. He says if Rolf Lenard doesn't want us to talk to his ex, that's all the more reason to do so. Zoe Wolpert and family live in Reigate. I'll pick you up at 9.00 tomorrow. Abbot will drive us, so we can talk on the way.'

The line went dead. Connor was obviously not sold on interviews with the Lenards. Or possibly he just disliked interference in his handling of the enquiries.

Thorneycroft went to bed, and dreamed that a claw-fingered woman in black robes and a tall hat was offering Luke a slice of Christmas cake. He screamed at Luke, 'run away, she's a witch, she'll send you to Coventry'. His voice was a reedy whisper. He could not move. He made a convulsive effort and woke, sweating and shaking.

He told himself that a nightmare was nothing more than an amalgam of his waking thoughts and fears. Reason didn't help. He got out of bed, pulled on a dressing-gown and went down to the study on the ground floor. Hauling the big dictionary from its shelf, he sat at the desk and looked up the word 'Coventry'.

'Coventry, a town of Warwickshire, England. To send to Coventry, to exclude from social intercourse.'

Higher up the page, he read:

'Coven, a gathering of witches, a gang of thirteen witches. (See covin).

'Covin' a compact, a conspiracy, a coven, 'covinous' or fraudu-
lent. 'Covin-tree, a tree before a Scottish mansion at which
guests were met and parted from'.

Just a bloody dream, he told himself. You visited a house called
Coventry Hall. Connor called old Mrs Lenard a witch. A couple of
weeks ago, Claudia nearly bought a Christmas cake from a
Bonbouche store. That's the mishmash that made up your dream.

His professional training reminded him, 'you know better than to
dismiss a dream. Dreams have buried content. You should try to
unearth that.'

He said aloud, 'I'm scared. I've been scared plenty before now, of
being injured or killed, of failing on a mission. I've had nightmares
but they never cracked me up like this one.'

The answer came at once. 'Now you are afraid for Claudia and
Luke. You are afraid you can't protect them.'

He returned to the bedroom and sat on the edge of the bed. He
wanted to call Claudia, but it was past midnight, a call would
frighten them all.

He thought, 'Claudia would pray. I'm no good at praying. The
words don't come out right.' He put his head in his hands.

'God,' he said, 'please look after them for me, and help me to do
whatever it takes to identify and arrest this poisoner.'

He fell asleep imagining Christmas at Appledore with Claudia and
Luke.

XV

LIKE COVENTRY HALL, the Wolperts' house stood on high ground overlooking a river valley, but there the likeness ended. There was no dark woodland here, instead there were exotic trees not yet fully grown. The drive meandered between rhododendrons cropped for winter, to a tennis court and swimming pool, and a modern building painted pale yellow. A BMW, a Mini Sports, and a battered camper were parked near the front door. A dark-haired girl was sitting on the steps, holding a beshawled baby. She raised an arm as the men climbed out of their car.

'Mr Connor? I'm Lynn, Zoe's daughter-in-law. She's in the sun-room. Follow the path that way.' She waved again, smiled and bent to croon to the baby.

Connor led the way along the path that brought them to a glassed-in verandah with a blue-tiled roof. Zoe Wolpert stood in the open doorway, arms folded. She was of medium height, slender but full-breasted, dressed in a blue tracksuit and trainers. Her face was tanned and rosy, without benefit of makeup. Her short greying hair had a natural wave, and her eyes were large and bright and hostile.

'Detective Chief Inspector Connor,' she said. 'And who are these others?'

Connor introduced Thorneycroft and Abbot, and she studied them, chin lifted.

'Three policemen,' she said. 'I must be a desperate criminal.' As Connor opened his mouth to speak, she held up her hand. 'Who set you on me? Rolf, or Eva?'

'No-one set us on, ma'am,' Connor said quietly. 'I'm in charge of the investigation into the Bonbouche poisonings. Three people have already been attacked, and it's possible that the poisoner is targeting the Lenard family.'

Her lips tightened. 'I am not a member of that family. I want nothing to do with them, or their problems. If my husband were here, he'd tell you to leave us alone.'

'I understand that Mr Wolpert is in Canada? The main speaker at an important architectural conference?'

'I see you've been snooping into our private affairs.'

Connor smiled. 'It was on late-night TV. By all reports, Craig Wolpert is a name to be reckoned with. He makes headlines.'

Her bright gaze flickered. She said tiredly, 'Well, you'd better come in.'

They followed her into the sun-room, which clearly was warmed by more than the wintry sunlight. Flowering plants luxuriated on low shelves and beyond them were wicker chairs and tables covered with yellow cloths.

Zoe Wolpert took her place in the centremost chair, and signed to them to sit down. Thorneycroft moved a rubber rabbit from a seat near the picture windows. They afforded a view of rolling lawns, and the valley below.

Connor cleared his throat. 'If I may just ask you a few questions?' he began, but Zoe was watching Abbot, who had taken a notebook from his pocket.

'I won't have you taking notes,' she said sharply. 'I haven't committed a crime. I won't put up with harassment.'

Connor nodded to Abbot to put the notebook away. 'Mrs Wolpert,' he said, 'we are not here to harass you, we're here to seek your help. There's a poisoner out there and we need to know why he's doing these things, why he's attacking innocent people.'

'The Lenards aren't innocent,' she said fiercely. 'Not to me, not to Craig. You're right, Craig's at the top of his profession, but it's no thanks to that pack of hyenas. They did everything they could to wreck his career. He lost important customers because the Lenards badmouthed him. They used their money and their influence to destroy him.'

'They didn't succeed,' Connor pointed out, and she made an impatient gesture.

'Not in the long run, but we had a hard time for ten years. It was Craig's merit that beat them. He was supported by folk who appreciate fine architecture.' Zoe smiled grimly. 'The house he designed for

Victor Lenard is recognized internationally as a splendid example of art deco. The Lenard money can't beat Craig's excellence. Now they have to shut their mouths and leave us in peace.'

Connor tilted his head. 'Tell me, why were the Lenards so hard on you and your husband? Marriages fail, people get divorced all the time. They move on, as you did.'

She raised her arms to hug her chest. 'Yes, I moved on. I married Craig and we have four fine children, five grandchildren. You saw Lynn … she's my oldest son's wife … they're staying with me while Craig's away. I have a fine family. But I lost my first two children to that wicked old bitch.'

'Who?'

'Eva Lenard.' Zoe closed her eyes and drew a long breath. 'You must think I'm as crazy as she is. I've spent twenty years getting her out of my mind and my life. I thought I'd succeeded, but now these poisonings … the stories in the papers … they've brought it all back.' She opened her eyes and stared at Connor.

'I've been over and over it in my mind, wondering if things might have been different. If Victor had lived, he might have controlled her. If Rolf and I had been older … wiser….

'Rolf was her favourite, you see. Eva adored him. And she and Victor raised him to take over Bonbouche. They … created him, you could say, in their own image.

'But Victor developed cancer of the throat. He died in 1973. Eva focussed on her darling Rolf, the king who was going to rule Bonbouche, with her as the Queen Mother.

'Rolf and I were married in 1974. He was 21 and I was 20. We didn't tell anyone, we just got married. Eva was furious. It interfered with her plans for Rolf, and she didn't approve of me. I wasn't rich or beautiful. I wasn't the sort of wife she considered would be useful to Rolf's career. She called me "Rolf's little golf-caddy".

'We started our married life at Coventry Hall. Rolf wanted that. I had Jason in 1975 and Fenella two years later. For a time the children seemed to make Eva happier. She was proud of them, enjoyed them. But as time went on I realized she was taking them away from me. She set the rules in that house, and the rules didn't favour me. She made the decisions about how my children were to be raised. She began to say and do things that put me in a bad light. I tried to keep my cool, but I was young and scared. I felt everything slipping out of my control. I felt helpless, and hurt, and angry.

'I decided that I must persuade Rolf to leave Coventry, and make a home with me and the children. He was very busy at that time, working his way through the Bonbouche structures, getting ready to take charge. That was what he wanted above all else ... to head the company. When I spoke about moving, he said no, it would upset Eva, and she was important to Bonbouche. That was true. Her money, her experience, her power, were more important to Rolf, than me or the children.

'Then Eva found out I wanted to leave Coventry. From that moment on, she set out to crush me. I could do nothing right. She manipulated, she lied, she bribed. Living in that house was like being in some Nordic movie, all darkness and misery. I was desperate. I didn't know what to do, until Craig came into my life.'

She paused, and none of the men breached the silence. 'Craig came to Coventry whenever there was work to be done on the house or gardens. Eva made it a royal command, and he was glad to obey, because Coventry was his creation, and he didn't want anyone else messing it about. Eva used to leave it to me to go round the property with him, and we used to talk about all sorts of things. Craig saw how Eva behaved towards me. She never bothered to hide her dislike of me. He understood what I was going through. He tried to talk to Rolf about it, but Rolf told him to mind his own business and that I was just being hysterical.

'Rolf never stood up for me or the children. You can't imagine what it meant to have someone supporting me and caring for me. I leant on Craig. Eva used to have spells when she wouldn't leave her bedroom. She'd stuff herself with rich food, then vomit it all up. When she was in one of those periods, and Hester Plum was taken up with looking after her, it was easy for me to leave the house. I'd sneak out, and go to meet Craig. We became lovers.'

'Did Mrs Lenard know what was going on?'

'Not at first, but of course she was bound to find out. People talk. I think, in the end, she knew all about Craig and me, but it suited her book. She saw it as a way to get rid of me. She set Hester Plum on to spy on me.'

'You have proof of that?'

Zoe said impatiently, 'Hester was the one who warned Eva that I wanted Rolf to leave Coventry. Hester had contacts in the area who fed her gossip. Hester's a manipulator. She had her plans laid from the moment she came to that house. She wanted money and power and she knew how to get them. She always took Eva's part, she sucked up to the Lenards. She's capable of anything. She was suspected of murder once, but she got away with it. Insufficient evidence, they said.'

Connor shook his head. 'That's a dangerous statement to make, if Miss Plum's name was cleared.'

'It wasn't cleared. They just couldn't pin it on her, but she had to leave her job. That's proof enough, I'd say.'

'Not in law. How did you come by this story?'

'I didn't "come by it", I made it my business to find out. After my divorce, and my marriage to Craig, I thought about what those two women did to us. I knew I couldn't fight Eva, but I could fight Hester. I made enquiries about her. I spoke to people I knew in the nursing profession, and to journalists.

'I learned that Hester had been a nurse in Liverpool, when she was young. She worked at a private hospital that specialized in the treatment of cancer. A patient in her care died. He had cancer of the stomach, it was very painful and he kept saying that he wanted to die. Hester Plum told people she thought people like him should be "helped out". She said euthanasia should be legalized.

'After the man died, other staff members remembered what she'd said. There was a post-mortem, and it showed that the man had taken a huge amount of painkillers. The question was, how did he obtain them? Hester Plum swore she knew nothing about that. She pointed out that the man had had a supply of the drug before he came into the hospital, and that they'd been kept in the bathroom cabinet at his home. His wife said she'd thrown them away, but she could have been lying.

'The hospital enquiry found that there was insufficient evidence to prove how the patient came by the pills, or that he'd taken them deliberately. The inquest declared his death a suicide. There was a lot of talk, and stories in the papers. Hester left nursing and came to Coventry Hall to care for Rolf and Silas, because Eva wasn't well. That was in 1958. She was 23 years old.

'When the boys no longer needed a nanny, Hester began to see to the running of the house. She became Victor's secretary. Everyone knew she was sleeping with him. Victor died and left Hester a lot of money. She stayed on at Coventry.'

Connor held up a hand. 'What was the cause of Victor Lenard's death?'

'He had cancer of the throat.'

'Did Miss Plum nurse him in his final illness?'

'No. He died in hospital. But Hester got the money she wanted. She owns Bonbouche shares, too.'

'Mrs Wolpert, have you discussed Miss Plum's history with anyone else?'

'No. I told Craig, of course. He said forget her, she's in the past, leave her to Heaven. It was good advice and I took it.'

Connor leaned back in his chair. 'So you left Coventry Hall, and went to live with Mr Wolpert.'

'Yes.'

Connor regarded her steadily. 'You left without your children?'

Zoe's shoulders sagged. 'Yes. I tried to hold on to them, while I was at Coventry, but I realized in time that I didn't have the love of Jason and Fenella. Eva had weaned them away from me. After I left to go to Craig, I tried to keep in touch with them, but it was useless. Any approach I made led to one of Eva's rages. Her anger is terrible. She said to me once, "I would rather see the children dead, than with you".'

'A divorce court almost invariably gives the mother custody of young children. Did you seek custody, Mrs Wolpert?'

'No, no, you don't understand. I knew I'd already lost them, I knew if I tried to regain them, the consequences would be horrible for us all.'

Connor looked disbelieving, but Abbot broke his silence, stretching a hand towards Zoe as if to pull her from a raging sea.

'Ma'am, when you left Coventry Hall, were you pregnant?'

Zoe stared at him. 'Yes. How did you guess?'

'You were abused,' Abbot said. 'What the old lady did to you was abuse, worse than physical blows. She abused your mind and soul, and I'm telling you, when we counsel abused women, we tell them to quit, get away from the abuser. You did that. You had another child coming. You didn't want him born in that house.'

Tears filled Zoe's eyes. 'Yes. I felt guilty, but I had no choice.' She rubbed her fingers across her cheeks, touched them to her temples. 'They didn't win, in the long run. Rolf and Eva lost, in the end. Rolf chose his business above me and the children, and now the children care nothing for him, and the business is heading for collapse.'

Thorneycroft spoke. 'Do you ever see Jason and Fenella?'

She gave a faint shake of the head. 'I don't see Jason. He's too busy competing with Rolf for control of Bonbouche. Fenella lives abroad, most of the year. She's married to a singer, a Jewish Italian. They seem happy together. She's made a life for herself. She comes to see me sometimes, when their group is in England.'

'Does she communicate with other members of the family?'

'With Jason, sometimes. She says openly that she doesn't get on with Rolf, or Eva.'

'Does she communicate with Hester Plum?'

'No. She dislikes her, but Fenella is never vindictive. She says that Hester is necessary to Eva, and when Eva dies Hester will be out of there quicker'n a cat can wink its eye. The Lenards won't let her stay on at Coventry.'

Zoe sighed, arching her back. 'I don't know why I've told you all this. You're here to investigate what's going on at the Bonbouche stores. I know nothing about that.'

'You've been very helpful,' Connor said.

She got to her feet. 'What's past is past. I have a good life, a wonderful husband, a happy family. I want no part of the Lenards' saga of misery.'

She accompanied them back to their car. They left her standing beside her daughter-in-law and the baby, who was asleep now in his pram.

As they drove away, Thorneycroft reflected that there were grains of gold in the broken rock of Zoe Wolpert's past. The picture she had painted of Eva Lenard and Hester Plum, biased though it might be, was illuminating. She described the Lenards as a group of people who had no love for one another, who were governed by ambition, greed, and the desire to dominate at all costs. Such a group might well arouse hatred in others, and a desire for revenge; might even incite someone to murder.

Connor echoed his thoughts. 'Zoe Wolpert gave us leads,' he said.

'Malherbe and Davidson must follow up on Nurse Plum's record. Koch can find out more about Rolf and Jason's stance in Bonbouche. If they're in competition, there're likely to be factions, and factions breed folk with grievances against one another, and against the system.' He stabbed a finger at Thorneycroft. 'I want you to tell me more about Eva Lenard's illness. It seems to have antagonized a lot of people. Can you talk to her doctor?'

'Serge Joliffe,' answered Thorneycroft, 'is a society practitioner who won't talk to me or anyone else about Mrs Lenard's problem. But her son Silas is also a doctor. He may be willing to confirm the nature of his mother's illness.'

'If you ask me,' Connor said, 'she's a nasty old bitch, spoiled rotten because she has a lot of cash. Wants her way all the time and doesn't care how she gets it. A mother-in-law from hell. The point is, is she crazy enough to poison a lot of strangers?'

Thorneycroft totalled in his mind what he'd seen, or had been told, of Eva Lenard. The depressions, the binge eating, the irrational anger, the resistance to medical advice, and above all the unstable personal relations, moods that swung her from total love of an individual to total hate and rejection, no grey areas. And there was the quetiapine in Hester Plum's medicine cabinet.

'She's ill,' he said, 'but one interview doesn't give me the ability or the right to diagnose the nature of her illness. It takes a specialist time and care to put a label on a problem of the mind. And the fact is, there are people who are sane in terms of the law, but are impossible to live with – unless, as seems to be the case with Miss Plum, one is driven by very powerful love, or self-interest.'

Connor sucked his teeth. 'I'll be checking up on Victor Lenard's last illness. When he died, Miss Plum collected a packet. I'd like to know why the Lenard crew put up with her.'

'Because she takes Eva off their hands,' Thorneycroft said. 'Hester is essential to Eva, and she looks after the Coventry Hall property, and its staff. I think Zoe Wolpert's right. When Eva dies, the Lenards will get shot of Hester pretty damn quick.'

'What a bunch!' Connor rolled his shoulders. 'All that money, and they don't know how to live.'

'It seems to be a dysfunctional family,' Thorneycroft said. 'That may well be the result of Eva's personality. She's alienated her descendants from herself and from one another. She's created a climate in which malice flourishes ... malice aforethought, perhaps, the deliberate intent to commit murder. But so far, talking to the Lenards hasn't provided us with the answer to who poisoned Jock Robins, Ben Tifflin, and old Mrs Murugan. Perhaps Silas Lenard can shed some light on the dark places.'

'I've been thinking,' Connor said abruptly, 'that it might be better if you spoke to him as one doctor to another. He might tell you things he wouldn't tell a copper.'

'That doesn't fit with the Super's definition of my role,' Thorneycroft pointed out. 'I'm supposed to be the silent observer, who speaks only on matters of forensic psychiatry.'

'This whole case is about forensic psychiatry,' said Connor testily, 'and that's not my field. I have work to do, there's a pile of reports on my desk, I need to talk to my team members, I don't need to waste time chatting up the Lenards. You and Abbot go and see the doctor. Maybe he's saner than the rest. Maybe he'll tell us something we can use.'

Thorneycroft knew that Connor's impatience was justified. The basic investigation had to be carried out with meticulous care; it must find and interrogate suspects, safeguard the chain of evidence, open enquiries, validate statements, and build up a case that would succeed in court.

A forensic psychiatrist, on the other hand, had a much more tenuous line to follow. It was his job to draw a profile of a killer, to think himself into a killer's mind and see the crimes through the criminal's eyes. He must attempt to understand a psychopath, and try to foresee where he would make his next attack.

That night in his empty house, he sat and studied his file of reports and notes on the Bonbouche poisoner. There formed in his mind the sense of someone who was cold, inventive, utterly determined to achieve his goal, and close at hand.

The countdown was proceeding. There would be at least two more victims, and each tick of the clock brought them a fraction closer to death.

XVI

ABBOT DROVE SLOWLY round the square and stopped opposite a solid Victorian façade crowned by a crenulated parapet. Light shone from its lower windows and glinted on fine streaks of rain.

'This is it,' Abbot said. He felt in his pocket and produced a page torn from a glossy brochure.

'From the paediatricians' conference in Berlin,' he said, handing the page to Thorneycroft. 'English one side, German the other. Silas Lenard led the main discussion group on day one.'

Thorneycroft studied the text. Silas Brampton Lenard, he read, was a product of Cambridge University, a specialist in paediatrics, an expert in the treatment of children with learning difficulties, a consultant at Great Ormond Street Children's Hospital. (Just round the corner from here, Thorneycroft thought.) He was married, wife was a fashion designer of note, they had two sons and a daughter. The older son was studying viticulture in France, the younger was on a gap year in the West Indies, and the daughter was married and living in Yorkshire.

There followed an impressive list of Silas Lenard's achievements as a doctor, an author, and a golfer. A success story, though not one in the Lenard tradition. A career that was right in the public eye, person-orientated, curative.

Abbot was peering at the house and its surrounds. 'Money,' he said, 'will get you everything except a blue plate beside your front door, and you have to be dead to get that.' He smiled at Thorneycroft. 'The plan is, I identify us, get us into the house, ask a few routine questions then edge it over to you. OK?'

'OK.'

They rang the front doorbell and were admitted at once by Silas Lenard himself. He was undoubtedly of Victor Lenard's get. He had the same slender build, black hair going grey, a narrow face seamed by sun and laughter, a presence that was immediately felt, a man used to authority.

'We'll talk in my study,' he said. 'We won't be interrupted there, unless you'd like tea, or coffee? No? Then let's get on with it.'

The study was large, equipped with mammoth desk, computer, and well stocked bookshelves. A fire burned in the grate, gas not coal. Over the chimney-piece hung an oil painting of a woman and three children. They looked happy.

The interview began as planned. Abbot asked routine questions which Silas answered comfortably. Then Abbot shifted ground.

'The three victims,' he said, 'have all been poisoned by food obtained from Bonbouche. We suspect that the poisoner is targeting not just the company, but the Lenard family. We're searching for a person, man or woman, who's aiming to settle old scores. Do you know of anyone who might fill that bill, sir?'

For a moment Silas hesitated, as if he searched his mind. Then he said decisively, 'no, but I'm not *au fait* with the affairs of Bonbouche.' He met Abbot's eyes, and said, 'I think I owe the police an apology. I should have got in touch with you as soon as I heard about the attacks.'

'Why didn't you?' Abbot asked, and Silas shrugged.

'I was busy in Berlin. I thought that what I was doing was more important. I phoned Rolf and told him it was up to him and Jason to handle things. It probably seems strange to you, but I'm a member of the family in name only.'

'Did Mr Lenard discuss the attacks with you?'

'Well ... he described what had happened to the Tifflin boy, and I read in the newspapers, some days later, of Mr Robins's death. Rolf is convinced that the attacks are the work of a serial criminal. Is that the official view?'

Abbot passed the reins of the conversation to Thorneycroft. 'The Doctor can answer that better than I can.'

Silas turned to Thorneycroft. 'I know about you, from the reports in the newspapers. You're not a policeman, are you?'

'I'm retained by the police as a consultant on forensic psychiatry,' Thorneycroft said, and Silas nodded.

'Rolf tells me you've been questioning all the Lenards. Did you include my mother in that process?'

'Yes, DCI Connor and I met her and her companion Miss Plum this week.'

Silas's eyes narrowed. 'And what did you make of my mother? Speaking as a psychiatrist, what did you make of her?'

'I can't give an opinion based on an hour's conversation, Dr Lenard.'

'But you do have an opinion?'

Thorneycroft took his time answering. This was, after all, typical Lenard behaviour, seeking to dominate the encounter, using aggression as his best defence.

'Let me ask you a question,' said Thorneycroft, 'does your mother suffer from borderline personality disorder? She displays many of its symptoms.'

'Very good! She was diagnosed as having BPD years ago. She wouldn't accept that she was ill and needed help. It suited certain of my relatives to ignore the diagnosis. I tried to convince her, and them, that she must have proper treatment ... not just medically speaking, but also as a member of a family. I was told to mind my own business. You know, of course, that it's essential in such cases that the illness be acknowledged by both the patient and her support group.'

'When did she begin to show the symptoms of BPD?' Thorneycroft asked.

'When she was a young woman in her early twenties. She was helping my father to build Bonbouche. She was also a society hostess, often in the news. In those early days, her temperamental oddities were regarded as whimsical and amusing. "Amusing" was a key word in the years before World War II. Drugs and wild parties were "amusing", crackpot politicians were "amusing". A dangerous word, as things turned out.

'I realized Eva was ill when I was still just a kid. By the time I was ten, I'd learned never to cross her, always to give her what she wanted. I was a witness to it all ... the spells when she wouldn't leave her room, her terrible bursts of anger, her over-eating and -drinking, She used to take laxatives to keep her weight down, but she still grew fat, and lost her looks.

'I saw the doctors come and go, the friendships wither, the family disintegrate.

'And there was Hester Plum. Rolf and I knew she was my father's mistress. They used a flat in Bayswater. It was terrible, watching her gain influence over him, and becoming more important to him than any of us. Without Hester, we might have been able to get my mother on to a proper regimen of diet and medication. Hester was and is a detestable woman, but now she's indispensable.

'My mother is terrified of losing her support, terrified of being abandoned ... another symptom of BPD, as you know.' Silas pressed a hand over his eyes, as if to shut the gates of memory. Then he looked up. 'By the time I was sixteen, I knew I had to leave that house. For my own survival, I had to get away.'

'When did you leave?'

'When I was eighteen. My father was very ill, unable to deal with my mother's behavioural problems, or control what went on in his own home. I'd always wanted to study medicine. I spoke to my father, and he agreed I should go to Cambridge. He knew that the family was breaking apart. He knew that Rolf could and would see to the business. He couldn't escape, himself, but he helped me to escape. He was in a kind of despair and it drove him to an early death; he just gave up.'

Silas fell silent, and Thorneycroft said quietly, 'did Miss Plum nurse him in his final illness?'

Silas straightened abruptly. 'No she did not. My father was removed from Coventry Hall by his doctors. He spent his final weeks in hospital in Cambridge. I was able to visit him, do what I could for him. I was twenty when he died. He left me a lot of money, in a trust fund. I had no need to return to the family. I ran out, if you like. I qualified, specialized, married and had kids. From time to time, I tried to intervene in family affairs, but it was wasted effort.

'Now I'm able to admit to myself and to the world that my mother has borderline personality disorder. It's caused a lot of suffering to a lot of people. It's broken our family. It's scarred all of us to some degree. But my mother is the chief sufferer. You know that patients with mental instability suffer acutely from depths of depression, the tumult of emotions, the lack of all the certainties that make it possible for people to live happy and productive lives. Of course, her suffering was partly her own fault. She refused to accept that she needed treatment. People like that give their friends and relations little choice.

They can stay and suffer with the patient, or they can break away completely. I broke away. So did my niece Fenella.

'What started out as my mother's "amusing" little whims, ended by costing her her family, and her influence within Bonbouche. My father realized that she couldn't possibly manage the international company that Bonbouche had become. He arranged that Rolf should take over, assisted by Jason when he was old enough. He left my mother a huge income, but saw to it that it would be administered by lawyers.'

Silas paused, then shrugged. 'The damage is done and can't be undone. The sins of her mother have been visited on the daughter, and the daughter's descendants.'

Startled by the strangeness of the comment, Thorneycroft said, 'do you mean that your mother was abused as a child?'

'Yes,' Silas answered, 'by her mother's brother. Her mother refused to believe "Eva's stories". Her parents were appalling people. They cared only about money and status, and spent months at a time out of England, leaving the child in her brother's care. My mother married my father when she was seventeen. Rolf was born in 1953 and I was born in '54. Mother's illness began to manifest itself a couple of years later.'

Thorneycroft saw that Silas would not be drawn further on that subject, and said, 'There is quetiapine in Miss Plum's medicine cabinet. She gave us to understand that your mother was on the medication for a short while. Has she ever attempted suicide, or self-mutilation?'

'No. She sometimes threatens to kill herself, but she's never to my knowledge made an attempt to do so. As for self-mutilation, that is out of her nature ... except that in a sense her behaviour mutilates her whole existence.'

'Were you aware she was on quetiapine?'

'No. I would have advised against it; it can have nasty side effects.'

'Your mother stopped taking it some time ago, but the drug is still in the cabinet.'

Silas's eyes narrowed. 'Indeed? That is a mistake. I'll tell Rolf to see the cabinet's checked, and medications not in use are disposed of. The woman's not to be trusted.'

'You mean Miss Plum?'

Silas gave a sardonic smile. 'My mother and Miss Plum. They both handle powerful drugs as if they were lollipops.'

It seemed that in the matter of medication, Silas was prepared to intervene in family concerns. Thorneycroft found that interesting.

'Dr Lenard,' he said, 'did you know that in her youth Miss Plum was suspected of providing a patient with the means to kill himself?'

'Yes, yes, I knew all about that. She's never tried to conceal the story. I don't hold it against her. She was cleared by a properly-constituted enquiry. And if you're asking if I see her as a serial poisoner, the answer is "no". Hester Plum is far too canny to endanger her very cosy lifestyle. All she has to do is sit tight, and kowtow to whatever goose is currently laying the golden eggs.'

Thorneycroft changed tack.

'Your father committed the Bonbouche empire to the charge of your brother Rolf and his son Jason. They've not broken away from the family, as you did. What's kept them on good terms with your mother?'

'I'd hardly call it good terms. They won't make an outright break with her. She owns too big a slice of Bonbouche shares.'

'To re-phrase; they've survived being part of her circle. How is that?'

'They never allow her to come too close,' Silas answered. 'Each of them has his own fortress. Rolf is totally committed to Bonbouche. Jason follows suit, and he also has outside interests ... sport and women.'

'It seems to me that they have very different ambitions for Bonbouche. Rolf says flatly that the company will remain unchanged in character. Jason seems intent on making changes.'

'Rolf's an administrator. Jason's a buyer and handler of food and wine. They're both brilliant at their jobs.'

'But what if their intentions clash?'

'Then I suppose they'll have to fight it out.'

'Do they fight?'

'Not that I know of. They argue, but I'm sure they both know which side their bread is buttered.'

Silas seemed not much interested in the topic. Thorneycroft tried one last question.

'Can you think of anyone, Dr Lenard, who has reason to make the attacks of the past three weeks?'

'No, I can't. Frankly, I'm too out of touch. My mother detests me, Rolf and Jason largely ignore me, and I close my ears to the gossip of their world.' Silas frowned. 'I think, if there are grudges, they are probably held against my mother. She's quarrelled with just about everyone she knows. But no names come to mind. You should speak to Fenella. She's the one who knows what's going on.'

'I understand she lives in Italy.'

'She's here in London, now. Her group is booked to do Christmas concerts. She'll be staying at a hotel, somewhere. Her agent is Cynthia Stopes, she's in the phone book, she'll be able to tell you where to find Fenella.'

'It's a spider's web,' Abbot said, as they drove away from the house. 'One strand leads to another. That family may be dysfunctional, like you say, but they're all part of the web, and a sensible fly keeps well away from it.'

Back at Concorde Street, they found Connor at his desk. He gave them a baleful stare.

'Negative, negative, negative,' he said, thrusting aside a stack of files. 'Thousands of questions, no answers. I spent the morning in the Murugan's neighbourhood. Nobody hated Granny Murugan, everyone says she's popular. The Hampstead Bonbouche where she bought her curry trashed all their stock of take-aways the moment they heard about Ben Tifflin's trouble, but they can't vouch for anything sold before November 18th.'

'Mrs Murugan bought her lot on November 7th, that's two weeks before Jock Robins and Ben Tifflin were poisoned. She remembers the date because it was her nephew's birthday.'

'So the perp started his campaign before November 7th,' Abbot said.

'Exactly. At least we're getting a time-frame.' Connor leaned back in his chair. 'Did you get anything from Silas Lenard?'

Abbot grinned. 'He spilled his guts to Doc Thorneycroft.'

Connor focussed on Thorneycroft. 'And?'

'He confirmed that Eva Lenard suffers from borderline personality disorder.'

'Which means she's loony?'

'Mentally unstable, disruptive and unable to maintain normal rela-tionships, but not insane. She functioned as a member of the Bonbouche Board of Directors for a large part of her life. She was capable of success in that area, but Silas says she's made a lot of enemies, and is the family member most likely to be the target of a revenge attack. He couldn't tell us who the attacker might be. He said we should talk to his niece Fenella. She's in London to stage Christmas concerts. I checked with her agent. She's now Signora Batista, married to an Italian singer. They're staying at the Towers Hotel, which is—'

'I know where it is.' Connor's green eyes were thoughtful. 'Silas Lenard's a doctor, he knows about poisons, he avoids his family, maybe he's the one with a grudge to settle.'

'I got the impression he doesn't give a stuff for Bonbouche or the family. He wants to steer clear of the lot of them.'

'He still has a lot of shares in the company. They all do. Bonbouche is the source of the Lenard money.'

'The shares are dropping, every day.'

'Sam Koch says that's temporary. He says, every time their shares come on the market, there's a feeding frenzy. He says Bonbouche may be suffering a set-back, but their top brass are confident it'll recover. The main shareholders in Europe and the USA are staying with the ship. Sam's keeping his eye on things.'

'Silas said that Fenella keeps in touch with Lenard affairs,' Thorneycroft said. 'She might be able to name the ill-wishers.'

'Then we might pay a call on her.'

Thorneycroft smiled. 'We?'

'Yeah. We three kings of disorient. Maybe the lady will sing for us, who knows?'

XVII

FENELLA BATISTA'S HOTEL was new, luxurious, and close to the Festival Hall. Connor, Thorneycroft and Abbot, arriving at the agreed hour, knocked on the door of her suite but got no response. The thick oak panels could not quite muffle the sound of a choir singing fortissimo.

'Is she rehearsing?' Abbot asked, and Connor snorted.

'Not with a choir, not in this hotel.' He raised a fist and banged several times. The music continued, but someone approached with rapid steps, flung open the door, and at once retreated to the far side of the room. Fenella Batista was listening to a CD, her back to the visitors.

Connor advanced and spoke her name. He was silenced by an uplifted hand. The music dwindled in volume to a tenor singing a verse of 'Joy to the World'. In the background, a choir chimed a carillon of bells.

The men moved closer, and Fenella turned. Her gaze fell on Abbot.

'It's no good,' she announced. 'It's wishy-washy and flat.'

Surprisingly, Abbot knew what she meant. He said kindly, 'what you have is OK, but you need a bass. There has to be a bass bell.'

Fenella stood clear of the music centre, arms folded. 'Show me,' she said. Connor opened his mouth to protest, but Thorneycroft muttered 'wait'.

Abbot relaxed his shoulders, drew a deep breath, and joined the choir's carillon with full deep notes. Fenella bestowed a delighted smile on him.

'You're right, that's it. Where did you learn to sing changes? How many do you know?'

Abbot grinned back at her. 'Everything from Oranges and Lemons to The Nine Tailors,' he said. 'My dad's a bell-ringer. I help him out sometimes.'

'You have a fine bass voice. That's hard to come by, outside Russia. Why in God's name are you a policeman?'

'It's what I want to be,' Abbot said. 'I sing for pleasure. Ma'am excuse me, but we didn't come here to talk music.'

Fenella glanced quickly at Connor and Thorneycroft. 'Oh heavens, I'm so sorry, my mind was on the concert. We're due to sing that carol, but I knew the arrangement wasn't right. I won't let my mind stray again, I promise.'

This was not a typical Lenard, Thorneycroft decided. Though she had her grandfather's cast of feature, her expression was mobile, her smile warm, and her large grey eyes were alert and amused.

'David's rehearsing,' she said. 'My husband. He wanted to be here, but he can't let the group down. I told him it's probably me you want to talk to. My uncle was with us last evening. He told us about his meeting with you.'

Connor, deprived of his usual introductory sentences, said brusquely, 'Dr Lenard advised me to speak to you. He said you know more about the Bonbouche company than he does.'

Fenella's eyebrows rose. 'That's not difficult. Silas takes care to ignore Bonbouche and its problems. You could say that's his second obsession. We're all obsessive in our family. It's in the genes, I suppose. Silas and I have tried to make our obsessions creative instead of destructive. He's a brilliant doctor, and I'm an OK singer. We both have jobs that bring us into contact with a lot of people, who value what we do. I still have my lows, but the music helps me through them. And I'm very happy in my marriage.'

She smiled at Thorneycroft. 'I've had counselling, you see. As a psychiatrist, you must understand why we Lenards need to free ourselves from our upbringing.'

'I know your grandmother suffers from borderline personality disorder, which doesn't provide the background for a happy childhood.'

'God, no. The worst was that she tried to turn us against everyone, even our own mother. She succeeded with Jason, not with me. I don't hate Zoe. I see her sometimes.' Fenella linked her hands tightly together. 'As a child, I withdrew into my shell. Eva prevented Jason and me from forming relationships outside the family circle. She impressed on us that friends were a fiction, just people after our money. Jason believed her, I didn't.'

Thorneycroft said quietly, 'did your father defend you against your grandmother's actions?'

'No. He was too busy. His obsession is the business. Bonbouche was and is his whole world. It's a lonely one. I pity him, but we have nothing to say to each other. We go our separate ways.'

'According to your uncle Silas, you keep up-to-date with Bonbouche affairs. Is that correct?'

'I have a spare-time interest, yes. I have enough of my grandfather in me to like the world of business. I also have a lot of money in Bonbouche. I keep an eye on my investments.'

'And now that those investments are under attack, what is your reaction?'

'Well, naturally I'm concerned for the company, but that's nothing compared to my concern for the people who've been poisoned. That is atrocious. Monstrous.' Her eyes were sombre. 'Silas told me that when the attacks started, you thought it was the work of a serial killer with a compulsion to destroy Bonbouche, but now you believe it could be a campaign against us Lenards.'

Connor leaned towards her. 'It's our job to consider all the possible motives for the attacks. One of them might be that the perpetrator's targeting a member of your family.'

Fenella grimaced. 'That's a frightening thought.' She paused. 'Silas thinks the most likely target is my grandmother. She's made so many enemies in her life. But I can't believe she's done anything bad enough to merit such terrible vengeance.'

'The killer is mad,' Connor said. 'He's killed a public benefactor, and endangered the lives of a child and an old woman. Are you on good terms with your grandmother?'

She shook her head. 'When I cut free, she wrote me off. If you don't toe the line, you're out. When my father married my mother against Eva's will, she turned against him. She had to find a new pet to fill the void. Jason's it. He sees her regularly.'

'How does he like being the blue-eyed boy?'

'Well enough, I'd say; it has benefits. Jason doesn't feel the weight of her tantrums. She's at her best with him. And of course there are material benefits. She's made it plain that he is to be her heir. Money's important to Jason, not just in his private life, but because of the business. He believes that a big chunk of the Lenard money must be ploughed back into the company.'

'You father and brother are at the head of British Bonbouche, aren't they?'

'Yes.'

'Does that make difficulties?'

Fenella's bright gaze sharpened. 'What do you mean?'

'Is there rivalry between them?'

'If you mean, will Jason challenge my father as head of the company, no, he won't. Jason doesn't want to be chairman. The position entails too much admin work, too many boring meetings. Jason likes to travel, initiate, experiment.'

Connor, mindful of the rules of interrogation, hesitated, but Thorneycroft had no such scruples. 'From what your brother told us,' he said, 'he would like to transform Bonbouche from a haven for gourmets to something more appealing to the *hoi polloi*. Your father, on the other hand, is adamant that there will be no changes in image or policy. Could that be a cause for dispute?'

Fenella looked amused. 'Dr Thorneycroft, there is always dispute in the business world. It's part of the dynamics. It brings in new ideas, and new blood. Of course, it has to be handled right. The strength of any company can be measured by its ability to turn dispute into profit.'

Thorneycroft sensed that she was deliberately playing down the differences between Rolf and Jason Lenard. He suspected it was Jason she wished to protect. He probed deeper.

'Have your father and brother reached a settlement of the dispute? Will Bonbouche change, or remain the same?'

Fenella met his eyes. 'You will have to ask them about that.'

Connor took up the cudgels again. 'We will ask them, Signora. My question to you is, do you know of anyone who might commit these crimes, either as revenge against the Bonbouche company, or against a member or members of the Lenard family?'

Fenella took her time answering. 'I'm not sufficiently in touch with the history and structures of Bonbouche to know if anyone would try to destroy it by murdering its clients. I agree with Silas that the most likely person to be targeted out of personal hatred, is my grandmother, Eva Lenard. She's made enemies.'

'Can you give me names?'

She shook her head slowly. 'I cannot think of anyone bitter enough, or crazy enough, to murder innocent people, just to get back at Eva. The people she's injured are mostly dead and gone, by natural process. She's an old woman. Why would anyone wait so long to take revenge?'

Connor eyed her steadily. 'Likely or unlikely, does any name come to mind, Signora? I must remined you that the poisoner may well be planning other attacks. We need you to be completely frank with us.'

Fenella closed her eyes. Thorneycroft guessed that she was debating whether to answer the question, or ignore it. At last she turned to face Connor. 'I have never been close enough to my grandmother to judge who liked and who loathed her.'

'Can you think of anyone who might have that ... insight?'

Again she hesitated. 'Perhaps, Peter Noble,' she said. 'As a young man he joined the firm of lawyers who acted for Bonbouche. That was way back, in Victor Lenard's time. Victor and Eva were very fond of him. In time he became head of the Bonbouche legal team. After Victor died, Peter had charge of the trust that handled Eva's personal finances.

'He did that job marvellously well. Eva had complete confidence in him, as did Rolf, and Jason, and I.'

'And your uncle Silas? How did he feel about Mr Noble?'

'Silas had ... has ... his own lawyers. But he liked Peter. Peter was a peacemaker and a counsellor to us all. He might be able to answer your question about Eva's potential enemies.'

'Do you have Mr Noble's current address?'

'The last time I heard, it was 17 Tekla Close Mansions, in Mayfair.'

If Connor saw significance in the word 'Mayfair', he gave no sign of it, merely saying casually, 'is Mr Noble still part of Bonbouche's legal team?'

'No. He retired in 2002. His health wasn't good.'

Fenella's tone warned that she would say no more on the subject of Peter Noble, and Connor didn't press her.

'One last point,' he said. 'Your grandmother has a companion, Miss Hester Plum. My information is that she has been a part of Mrs Lenard's household for many years. She also has shares in Bonbouche. Does she influence the policies of the company?'

'I have no idea.'

'Are you on good terms with Miss Plum?'

'I'm not on any terms with her. I don't much like her, but she's essential to my grandmother's well-being. I'm grateful for her presence.'

Abbot, who had been sitting in the background, taking notes, suddenly spoke:

'Ma'am, Miss Plum was once your grandfather's secretary. She must know a lot about the company. If there was a dispute between your father and your brother, would she take sides?'

Fenella smiled. 'Miss Plum doesn't take sides, Sergeant. Or rather, for Hester there's always only one side, and that's her own. At the moment, her interest lies in keeping Eva happy. Which means, she stands by Eva at all times. But if that interest were to change, she'd change with it.'

'An opportunist?' Connor said, and Fenella shrugged.

'Aren't we all?'

Connor posed a few more questions, about Fenella's own activities over the past few weeks, then brought the interview to an end.

Fenella saw them to the door. Her last words were for Abbot. Stabbing a finger at his chest, she said, 'you're right about the bells, I'll bring in a bass. As for you, you should be a singer, not a cop. If ever you want to change your profession, let me know.'

Riding down in the lift, Connor said, 'Mr Peter Noble lives a hundred yards from the Bonbouche where Jock Robins acquired his last meal. He's been mixed up in the Lenard/Bonbouche affairs for half a century. What's more, La Batista knows something about him that she didn't tell us. They all protect one another. Don't they realize there's a murderer out there, and maybe one of them's at the top of his hitlist?'

Thorneycroft made no answer. He shared Connor's frustration and fear, but he saw no way to break down the Lenard reticence. They were programmed to live to themselves. They took no advice, answered no unwelcome questions, and made their decisions with an unbelievable and foolhardy arrogance. They would not depart from that pattern, not even to save their own lives; and the sands in the timer were running very low.

*

As they entered the ops room at Concorde Street, Connor button-holed DC Davidson.

'Check if there's a Mr Peter Noble at 17 Tekla Close Mansions, Mayfair, and get me his contact numbers. If he's moved trace him.'

Davidson moved off and his place was taken at once by Sam Koch, brandishing a sheaf of computer print-outs.

'Answers to my queries about the management structures of Bonbouche and Company,' he announced.

Connor eyed the sheets with misgiving. 'Get to the point, Sam, time's short.'

The men sat, Koch perching on the edge of a desk. 'My first question,' he said, 'was "how secure is the hierarchy of the company in the United Kingdom?" Answer, "very secure; the London Board is senior to all other structures, here in Europe and in the USA, Rolf Lenard is in the driving seat of the London Board, and there's no move to eject him".'

'Says who?' demanded Connor.

'Reliable witnesses,' Koch answered. 'Commercial Division spoke to banks, business leaders, people who know the movers and shakers. Rolf Lenard is supreme at his job, and he also happens to be one of the richest men on earth. No-one's keen to jostle his elbow.

'However,' Koch raised a cautionary hand, 'in the USA he's not quite so popular. There are tycoons there who'd like a bigger slice of the Bonbouche cake.'

'Do they aim to get rid of Rolf?'

'Not that, precisely. The wiseacres say, "don't quote me, but the fight's not about top position, it's about policy". The European interest groups want Bonbouche to stay the way it is, supplying the beautiful people with the best food and drink in quiet elegant surroundings.

'The USA buffs, on the other hand, fall into two camps. Some of them support the present style of Bonbouche, but there's a body of younger shareholders who want to diversify, they want to set up outlets for fast foods for the masses, wines that are good but within the reach of the middle-incomes. In other words, they favour a style that's modern, cool, and very lucrative. Jason Lenard favours this second option.'

'But will Jason cross swords with Rolf?'

'Some say he will. He has a following on both sides of the Atlantic. But the poison attacks have produced the result you'd expect. Bonbouche is under threat, so everyone has had to pull together and not rock the boat.' Koch tapped the print-outs. 'The facts and figures show that, for the moment, there are no cracks in the Bonbouche façade. Which means, doesn't it, that the perp's failed in his objective. Bonbouche won't go down. Staff, office-bearers and shareholders will stick together and see the company right.'

'Do you have the names of these movers and shakers, in Europe and the USA?'

'The ones we've identified are here, in the reports.' Koch rubbed a finger down his nose. 'I don't have the Deep Throats, here or over there.'

'What d'you mean, "deep throats"?'

'In all these world-wide operations,' Koch said, 'there are facilitators, advisors, information sources and seekers, spies who pass info. for love or money. I'd be surprised if Bonbouche is any different. If we can find who ferries the crap across the Atlantic, we might learn what's going on at the bottom of the deep blue sea.'

'So tell Commercial to get on with it.'

Koch sniffed. 'I asked them politely, sir, and they told me it's easier said than done, secrecy's the name of the game, they're working on it but it takes time.'

'Time, time,' muttered Connor, 'time for more people to die.' He saw Davidson approaching, and waved Koch away. 'I'll chivvy Commercial, you keep up the good work.'

Davidson handed Connor a slip of paper. 'Mr Noble's still in residence,' he said. 'I called the apartment. Some kind of watch-dragon said I couldn't talk to him, and slammed down the receiver.'

Connor pulled a telephone towards him, and punched numbers. A high, quacking voice answered, loud enough to be heard across the room.

'Mr Noble's residence.'

Connor shifted the receiver further from his ear. 'I am Detective Chief Inspector Liam Connor of the Metropolitan Police, ma'am. May I please speak to Mr Peter Noble?'

The quacking rose to a shriek. 'No you may not. He is ill.'

'Indeed? I'm sorry to hear that. Would you please give him a message ... no, no, I understand, but this is an urgent matter. Kindly ...'

The quacking became incoherent, and then, surprisingly, stopped altogether. Listening, Connor smiled.

'Mr Noble? I'm very sorry to disturb you, sir. I was not aware of the circumstances ... yes, that's correct, I'm in charge of the investigation. Mrs Fenella Batista suggested you might be able to assist us ... yes, it is vital. We fear there may be other attacks ... of course, I understand, but any information you can give us will be very much appreciated ... yes, whenever and wherever it's convenient for you. Yes, that will be fine. We look forward to it, and thank you for your co-operation.'

Connor replaced the receiver, wry-faced. 'He'll see us, but don't get your spirits up. Noble had a triple heart-bypass, the first week in November. He returned home from convalescent hospital three days ago, and he's still recuperating. There's no way he could have committed or even organized the poison attacks.'

'He may be able to supply us with the names of the key people in the USA,' Thorneycroft suggested, but Connor shook his head.

'According to Davidson, Noble stopped practising law six years ago. He broke all ties with Bonbouche. In big business, six years is a long time. I doubt he can tell us anything about Bonbouche's present operators, or their undercover deals. Still, he's better than nothing. We'll be in his area tomorrow morning for the Robins inquest. Mr Noble will see us at two o'clock tomorrow afternoon.'

XVIII

CONNOR AND THORNEYCROFT arrived early at the back door of the building where the inquest on Jock Robins was to be held. They had to push their way through a crowd of officials and onlookers to reach a place in the courtroom. The press gallery was already full, and two of the observers' seats were occupied by Rolf and Jason Lenard. Rolf sat quietly, head bowed. Jason, seeing Thorneycroft, raised a hand in greeting.

Thorneycroft was no stranger to courts called to pronounce on violent or unnatural death. He always found the experience distasteful, not because of the legal process involved, but because of the ghoulish interest it aroused.

Glancing along the rows of seats, he saw that Ben Tifflin's parents were present, seated next to Helen Robins. There was no sign of the Murugans. Sensible of them, he thought. Inquests didn't give closure. They simply described in cold words the events that had led to the death of a victim, whether by accident, suicide or murder. The bereaved, who asked the questions 'by whose hand?' or 'why?' very seldom got answers.

Connor sat with shoulders hunched, looking often at his watch. 'Carolus is a good man,' he said, 'he won't beat about the bush.'

The coroner Carolus was small and gnomish, entirely bald, with a sharp dry voice and a down-turned smile. He opened proceedings by expressing his condolences to Helen Robins, and commending her for her promptness in bringing the circumstances of her brother's death to the attention of the authorities.

He then set the parameters of the inquiry, and set it in motion.

Primary facts had to be established. Witnesses from Bonbouche testified that on Friday, 17th November, Mr Jock Robins had been served and had consumed a meal of Bonbouche food and wine. Helen

Robins described how he had been taken ill that same night, and several doctors reported on his original symptoms and medications, his brief recovery, relapse and death in the clinic on Wednesday, November 22nd. Those present in the court, being already in possession of these facts, sat with quiet attention.

But when Helen Robins related how, a few days later, she had read of the poison attack on Ben Tifflin, and had decided she must seek an autopsy on the body of her brother, there ran through the courtroom that frisson that Thorneycroft detested; the excitement aroused by the scent of blood.

Mr Duncan Brews, pathologist, gave details of the autopsy he had performed on the dead man, and delivered, first in medical jargon and then in plain English, his observations, tests and final report. He gave it as his opinion that Jock Robins had died as the result of consuming poisonous mushrooms, allegedly contained in the meal supplied by the Mayfair Bonbouche, which was located in the same building as Mr Robin's flat.

Up to this point the coroner had contented himself with clarifying statements made by witnesses. Reaching the subject of the mushrooms, however, he became much more punctilious, making sure that the mushrooms had been brought to Mr Robins's apartment from the Mayfair Bonbouche kitchens, by Bonbouche employees; he verified that Robins had consumed the mushrooms, and was poisoned by them.

Was there any chance, Carolus asked, that Mr Robins had obtained the mushrooms from some other source? No, said the Bonbouche chef, he had personally placed them on the tray, lifted them from the serving dish to Mr Robins's plate, and watched him eat them.

Lawyers rose to repeat questions and make points. Duncan Brews was recalled, and asked if by any possible chance he might interpret the death as accidental ingestion of a potentially poisonous substance. He answered bluntly, 'it is not my job to say if it was accident or no. I have just to identify the cause of death.'

'Which was?' prompted Carolus.

'The collapse of the patient's kidney – and heart-function, brought on by the ingestion of poisonous mushrooms, probably Gyromitra esculenta. My initial view was that Mr Robins might have come by the mushrooms by accident, but three days after his death, there was wide publicity about the serious illness of a boy who had swallowed aspirin in a Bonbouche sweetmeat. Miss Robins reminded me of the story, and indeed I needed no reminding. The circumstances of the Tifflin incident made me consider very carefully what I wrote in my report. I could not in good conscience suggest that Mr Robins's death was accidental.'

A buzz went round the courtroom, and under cover of it, Connor murmured, 'I'd have thought the Lenards would have got their legal eagles to push the idea of accidental ingestion, but they don't seem to be trying to do so.'

'Better not,' Thorneycroft said. 'They acknowledge they've been used as a vehicle. That doesn't make them guilty of a crime.'

Next to take the stand was the police pathologist, Dr Prout. Asked to report on the forensic tests run on the sherbet eaten by Ben Tifflin and the curry eaten by Mrs Murugan, he confirmed that the sherbet had been heavily laced with double-strength aspirin, and the curry with cortisone. It was his view that the alterations had been deliberate, and malicious in intent.

'Ben Tifflin and Mrs Murugan might have died,' he concluded, 'had there not been doctors on hand to pull them through.'

At the end of a long morning, Connor took the stand. He reported that in each of the three poison attacks a card had been delivered to the victim's family and that the cards had been numbered in countdown order, namely; 5, 4, and 3. He related that shortly before Mrs Murugan ate the poisoned curry, an unidentified person had called The Challenger newspaper promising a 'hot and spicy story', and that an anonymous letter had been sent to the Concorde Street police station, threatening further attacks.

The verdict delivered by the coroner was that the death of Mr Jock Robins was murder by person or persons unknown.

Once the hearing was over, the press and public galleries emptied quickly. Connor and Thorneycroft lingered to talk to Dr Brews, who had a question for Thorneycroft.

'Why,' he asked, 'would anyone choose mushrooms as a means of committing murder? So unreliable. Mushrooms don't contain a regulated amount of toxin, they're of different sizes, they vary in the strength of the toxin they contain. Why did the poisoner choose mushrooms?'

'I think, for the publicity value,' Thorneycroft said. 'The story's been on the front page of every important paper.'

'You think the killer is just a publicity-seeker?'

'No, but if we know why he wants publicity, we'll know who he is.'

Leaving the building among the tailenders, Connor and Thorneycroft found Mr and Mrs Tifflin waiting on the pavement. Mrs Tifflin came to bar Connor's path.

'I want to talk to you,' she said. 'I want to know what you're doing to catch that murdering swine. The police are useless. You let him get away with murder, you let him poison innocent people.'

Her husband put an arm round her shoulders, but she shook herself free and struck Connor's chest with her fist. 'Why don't you catch him? I can't sleep. I can't think of anything but him. He could come back and try again, he could try to kill my child, my only child. You don't know what it's like, you don't care, useless, useless....'

Tears were streaming down her face and she was trembling violently. Connor tried to catch hold of her hands and she kicked his shins, threw back her head and screamed. Paul Tifflin called her name and she turned and struck him across the face.

Thorneycroft stooped, lifted her bodily off her feet, and carried her to the steps of the court-house. Setting her down, he held her shoulders, forcing her to face him.

'Linda, listen. Listen to me. Ben is safe. You are all three safe. It's all right Linda. It's all right.' He kept on repeating the words until she stopped screaming and dissolved into shuddering sobs. He found a handkerchief and mopped her eyes and nose. She pushed his hand away.

'Nobody's doing anything,' she sobbed. 'Paul promised he'd take those shop people to court. He hasn't done it. Nobody cares. I read the papers, there's nothing, no-one's been arrested. No-one. Nothing.'

'They will be,' Thorneycroft said. Paul Tifflin came and stood behind his wife, putting his arms round her. To Thorneycroft he said, 'I'm sorry. She doesn't mean it. We know the police are making every effort, but she can't sleep, you see, not even with sleeping pills.'

'She's suffering from stress,' Thorneycroft said. 'It's understandable.'

Paul Tifflin murmured to Linda, coaxed her to walk with him to their car. She sat slumped in the passenger seat, covering her face with her hands.

Connor came to join Thorneycroft. 'Why did she have to go off at us like that? Doesn't she know we have kids of our own.'

'She should be in hospital,' Thorneycroft said. 'Post traumatic shock, the anger stage.'

They started to move towards their own car, when they heard a voice calling them.

'Dr Thorneycroft … Inspector …'

Turning, they saw Helen Robins walking towards them. 'I wanted to thank you,' she said, 'both of you, for your efforts during these past dreadful weeks. James French-Holly has told me how hard you've been working to bring this man to justice.'

Connor took her outstretched hand. 'Thank you. I know this has been a very hard time for you. And today must have been hard, too, bringing it all back to you.'

'Yes, it was hard, but it's a comfort, knowing that the law is there to support us. I spoke to Mr Carolus, afterwards. I wanted to know when I'll be able to hold the funeral service for Jock. He said, not too long now. We will have the service at Abinger Hammer, in our family church. That's another comfort, my church, and all our friends.'

They had drawn level with a Daimler sedan and a uniformed chauffeur stepped out and held the rear door for her. She settled in comfortably, smiled and raised a hand in salute, and was driven slowly away.

Connor said, 'rain or shine, I'll be attending that funeral.' He glanced at the court-house clock. 'We've time for a bite before we're due at Peter Noble's.'

XIX

PETER NOBLE RECEIVED Thorneycroft and Connor on the enclosed balcony of his apartment. A narrow street afforded a glimpse of the park, bare and purplish trees shrouded in rolling mist.

Lying on a lounger, wrapped in rugs, he looked frail, but his hazel eyes were full and bright, and his smile was challenging rather than welcoming. He waved aside Connor's appreciation with a flick of thin fingers.

'I'm glad you're here,' he said. 'I've been deeply disturbed by what's happening at Bonbouche. I'm afraid Hannah gave you a hard time. She can't understand that I find it much more stressful to be kept in the dark, than to know the truth. Let's get straight to business, Chief Inspector. Bring your chairs closer, it saves me effort. What can I do for you?'

Connor said, 'how much have you been told about the poison attacks, sir?'

Noble pursed his lips. 'I read the newspapers, and I spoke to Rolf Lenard as soon as I could get my hands on a telephone. Rolf brought me up to date, described the three attacks and the progress of your investigations. He said you fear further attacks, following this countdown pattern.' The bright gaze shifted to Thorneycroft. 'I imagine the guilty person is insane?'

Thorneycroft nodded. 'Yes. Which doesn't mean he's short on intelligence.'

Noble smiled. 'Thank you. I see that a forensic psychiatrist is a useful addition to a police team. Tell me, then, Rolf insisted that we are dealing with a serial killer, but reading the reports, it struck me that there's been only one death and a singular lack of blood-letting. Does that square with Rolf's definition?'

'I don't think he's a serial killer in the accepted sense. He's planning and committing a series of poison attacks on people who patronize Bonbouche. It's not clear whether he's targeting the company, or its owners. Nor is it certain that he has murder in mind. Jock Robins's health was poor. The mushrooms he ate might not have killed a man in better physical condition.'

'Robins did die,' said Noble grimly. 'A man of value to the community was poisoned at random, like a rat.'

'Did you know him?'

'Not personally, but by repute. His death is an offence against humanity.'

'Isn't all murder?'

'I suppose so, if you're considering ethics. Some victims are a greater loss than others. But you're not here to listen to my views on the value of human life.'

Connor spoke. 'You worked for many years with Rolf and Eva and Jason Lenard. Powerful individuals, with an overriding interest in the Bonbouche company. Could they perhaps be targets for a killer?'

Noble ducked his chin on to his chest, considering his answer.

'The Lenards,' he said, 'have a genius for alienating people.'

'Can you name any of those people, Mr Noble?'

Noble sighed. 'I can name dozens of folk who resent or dislike the Lenards, but I cannot think of one who would poison a public benefactor, a child, and an old woman, just to get back at the Lenards.'

The words raised an echo in Thorneycroft's mind, but he couldn't for the moment think why. He said:

'You worked for a long time with Rolf and Jason Lenard ... who have, according to Fenella Batista, an obsessive interest in the Bonbouche company. They must surely have some enemies in the business world?'

'Rolf and Jason are entrepreneurs,' Noble replied. 'The type isn't uncommon, men to whom the business world is all-important, who pour their talents and their strengths into their work, and have little time for normal pursuits, wife, girlfriend, child even.'

'I asked if they have made enemies.'

Again Noble hesitated. 'They are both products of a broken family,' he said at last. 'They learned young that to survive they must be thickskinned, ruthless and use their survival skills.'

'How would you describe those skills?'

'Constant watchfulness, the ability to detect and forestall hostile moves, the ability to think and react faster than one's opponents, the ability to bear loneliness ... even to seek it deliberately.'

'Qualities like that are liable to attract enmity.'

'Yes.' Noble's voice was sad. 'I've known a number of tycoons in my time, and the majority of them have been brilliant at the job of making money and handling power. Most of them have been ruthless, manipulative, and abusive of the rights of others. Most of them have had enemies.'

'It's been suggested that Mrs Eva Lenard might be a prime target for a revenge attack.'

Noble's smile was sardonic. 'There are certainly droves of people who've crossed swords with Eva ... I'm one of them ... but none of us has ever tried to kill her.' He paused, scrutinizing Thorneycroft's face. 'Are you aware of the nature of Mrs Lenard's illness?'

'Yes. She suffers from borderline personality disorder. Not a sociable condition. You say you crossed swords with her?'

'Only in self-defence.' Noble seemed to be recalling events long past. 'When Bonbouche was in its infancy,' he said, 'I was a junior lawyer in the firm retained by the company. Victor and Eva Lenard took a shine to me. As time went on, I became leader of the legal team, and after Victor died, I was also in charge of the trust that administered Eva's personal fortune.

'You could say that I grew old in the service of Bonbouche and the Lenards. The trouble came with the arrival of the millennium. Bonbouche had always catered for prestigious events, and as 2000 AD drew near, its branches all round the world made plans to be part of the celebrations.

'Here in London, Bonbouche was contracted to provide the food and wines for a magnificent banquet, which was to bring together the cream of society: royals, film stars, sports stars, politicians, business leaders, etcetera.

'Eva was still at that time on the London Board of Directors. It was a courtesy membership. She seldom attended meetings, but as the century turned, she developed a burning ambition to be queen of the ceremonies. She not only came to meetings, she tried to dominate them. When she wasn't listened to, she threw furious tantrums, called names, and issued threats, the most inflammatory being that she would sell her very large slab of Bonbouche shares, or give them away to Jason.

'"Jason won't have to wait till I'm dead to get my money" she said, and she started a campaign to dictate what entertainment was to be provided at the banquet.

'Rolf did his best to calm her down. He pointed out that Bonbouche would provide the menu that the sponsors wanted, but would have no say whatsoever in how the guests were entertained.

'Eva flew into a screaming rage. She slated Rolf, and me, because I upheld Rolf's opinion. I went to see her at Coventry Hall. I warned her that if she continued to behave so hysterically, she would not be voted on to the Board at the forthcoming AGM. I urged her to leave the millennium problems to younger folk. I reminded her that the doctors wanted her to stay home and rest.

'Eva not only ignored my advice, she threw me out of the house. And when, as I'd warned, she was dropped from the Board, she accused me of influencing the vote, of treachery, and of attempting to embezzle money from her trust fund. She took me in huge hatred. She does that when she's thwarted. She even tried to get my firm dropped from the Bonbouche consultancy.

'She wasted her breath, of course. People knew her well enough to ignore her outbursts. My job and my reputation remained intact, but I confess that I was deeply hurt, and my wife refused to have anything more to do with Eva.

'In 2001 my health deteriorated, and I resigned from active business. I retired to this flat with my wife. She died in 2003. I've stayed on here. Mayfair is my village. I'm happy here.'

Noble made a fluttering movement of his fingers, as if to brush away a trivial irritant. He looked very tired, and Thorneycroft thought he should not be questioned further, but Connor persisted.

'Mr Noble,' he said, 'during this millennium hoo-ha, was Mr Jason Lenard on the London board?'

'Yes he was.'

'Did he back his father, or his grandmother?'

Noble frowned slightly. 'Neither. Jason refused to believe I was at fault in any way, but he wanted Eva to remain on the board. He said publicly that he did not want her money, her health was all that mattered to him. He told her she must take things more quietly.'

'A diplomat's answer.'

'Yes.'

'Did it cause dissension between Jason and his father?'

'No. They were both trying to find a way out of a tricky situation.'

'You were grossly slandered. Did you take any legal action against Mrs Lenard?'

'Good God, no. I knew her actions sprang from her illness. One can't hold such patients responsible for their outbursts. Eva was … is … a sick woman. She had done unpleasant, unkind things, but she's not a criminal to be dragged through the courts … or to be put down like a mad dog by an insane poisoner.'

The old man was patently sincere in what he said, and Connor changed his approach.

'Do you retain an interest in Bonbouche?' he asked.

'I have some shares, nothing exceptional. I take no part in Bonbouche operations. I left the business world years ago and since I left there've been changes in the company's structures and personnel. The electronic age has left me behind. I'm retired and, frankly, I thank God for it.'

'Out of the rat race,' said Connor sympathetically. 'A big organization like Bonbouche, with networks in Europe and America … a man has to be tough to survive. Has to know what's going on under the surface, so to speak.'

Noble made no answer, and Connor's tone became deferential. 'One of my tasks, one I'm not really trained for, is to try to understand how the Bonbouche machine works, here in Europe and in the United States. Our experts tell me that on this side of the Atlantic things are going smoothly, but they suggest it may be different in the States. There could be private agendas, power struggles, people who are working to change company policy or advance personal interests.'

Noble smiled as if at a naïveté. 'It happens.'

'And there could be others who know of these … goings-on?'

'Probably.'

'There might be someone who's planning to derail the Bonbouche gravy train, wreck its sales, in order to promote a private strategy?'

Noble said firmly, 'If you mean is someone poisoning innocent people in order to obtain a stranglehold on Bonbouche, that is a ludicrous notion.'

'It may seem ludicrous to you.' Connor's eyes were diamond bright. 'But a man's dead, Mr Noble, and a little kid and an old woman are lucky to be alive. We have to stop a poisoner, and to do that we have to follow every lead we can, no matter how ludicrous it seems to normal folk.'

'Why don't you consult the American experts on their knowledge of Bonbouche?'

'We have, sir, but experts work slowly, and this poisoner has promised to make further attacks. So far the intervals between his hits have been short … a matter of a few days. That means his next attack could be only hours away. If we're to prevent it, we need short cuts.'

Noble said wearily, 'I told you, I'm out of touch with Bonbouche affairs. I don't see how I can help you.'

'You may be out of touch, but you may know somebody who isn't. Someone in the USA who's aware of the undercurrents, the secret networks, the private agendas. Time's not on our side. We need the help of every decent-minded citizen. If you can give us the name of a possible informant, we can work with speed. Speed may save lives.'

Noble shook his head. 'Even if I could give you a name, you would not be able to reach its owner. Informants such as you speak of do not talk to policemen.'

He leaned back against his pillow, drawing in deep breaths. Alarmed, Connor got to his feet.

'I'm sorry,' he said, 'I've overtired you. I'll say no more, except that if you can think of anyone who can give us even a suggestion why Bonbouche customers have become targets for a murderer, then I beg you to let me know at once. I'll leave my contact numbers with your housekeeper. John, we're leaving.'

Before he could start for the door, Noble raised a hand. 'Wait, man. I never said I wouldn't try to find a name for you. Sit down and listen.'

As Connor resumed his seat, the sick man reached towards the table at his side, picked up a leather-bound notebook, and slowly turned its pages.

'You are right,' he said, 'in thinking that there are networks within Bonbouche … as in every international company. Those at the top have outside contacts who don't have links to people lower down the scale. They don't identify themselves as part of the official company web. They don't concern themselves with the lives of ordinary mortals. They tend to think in billions, not millions. They are not approachable by the likes of you and me.

'But it is possible to tap into the lower strands of the web, where there are people who gain an inkling of what goes on in the big spider's mind, so to speak. Those lower people pass information up to the spider … and down again, if the spider so wills it.'

He laid a finger on a page of the notebook. 'When I worked with Bonbouche, I kept in touch with a man named Eli Fishburn. Sometimes … not often … he was able to tell me which way the wind was blowing. He watched the web. He made money by doing so.'

Connor said eagerly, 'how do we reach Mr Fishburn?'

'You don't,' Noble answered. 'I've told you, such people do not talk to policemen. Fishburn may simply ignore me. All I can do is set the enquiry going, and hope he'll respond.' Noble's gaze became icy. 'And I warn you, if you intervene, if there's the smallest hint that the law is breathing down my neck, you will get nothing but silence. Do you understand?'

Connor hesitated, unwilling to surrender what was his right and his duty, but Thorneycroft said quickly, 'Yes. Perfectly.'

'Good.' Noble's mouth curled. 'In any case, I doubt if the police budget could meet Eli's prices.'

'Can you?' Thorneycroft said, and Noble's smile broadened.

'Yes. I can. Just.'

Leaving the property, Connor said sourly, 'That's a man with a grievance against Bonbouche.'

'He denies he ever felt one.'

'He would, wouldn't he, if he's guilty of the attacks.'

'Why would he resort to violence after a delay of seven years?'

Connor scowled. 'I had Koch check him out, right after Fenella Batista gave us his name. In 2000 he had a very big stock of Bonbouche shares. Over the past five years he's sold most of them. Damaging Bonbouche wouldn't affect his pocket. He knows the Bonbouche routines, the geography of their stores. He may still have keys, and he could obtain the uniforms.'

'He's in no shape to commit the crimes, Liam. He's had major heart surgery, he's been in hospital or convalescence over the whole period the crimes were committed. It would have been physically impossible for him to access the storerooms, switch the food-packs, and send the cards.'

'If he's rich enough to bribe a top financier, he's rich enough to hire a hitman.'

'If he's the poisoner, why has he agreed to approach Fishburn?'

'Maybe Fishburn's in it with him, maybe Fishburn's a figment of Noble's imagination.' Connor chewed his lip. 'You know what's the worst in this job, it's the waiting, waiting for some bastard to kill someone, not being able to prevent it. It could happen at any time now. Jock Robins was poisoned on Friday, November 17th, Ben Tifflin the day after. Then there was a gap of 12 days. Mrs Murugan ate her curry on 30th November.'

'She bought the curry in mid-October,' Thorneycroft pointed out. 'If she'd taken it out of her deep freeze sooner, she could have been the first casualty.'

'But she didn't. The perp knew that there was a notice on all the curry cartons that the food shouldn't be frozen for longer than three weeks. He knew someone would eat the poisoned curry within a few days. He called *The Challenger* and told us to expect something hot and spicy in the news. That pattern could be repeating itself right now. Another curry in someone's freezer could be close to expiry date.'

'Or someone's Christmas pudding,' Thorneycroft said.

Connor looked sick. 'The idea's obscene. I've been hoping, with this gap in the attacks, that the bastard's fallen under a bus.'

'Can't bank on that,' Thorneycroft said. 'Maybe this Fishburn will come up with something useful.'

'I don't like it,' Connor growled. 'Noble's a wild card, he's going to bribe Fishburn. I don't like working that way.'

'He's going to pay for information,' Thorneycroft said, 'and don't tell me you've never done that.'

They emerged from the tall building into the lane that led towards the park. Away to their right was a row of shops and restaurants, and the pink and gold awning of Mayfair Bonbouche.

'They were practically neighbours,' Connor said, 'him and Jock Robins.' He squinted at the building above the awning. 'Unless we can make a breakthrough, someone else is going to be poisoned, so

I'll forget about my good record and my pension, and trust to God that Nobel or Fishburn or some other bloody chancer is going to give me a lead to the killer.'

When Thorneycroft phoned Claudia that night, she had just returned from choir practice.

'We did the old favourites,' she said, 'plus a Caribbean carol, and a mediaeval lullaby I'd never heard before.' She chatted on about her day, and Thorneycroft listened, soothed by the happiness in her voice. Claudia and Luke and Claudia's parents provided a normality that for a brief space washed away the ugliness that surrounded him.

When at last Claudia asked him how the case was going he was tempted to lie, to say that the police had succeeded in blocking the poisoner's path, that an arrest would soon be made, but he couldn't deny the anxiety that possessed him.

'There's been no attack for eleven days,' he said. 'I think it's a remission, not a termination. The poisoner won't be deterred. He may choose other routes, other areas.' He fell back on the old police formula '… we're following every avenue.'

'I see,' Claudia said quietly. 'It's horrible for you all, but you will succeed. You're in all our prayers. Take care, my darling.'

'You too,' he said. He tried for a lighter note. 'We'll have champagne for Christmas.'

'Yes.' He could hear the smile in her voice. 'Luke went to his first Christmas party this afternoon. The host's spaniel has just had puppies. For Luke it was love at first sight. We'll have to buy him a puppy, when we get home.'

'Yes,' he agreed. 'Love you. Sleep well.'

He fell asleep thinking about suitable breeds of dog for a one-year-old London boy.

XX

ON TUESDAY, DECEMBER 12th, Thorneycroft was woken at 6.00 a.m. by the jangling of his bedside phone. It was Connor, speaking from Concorde Street.

'I've just got here,' he said. 'A fax came through from Peter Noble, he's hit pay-dirt. Abbot and Koch are here, join us a.s.a.p.' As an afterthought he added, 'drive carefully, the temperature's way down and there's ice on the roads.'

Thorneycroft dressed quickly, drove carefully, and arrived at Concorde Street without mishap. The parking lot was arctic, but the air in the incident room was warm. Connor, Abbot and Koch were seated at the centre table, with a tray of canteen coffee and sandwiches between them.

As Thorneycroft took his place, Connor handed him a computer print-out.

'Noble phoned me at five o'clock this morning,' he said. 'He'd had a fax from Fishburn. I asked him to relay it to me, here. He said no, first he'd have to decode it, and second, he wouldn't fax it, I must send someone to collect it in person. Koch obliged. I've informed the Super of the message.'

Thorneycroft studied the printed page. It read:

Eli Fishburn to Peter Noble. 12/12/2007
In response to your queries, I have to report as follows:

On October 18th 2007, I communicated by telephone with Rolf Lenard at his home address in Ennisdale Square, London, and informed him that a majority of the New York Bonbouche management was in favour of modernizing the structure, outlets and sales methods of the company. They, together with controlling elements in Los Angeles, Chicago, and other main centres in the USA, will support a resolution to be proposed by Berlin Bonbouche at the March 2008 AGM of Bonbouche, in London, to the effect stated above. I attach a copy of the proposed resolution, with details in a formal motivation.

Rolf Lenard agreed to convey this information to the members of the London board without delay. I hope this information will be of use to the UK police in their present investigations.

signed Eli Fishburn.

Thorneycroft turned to Koch. 'Noble said he had to decode the message. That means he's still in close touch with Fishburn and they share a code. So the connection is secret, right?'

'Secret in the sense that neither Fishburn nor Noble wants the wrong people to read this message,' Koch answered. 'But what interests me is that Fishburn, while he doesn't indicate where he stands on the question of changes to Bonbouche, wants the matter brought out in the open. He warned Rolf Lenard of what was being planned, and he states that Rolf Lenard agreed to tell the London board about the plans.'

Connor said angrily, 'this is what they've been hiding, Rolf and Jason and all the other members of bloody Bonbouche. Fishburn warned them in mid-October that the resolution would be put forward at the AGM. It would be proposed by Berlin Bonbouche, which is a big wheel in the company, and it would be supported by a lot of the USA delegates. Fishburn knows that the resolution if it's moved will split not only individual members of the company, but boards around the world.'

'And the Lenard family,' commented Thorneycroft, and Connor nodded.

'Exactly. Rolf against Jason. Elitist against populist. And putting aside the personal squabbles, there's a vast amount of money involved ... their own, and the company's. We have a whole new set of questions to ask. The Super agrees that the first to be questioned must be Rolf and Jason Lenard. I want to know why they kept from telling us about Fishburn's warning.'

'Thought to keep it in the family, maybe,' Abbot said.

'They wouldn't dare,' Koch said bluntly. 'Fishburn is the sort who keeps his ear to the ground. He'd know if his message didn't get through to all the Bonbouche branches, and he'd take his info elsewhere.' He looked at Connor. 'You'll be meeting with the Lenards, sir. I imagine they would aim to handle the resolution in legitimate ways. They would at least have notified senior office-bearers in key cities that it was on the cards for the AGM. We need to know what's in the company rules ... how much notice must be given for a resolution to be put on the agenda, whether there's a formal body that considers the resolutions, and who sends the agenda out to all the delegates. In other words, did the Lenards see that procedure was properly followed?'

Connor said impatiently, 'you can go into all that, Sam. My query is, why would a resolution to be debated next March, cause a madman to try and bring down the whole Bonbouche operation? I just can't make the connection.'

Koch hunched his shoulders. 'The resolution can divide the company into camps. The poison attacks are focussing attention on the Lenards, who control the central board of the company. The death of Jock Robins, the public panic, the drop in Bonbouche shares, can ultimately be blamed on the Lenards. Discredit them, get them out of office, and there could be a chance of a takeover of the entire company.'

'Maybe.' Connor was shrugging into his fleece-lined jacket. 'I'm going to have a word with Mr Noble,' he said, 'and then I'm going to have Mister Rolf and Mister Jason Lenard for afters.'

Rolf Lenard received Connor, Thorneycroft and Koch in the boardroom of the Chelsea Bonbouche. Connor handed him the text of Eli Fishburn's fax, excluding the mention of Peter Noble's name. Rolf read it, frowning slightly, then laid it aside.

'You appear to have made a backdoor approach to Mr Fishburn, why did you not apply to me first?'

Connor's eyes held a dangerous glint. 'Is the information on that page correct, sir?'

Rolf's eyebrows rose. 'Yes. Eli called me on the phone on the evening of October 18th, six o'clock our time. He told me about the proposed resolution, and later sent me a written copy of it, with its motivation. I presume you've seen that too?'

'I'll ask the questions, sir. Why didn't you think to mention Mr Fishburn's warning to me?'

Lenard spread his hands. 'I didn't think it relevant to your investigation. If I erred in that, I apologize.' He leaned forward and pressed a button on the intercom machine.

'Miss Reeves, please bring me the file for the March AGM,' he said. He met Connor's stare. 'You may wish to study the response I made to Mr Fishburn's communication.'

'Give me a précis,' said Connor silkily.

'Well,' said Lenard, 'it came as no surprise to me to know there was a move to raise the subject of reorganization, at the AGM. I have my sources in New York, Inspector. They keep me up to speed. However, what did trouble me was that those seeking to change things were not doing it in an open manner. They were not discussing it at branch level, nor at interim meetings in the major cities. It was to be sprung upon us at the last minute. There was a great deal of secret lobbying, and that always leads to dissension and division.'

There was a knock on the door, and a secretary came in, laid a bulky file before Lenard, and left. Lenard pushed it across to Connor. Connor handed it to Koch, who began to leaf through its pages.

'You received Fishburn's warning on October 18th,' Connor said. 'What did you do about it?'

'I at once informed Jason and the other members of the London board. We met next morning and discussed the matter at length. Our unanimous decision was that it was the proper course to inform our CEOs in Europe and the USA of the proposed resolution and seek their response to it. Our opinion was that before being tabled at the AGM, the resolution must be debated at branch and higher levels, as is required by our company rules, and if it were democratically accepted at those levels, it should proceed to the AGM.'

'You didn't attempt to block it?'

'Certainly not. We requested the instigators to legitimize it, that is all.'

'And did they?'

Lenard folded his hands. 'Chief Inspector, to take an instruction through all the levels of an organization spread across two continents, takes time. We were satisfied that the work was being done, and that ordinary members of Bonbouche were being given the chance to express their views on whether or not company practice should change. We could count on having clarity well before

Christmas, but on November 18th the Tifflin boy was poisoned, and the following Wednesday we learned of Mr Robins's death. Those events altered the whole situation.'

'How?' Connor said.

'There was extreme shock and concern at all levels of the company. The resolution was at once withdrawn, and there was total agreement that any existing divisions must be set aside, and that Bonbouche, in the face of such a wicked and virulent threat, must be in total unity of purpose.

'As you know, from November 18th, we did our utmost to protect our customers, and we co-operated in every way we could with the police investigations.'

'But you didn't tell us about Mr Fishburn's message, or the resolution.'

Lenard appeared nonplussed. 'Fishburn's message was received by me on October 18th. The poison attacks followed a full month later. We had no reason to connect them with what Fishburn reported. That, I must remind you, concerned company policy, it was an internal affair. Had we publicized the resolution in October, it would have caused distress to our shareholders and customers. I must point out that the Murugan attack could not have been prevented by our telling you what Fishburn told us. The curry Mrs Murugan bought was sold to her in October, before we had any notion that we would be targeted by a poisoner.'

Connor's mouth tightened. 'You withheld information, Mr Lenard. No doubt you did it to protect your company, but you were not and are not competent to decide what will or won't be of importance in a murder investigation. I have asked you repeatedly to identify anyone who could have a motive to attack Bonbouche as a company, or your family as its main operators.

'You should have informed us of the dissension within Bonbouche, when first I spoke to you, on November 18th, after the Tifflin attack. Jock Robins was already dying of poison, Ben Tifflin had already been attacked, and had we known at once of Fishburn's report, we might have had more time to put out warnings and to prevent Mrs Murugan from eating that curry.'

Rolf Lenard's face was dark red. 'I did what I thought was right,' he said stiffly.

'And as they say,' retorted Connor, '"the road to hell is paved with good intentions".' He turned to Koch. 'Sam, do you have any questions for Mr Lenard?'

'I'd like copies of these,' Koch answered, fingering a wedge of papers in the file before him, 'and we'll probably need to talk again.'

Lenard stood up. 'My secretary will make copies for you at once,' he said, 'and I shall be glad to meet you, at any time.'

In the corridor Connor paused to glower at the portrait of Victor and Eva Lenard. 'I wonder if anyone mentioned Fishburn's little bombshell to the old witch.'

'I imagine she was told at once,' Thorneycroft said. 'Stories like that leak fast, and she's not a woman who likes to have things sprung on her.'

'Who would she back, in a fight?'

'Well, Jason's her blue-eyed boy, but Rolf's the head of the firm that she and her husband created. She could have gone either way. I think she'd have been very upset by any threat of a split in the company, and by the fact that her son and grandson took different sides. If she wasn't informed and found out later her reaction might well have been stormy.'

'Violent?'

Thorneycroft hesitated. 'I think heads would have rolled, symbolically speaking.'

'How about literally speaking?'

'I don't know,' Thorneycroft said. 'One can't predict how a woman with her illness will react under stress.

Jason Lenard arrived exactly on time at the Concorde Street police station. He was wearing an Armani suit and carried a lap top computer. As he sat down he said, 'you were lucky to catch me. I'm going abroad this afternoon.'

'Where to?' Connor asked.

'Rome, for a week. A conference and some business meetings. Then I hope to spend a couple of days in Tuscany, with wine merchants. Why do you want to see me? Have you made any progress on the case?'

Connor ignored the question. 'I need to talk to you about the information sent to your father by Mr Eli Fishburn on October 18th last.'

Jason tilted his head. 'Oh? What about it?'

'Mr Fishburn warned of a move, in the USA and Europe, to alter the structure and policies of Bonbouche et Cie. Your father received the message on the evening of the 18th. When did he inform you of it?'

'Immediately,' Jason said. 'That same night. He was very steamed up about it.'

'And what was your reaction?'

Jason sniffed. 'I was irritated. The subject has been chewed over for months. If people want to change company policy, they must do it in the proper way; it needs to be aired from grassroots to heaven, no secret agendas. Those always get found out.'

'What's your attitude to the resolution, sir?'

Jason's smile was mocking. 'As I remember, Chief Inspector, when we met in the warehouse, I told you that I believe in change, but it has to come about by persuasion, not threat.'

'How would you ... er ... exert persuasion?'

'By producing the facts for members to consider. The facts are that Bonbouche has, and will continue to have, a reputation as the purveyor of fine foods and wines. We must not sacrifice our hold on that market, but in the modern world, a lot of purchasing power lies with the young middle-income group. They want pizzas and sushi and affordable wines. Bonbouche must create outlets for those goods, still with the aim of excellence. We must open a few places, in the big cities, to test demand – if I'm right, it will be great, and so will our profits.'

'If the resolution cited by Fishburn had come under discussion at the AGM, would you have supported it?' Thorneycroft asked, and Jason smiled.

'I'm not required to answer hypothetical questions, am I, but I'll answer this one. I would have opposed the resolution in its present form, because it would have caused division, and would not have achieved the desired result.' His expression hardened. 'The changes I favour will come, Doctor, because they are dictated by economic circumstances and popular demand. I intend to see that they come peaceably, and with good effect.'

'That may take time, surely?'

'I can wait.'

Meeting Jason's cold eyes, Thorneycroft thought that here was a man with the patience of a predator. He would indeed wait hidden at the waterhole for the chance to make his kill.

Connor and Koch posed other questions, which Jason answered with the same unruffled calm. As he was about to leave, Connor said, 'Mr Lenard, I have to warn you that in my view, you and your father may be targets for the poisoner.'

Jason sighed. 'Yes, Inspector, the thought has crossed my mind.'

'Then take precautions. Don't visit dangerous places, stay with people you can trust, and watch what you eat and drink. Perhaps while you're in Italy you should engage a bodyguard.'

Jason's mouth curled in genuine amusement. 'Thanks for the advice,' he said. 'I might try for a blonde with a black belt.' He met Connor's eyes. 'Don't worry, I'll have my personal assistant along with me on this trip. He's male, and a black belt. I'll make him taste everything I eat or drink.'

When Jason had left to catch his plane to Rome, Koch spoke his mind.

'Say what you like, my bet is he was part of the plan to set the cat among the pigeons at the AGM. The text of the resolution and the motivation supplied by Fishburn, tally exactly with what Jason Lenard said to us. I'd say there was a secret agenda and he helped to draw it up, but when Jock Robins died, he and his mates saw the warning light, and cancelled the plan. It won't be a permanent withdrawal. They'll regroup and next year, there'll be a new plan ... with Jason Lenard at the head of it.'

'I'm not interested in the future,' Connor said. 'I want to know how the Fishburn faxes are linked to the Bonbouche poison attacks. What do you think, John?'

Thorneycroft said slowly, 'I think that the Fishburn fax may well have triggered the poison attacks. The poisoner aimed to gain publicity, disrupt the Bonbouche organization and force the factions within Bonbouche to unite. He was successful. The factions did unite, the resolution was scrapped. The perp saw no need for further attacks. That would explain why there've been none since the one on Mrs Murugan.'

'You're saying the danger's over?' Connor's tone was derisive, and Thorneycroft said quickly:

'No I certainly am not. As Koch said, the squabbles inside Bonbouche aren't settled, they're merely delayed. If there's any attempt to change company policy, the attacks could begin again.

'There's another point to consider. We've been working on the theory that the poisoner was motivated by some personal grievance but if the attacks are linked to some kind of power struggle in the company, then the field of possible attackers widens to include the whole of Europe and the USA. There could be thousands of possible suspects.

'For what it's worth, I don't think the poisoner is likely to be one of the Bonbouche food-handlers. We should be thinking of someone higher up the company ladder.'

'Like Jason Lenard,' Connor said, and Koch nodded vigorously.

'Jason's one of the possibilities.'

'Ray of sunshine, you are,' Connor said. He rubbed a hand over his jaw. 'If it's not a handler, who did switch the food packs, and how?'

'You've examined the video tapes at the Chelsea, Mayfair and Hampstead stores, watching for handlers' activities. I think you should check the tapes for all the London outlets to see if you can pick up people purchasing mushrooms, sherbet or curry. It could be that a customer bought a pack, took it home, doctored it, and returned it to a sales counter or storeroom. A purchaser might be recognizable as someone concerned in the Bonbouche power struggle.'

'Pigs might fly,' Connor said wearily. 'The long and the short of it is, Fishburn's fax has changed the whole case. It's no longer a London crime for personal revenge; we're now looking for a different kind of criminal, with different motivation. We have to start over. We'll do what we can, we'll check the video tapes, we'll inform the international law enforcement agencies of the Fishburn angle and we'll ask them to hunt for past and present offenders. It's a mountain of work, and it'll take time.'

Thorneycroft said, 'you should ask Rolf Lenard to inform all Bonbouche branches that the management has no intention of making any changes in Bonbouche policies. That may give us some breathing space.'

'Yeah.' Connor picked up the bundle of papers supplied by Rolf Lenard's secretary. 'I have to talk to the Super. I'll ask him to speak to Lenard. You better come with me, Sam.'

As the two men headed for the door, Thorneycroft sat hunched in his chair thinking of what Connor had said.

It was indeed an altered case they faced. A different perpetrator with a different motive, yes, but still the same essential man – still clever, well-educated and deft with his hands. Still arrogant and callous enough to endanger innocent people.

In the end though he was still stupid with the stupidity of most amateurs; he was monkey-clever, too fancy in his methods, contemptuous of the skills of the law and the people who upheld it.

He would make mistakes. He would be caught, but time was desperately short.

Thirteen days to Christmas.

God, let it be lucky thirteen for us.

XXI

'THE POLICE HAVE been harassing Rolf and Jason. They've been questioning them, Rolf says. What about? What's happening?'

Eva Lenard was seated in her wheelchair, close to a fire of apple logs. Her two dogs dozed at her feet, and Hester Plum lounged half-asleep on the other side of the hearth, a book unopened on her lap.

Eva slammed a fist on to the arm of her chair. 'Hester! Are you listening?'

'Yes dear, of course.' Hester Plum sat upright. 'Rolf called this evening. The police spoke to him and Jason. It seems they've got word of the ructions back in October.'

'How did they do that?'

'They spoke to Peter Noble. He spoke to Eli Fishburn, who reported back to Noble, and Noble told the police.'

'How much do they know?'

'They know about the proposed resolution to change our structures and policies. Inspector Connor is furious that Rolf didn't mention it to him.'

'Why should he mention it? All that squabbling was months ago, long before these poisonings. It was an internal matter, nothing to do with the police.'

'Connor thinks differently.' Hester hesitated, gazing thoughtfully at her companion. She said carefully, 'he thinks the man may be aiming to harm the family.'

Eva blew out her lips. 'That's nonsense.'

'It is a possibility, Eva. We should take it seriously.'

The old woman pouted like a child. 'It's just that creep Peter Noble, trying to make trouble for us, bringing up the Fishburn affair. Peter hates me, he wants to frighten me. I wouldn't be surprised if he's behind these attacks.'

'That's impossible. He's a very sick man. He's had a triple by-pass and can't leave his apartment.'

'He could pay someone to do his dirty work ... just as he pays Fishburn to snoop for information.'

Hester got to her feet. 'You mustn't work yourself up over Peter Noble. He's out of our lives. Forget him. Let's think about your birthday, it's only four days off. Cook's been asking about the menu, and the number of guests. Rolf and Minette, of course, and Jason, but do you want to invite anyone else.'

'Jason won't be here. He phoned me this morning, from Rome. He'll be away for a week.' Eva's face crumpled. 'I hate it when he goes away. He might have stayed for my birthday.'

'He's sent the wines,' Hester said, 'Your favourites. Two bottles of Shiraz and one of Dom Perignon.'

'It's him I want to see, not a lot of bottles.' Eva stared at the fire. 'We'd better have lamb as the main course. It will go well with the Shiraz. You think of the rest. We'll have drinks here before dinner.'

'Do you want the champagne then, or with dinner?'

'I don't mind, ask Rolf what he prefers. And I want the Christmas decorations up in time for the party. You'd better get the tree in. Thomas and René can dig one up and put it in the big tub so it has time to settle.'

'I'll see to it.'

'And the bonfires,' Eva said. 'I want all the leaves and litter burned before Christmas.' She smiled sideways at Hester. 'They burned the witches, did you know? A week before Christmas.'

'So you've told me,' Hester said shortly. 'A horrible pagan custom, burning poor old women who grew herbs and kept cats.'

'They poisoned people,' Eva insisted, 'and cattle died.'

Hester rose from her chair. She knew when Eva was baiting her, working off her own unhappiness on whoever happened to be at hand.

'Are you ready for your Horlicks?' she said, and Eva smiled.

'Yes, and I'll have a chocolate biscuit.'

Hester went to her own apartment, prepared the Horlicks and arranged biscuits on a plate ... although not of Bonbouche's providing. Eva would grumble about that. She knew about the happenings of the past few weeks, the embargo placed on Bonbouche goods, but the reports skated on the surface of her mind. She did not absorb them. It was better that way.

Hester carried the hot drink and biscuits back to Eva's living-room, set the tray down, and left Eva feeding biscuits to her dogs.

At nine the next morning, Hester Plum rose from the breakfast table and went to the utility room where waterproofs, boots and gardening gear were stored. She drew on a fleece-lined jacket and leather gloves, and exchanged her shoes for Wellingtons. She tucked a paper bag, small clippers and a trowel in the pocket of the jacket. There might be Christmas roses that would do for the table at Eva's birthday dinner.

The gardeners, Thomas and René, were waiting at the kitchen door. René carried the big square tub which would receive the Christmas tree. Thomas was in the driver's seat of the truck that would transport the tub and tree back to the house.

The cold weather continued, the air striking hard at the lungs, but there was no wind. They took the truck the short distance to the woods behind the house. There the track was barred by a gate that was always kept locked.

Thomas produced his ring of estate keys and unlocked the gate. In a few minutes they reached the rise where Victor Lenard had planted young pine trees, now the only patch of green among the winter oak, ash, and chestnut.

Each year, a tree was selected from this ridge, to deck the house. In Victor's time, Hester remembered, it had been a big tree, which stood in the drawing-room where the guests could enjoy its lights, trimmings and wrapped presents.

Now it would be a small tree. There would be only two guests for dinner, and the table in the dining-room would not be extended by extra leaves.

Thomas and René walked away through the spinney, to find a suitable tree. They would dig it up with care so as not to damage its roots, and plant it in the tub, packing in stones and soil to hold it upright.

Hester had seen the process many times. It bored her. Christmas meant nothing to her in religious terms, and she had no family to share it with. This year would be like the last and the next. Her job was to see that the birthday dinner pleased Eva, Rolf and Minette. She had already bought and wrapped presents for Eva and herself to give.

She stood on the track, arms folded against the cold. The silence of the woods pressed down on her, as it always did. Turning her head, she scanned the skyline, searching for the tallest of the trees, the oldest, the one that had marked the place where Coventry Hall had stood in the seventeenth century. The tree must have been full grown, even then. Now its gnarled branches still dominated the woods.

It had been the covintree of welcome and farewell. Eva liked to deny that good name and call it the coventree, where witches met, to hobnob with Satan and plan evil deeds.

Victor hadn't liked the site. Too dark, he'd said, and damp as well. He'd pulled down the ruins of the old house, and built the new one to his taste, as he'd built Bonbouche et Cie.

On impulse, Hester called to the men that she was going for a walk. She followed the track, to the narrow path that branched away westwards to the big tree. Job-gardeners came every month to keep the woods tidy, and she had no difficulty reaching the massive bole, still sound though deeply scarred by age. She did not stop there, but walked on, to the dell beyond. The ground was mottled by patches of sunlight. She crossed to the far bank, stooped down, and brushed away the fallen leaves and mast.

She stood motionless, staring down at the bank. Someone had dug out a square of undergrowth. Next to the bare patch, the loam was pierced by dried stalks and withered leathery discs. Hester compared the two areas, thinking.

She took the trowel from her jacket pocket, and carved out a second square of earth, digging deep to reach the subsoil. Lifting the square in her gloved hands, she slid it carefully into the paper packet she had brought, folding over the top so that no earth could escape.

She returned packet and trowel to her jacket pockets, dusted off her gloves, and walked back to join the gardeners. They were still busy putting the Christmas tree into the tub, and she waited quietly for them to finish.

When at last they were driving back to the house, Thomas voiced his yearly complaint.

'Proper waste of time, this is. Quicker to buy one from the market, I'd say.'

But that wouldn't satisfy Eva, Hester knew. Eva desired everything to be done the way Victor had done it, and the one unchanging rule was that what Eva desired, Eva got.

Hester carried the paper packet to her private kitchen, and laid it on the sink, She sat in a wickerwork chair and thought about what to do next. She was, for once, unsure of where her best interests lay.

She could do nothing, say nothing, but that was dangerous. If by some chance it occurred to someone to search the woods, then her silence could be taken as proof of her guilt.

Yes, silence was dangerous, but not as dangerous as going to the police. Most likely the police knew about her past. They knew that one of her patients died of an overdose of a potentially dangerous drug. They knew there'd been an enquiry. She couldn't go through all that again. She wouldn't risk losing everything she'd worked for, all these years.

But someone must be told, someone safe. Not the police, but someone who could tell the police without naming her.

She must not use the Coventry telephones, calls could be traced. She would use a public pay phone, tomorrow first thing, that was the answer.

She carried the packet through to her living-room. She found a Koki pen and wrote on the packet the date, and the words, 'Coventry woods'. Then she sealed the packet with tape, and placed it in her wall-safe, behind the Modigliani.

That done, she removed her gloves and washed her hands, then went to the attic to collect the boxes of Christmas decorations which she would hang on the tree, around the dining-room and Eva's apartment, to mark another joyless Christmas.

The morning after the interviews with Rolf and Jason Lenard, Connor and Thorneycroft met in the incident room at Concorde Street.

'We've made some progress,' Connor said, 'Koch has confirmed that there was a policy conflict in Bonbouche in mid-October and that it was quashed as soon as the poison attacks started. Malherbe and Ayusha Ramiah have established that it would have been possible for dozens of people to access the Bonbouche storage area at any time up to November 18th, when Ben Tifflin was poisoned.

'After that date, security at all the London outlets was tightened, but it would still have been possible for a determined person to plant more poisoned packs. And despite all our warnings, there could still be poisoned food packs in freezers and fridges.'

He spread his hands flat on his knees. 'Theories are all we have. I don't like this silence. I don't think he's given up, do you?'

Thorneycroft shook his head. He remembered from his army days the hours and days of silent waiting. You never trusted silence. Maybe the fight was over, but more likely the enemy was working on a new plan, taking up new positions, waiting for you to drop your guard so they could make a new attack.

'Are you watching the Lenards?' he asked.

'As best we can,' Connor answered. 'We can't give them twenty-four hour protection. We can't justify that because all we have are theories. I've warned them to be careful, to see themselves as possible targets, but they don't believe me. They all have this sense of immunity. Little gods and goddesses who can't be reached by mere mortals.'

Thorneycroft moved his shoulders uneasily. 'They need protection.'

'This one of your gut-feelings?'

'No. Something I learned at medical school.'

Connor made a hissing sound. 'All right, I'll see what I can do, but I warn you, it won't be much.'

Early on the morning of December 14th, Hester Plum drove to a public phone booth in Richmond and made her call. She spoke for just under three minutes, ending with the words, 'I think the police should be informed. I leave that in your hands, as always.'

On December 14th, Peter Noble phoned Fenella Batista. 'I listened to your concert last night,' he said. 'I wish I could have been there. It was splendid. Your group has technique and musicality. World-beaters all.'

'Thank you, Peter,' Fenella said. 'Your opinions are always welcome. Are you feeling better?'

'A little each day. Will you be here for Christmas?'

'No. We go back to Italy on Monday, to take part in the Christmas Messiahs.'

'I hope,' Noble said, 'there will be peace on earth to men of good-will.'

'Don't bank on it,' Fenella answered.

Silas Lenard put through a call to Jason Lenard in Rome. 'I had a call from Hester,' he said. 'Eva's upset that you won't be with her for her birthday. Do you have to be away for so long?'

'Why the concern?' Jason sounded amused. 'You don't care a stuff about Eva.'

'In view of what's happening,' Silas said, 'even my hard heart is touched. You should be here, Jason. For your own sake as well as hers.'

'I've provided the festive wine,' Jason said, 'and I've promised to phone her at eight on her birthday night. I'll bring her back something splendid from Tuscany. Satisfied?' As Silas made no answer, he laughed. 'Go and see her yourself, why don't you?'

'She wouldn't find the visit welcome,' Silas said.

Jason phoned Rolf.

'I've just had a call from Silas,' he said. 'He was moaning because I won't be at Eva's birthday bash. I've already sent the festive wines, two Shiraz and one Dom Perignon. I wrote messages on the bottles, be sure and show them to her.'

'I will,' Rolf said, 'but it would be better if you were here to do it yourself.'

'You know I can't be. The negotiations here are tricky. If I can get Gianelli to accept our terms, it'll be a major breakthrough. And we need the Tuscany deals.'

'Yes. Well. I'll see you on your return.'

'I'll be back at the office, Monday morning.'

At Concorde Street, Connor conferred with Thorneycroft.

'Saturday's Eva Lenard's birthday,' he said. 'Rolf and Minette Lenard, and their dogsbody Arnold will be visiting Coventry Hall. Hester Plum's invited, but Jason's still in Italy. I spoke to Rolf Lenard and said I'd like a police presence at the house that evening, he hummed and hawed ... said it wasn't necessary, the place is secure, he didn't want his mother frightened, but he agreed to let a copper sit in the downstairs hallway. The Richmond nick will supply a reliable man. Best we can do. I hope it's enough.'

'What's on the menu?' Thorneycroft asked, and Connor grimaced.

'Home cooked food, and wines supplied by Jason a month ago, before the attacks started. The wine will remain corked until the meat course is served.'

'What about drinks before dinner?'

'Everything from Mrs Lenard's drinks cabinet. The house has good security: a burglar alarm, and electric fence all round the property. The Richmond nick will be on alert. I don't think any uninvited stranger will join the party, on Saturday night.'

XXII

AS THE LENARDS' Rolls reached the gate of Coventry Hall, thunder crackled over the Thames estuary, and lightning split the eastern sky. Rolf Lenard pressed the button of a remote and the gate slid open. They started up the drive. The house blazed with light, and bonfires burned among the boles of the leafless trees. Rolf raised a hand in salute to the two gardeners tending the fires.

'It's good to see the old custom upheld,' he said.

Minette shot a venomous glance at the building ahead. 'They burned witches, once,' she muttered. 'Pity they don't, any more.'

'The fires have nothing to do with witchcraft,' said Rolf. 'We light them to clear away the dead leaves and rubbish, before Christmas. In my father's time—'

'You had fireworks and a band and a hundred guests,' said Minette waspishly, 'now it's us and fat Miss Plum.'

Rolf looked at the stiff back of Terry Arnold in the driving seat. 'We must make the best of it,' he said. 'What did you get for mother?'

Minette tapped the parcels on her lap. '"Joy" perfume and Lindt chocolates.'

Rolf nodded approval. 'I bought her a block of platinums,' he said, 'she'll enjoy watching them appreciate.'

The car drew up at the open front door and Rolf and Minette alighted. The car moved on to the parking yard at the back of the house.

'Terry should dine with us,' Minette said. 'He's not a servant.'

Rolf pursed his lips. 'He's an employee, my dear, and I'm sure he'll be happier dining with Thomas and René and two pretty house-maids, than with us old fogies. Cook will see to it that he eats like a prince.'

As they entered the hall, a uniformed policeman standing at the foot of the stairs, saluted them. Rolf returned a nod, but did not stop to talk to the man. They made their way past the stairwell to the main corridor, and were met at the door of Eva's salon by Hester Plum. She gave Rolf a welcoming smile, and said to Minette:

'You needn't worry about the dogs, I've shut them in my flat.'

'They jump up,' Minette said, 'with muddy paws.' She brushed past Hester and walked to where Eva sat in her wheelchair. Dropping a peck on Eva's cheek, she held out the parcels. 'Happy birthday, Eva. They can be changed at Harrods.'

'I'll open them later,' Eva said. She was watching Rolf who stood talking to Hester. 'What is it?' she called. 'What's happened, is it more trouble?'

Rolf crossed to her side. 'No, all's quiet.' He kissed her hand and cheek. 'I spoke to Jason today. He'll be phoning you at eight o'clock, so keep your mobile handy.'

'That'll be right in the middle of dinner,' Eva complained, but her expression softened. 'Jason's so good to me. He sent the Shiraz and champagne. Do you want the fizz now, or later?'

'Let's have it with dessert,' Rolf said. 'What would you like in the meantime? Sherry? Something soft?'

'Soda pink. I can't take red wine, it gives me gout. The Shiraz is for your enjoyment, not mine.'

Rolf moved to the drinks trolley and poured angostura and soda for Eva, vodka and lime for Minette, Amontillado for Hester and whisky for himself.

They settled round Eva and talked not of the present but of the distant past, for that was where the shreds of Eva's happiness lay, and no-one wished to speak of the dangers that threatened now.

At 7.30 the dinner gong rumbled at the far end of the house, and they set out along the corridor to the dining-room. Reaching its doorway, Rolf stopped and gazed about him. He gave Hester a nod. 'Very nice, my dear. You've done us proud.'

Hester's decorations chimed with the style of the house. The Christmas tree stood against the opposite wall, lights winking, branches loaded with exquisite baubles and gold-wrapped bonbons. The stained-glass panels of the vast central light threw prisms of scarlet, green and royal blue on the plain damask tablecloth, and scented candles burned between two vases of hothouse flowers.

Rolf rubbed his hands together. 'I'll open the wine,' he said. 'Let it breathe.' He strolled to the sideboard, and while the women took their places at the table, he drew the cork from the first bottle of Shiraz. Jason had scrawled a message across the label, and Rolf brought the bottle for Eva to see. She touched the writing with a fingertip.

'"Happy Days, favourite Gran",' she said. She shook her head, smiling ruefully. 'Not much hope of that, the way things are.'

Rolf carried the bottle back to the sideboard. As he set it down, thunder crashed overhead, and rain spattered the windows. Rolf went to the centre window, raised the sash and leaned out, waving and calling to the gardeners to come inside. He closed the window and drew the long curtains. 'It's snug inside,' he said.

Returning to the sideboard, he picked up two sherry decanters – one of sweet and one dry. He served Eva, Hester and himself, but when he came to Minette at the end of the table, she waved him away.

'I'll stick to vodka,' she said. 'Bring me the bottle, and the lime and ice. I'll fix it myself.'

Rolf hesitated. 'There's wine and champagne to come,' he warned.

She said between her teeth, 'bring me the bloody Vodka.' He shrugged and did as she commanded.

He took his place at Eva's right, and a housemaid brought in the first course: consommé and blintzes. Rolf and Eva, to whom food was of supreme importance, ate and drank in silence. Hester finished her soup, then tried to engage Minette in conversation.

'I'm going to Austria after Christmas,' she said.

Minette's eyes roved over Hester's ample flesh. 'Winter sports?' she asked. 'Or do you prefer the indoor variety?'

Hester ignored the rudeness. 'I'll be in Vienna with the Hasselts for the New Year celebrations,' she said, 'then I go to Madeira for a fort-night.'

Minette squinted over the rim of her glass. 'Who's going to look after Mumsie and the mausoleum while you're away?'

'That's all arranged. She'll have the same nurse-companion I engaged last year. They got on very nicely, and Rolf and Jason will keep an eye on things. I don't have to worry about the staff. They could run the place blindfold.'

Minette shivered. 'I wish we could go somewhere sunny, meet people who aren't important to the business, get a life.'

The soup plates were removed and replaced by ramekins of *Sole Veronique*. Rolf launched into a discussion of an art exhibition he had visited two days before. Eva half-listened to him, her eyes shifting often to her wristwatch.

On the stroke of 8.00 her mobile jangled. She snatched it from the side pocket of her chair and held it to her ear, calling 'Jason? Jason, I can't hear you.' She shook the phone. 'It's not working!'

'Switch it on,' Minette yelled, and Hester got up and adjusted the instrument. The maid and cook appeared in the kitchen doorway with the dinner-wagon, but Rolf waved them back. Eva was cooing into the phone, listening to what were obviously birthday greetings.

Rolf began to make signals to her, and she said, 'your father wants to know how it went with Gianelli? Did he sign? Really? That's marvellous, darling, you're a great negotiator.' Rolf tried to take the phone from her, but she thrust him away and went on talking. 'When do you go to Florence? ... Where will you be staying? ... Phone me from there, I want to know all about it ... What? Oh, no, there's no need for presents, darling ... well, if you insist, shoes, brown, you know what I like ... yes ... yes ... goodnight. Sleep well.'

Rolf was snapping his fingers, wanting the phone, but Eva had already switched it off.

'He's in a restaurant,' she said, 'about to meet the Gianelli tribe. He says he's struck a fantastic deal. He'll be back here next Tuesday.'

'I'll call him tomorrow,' Rolf said resignedly.

The cook and maid appeared again, and served the roast lamb, vegetable, gravy and sauces. Rolf fetched the open bottle of Shiraz, poured a little into his glass and sipped it. He nodded, and looked questioningly at Eva, who shook her head. He served Hester, and moved towards Minette. Before he reached her, she surged to her feet and stood swaying and glaring at him, her face contorted.

'I'm not going to sit here stuffing my face and slurping that muck while Terry's downstairs in your Edwardian dungeon. I'm going to join the lower classes. That's where I belong.'

Rolf put a hand on her arm. 'Sit down at once. You're drunk. It's my mother's birthday, try to behave yourself.'

She shook him off. 'No. I've made up m' mind. I'm outa here.'

She headed unsteadily for the door. Rolf would have gone after her, but Eva said sharply, 'no, Rolf. Let her go.'

He turned to face Eva. 'I apologize. She's up to her gills in Vodka. She's behaving like a slut.'

Eva's eyes sparkled with rage. 'And whose fault is that? You're a great fool! You're driving her straight to the arms of that batbrained muscleman. You pay her no attention, so of course she turns to someone who does.'

Rolf's face was set in an icy smile. 'It would be foolish, Mother, to imagine that Minette would leave me for a toyboy without brains, money, or professional skills.'

'You never learn, do you?' Eva said. 'You lost Zoe, but at least it was to a man of standing. Don't lose Minette to a mere stud. And remember, she'll bleed you white.'

Rolf drew a long breath, visibly struggling to control himself. At last he said, 'let's not quarrel. Let's enjoy your birthday, Mother. A toast.' He raised his glass towards Eva. 'Happy birthday to you. May we share many more with you.'

He settled in his chair, sitting hunched over his plate, stabbing at food with his fork, his left hand clenched on the table. Eva was making no effort to eat. Her face was dark red, and when Hester tried to talk to her, she was silenced by a wave of the plump hand.

Hester drained her glass of wine, reached for the bottle and refilled her glass.

Disasters, she thought, we are surrounded by disasters. We live with rage, and hatred and poison. Minette will leave, one more disaster, and there is nothing I can do about it.

Tears came to her eyes and she made no effort to wipe them away. She gulped the Shiraz, not tasting it. No-one was eating, Eva should put an end to this ghastly meal, call for the cold food to be taken away. But Eva's face was set in a basilisk stare. She had retreated to her own dark place, and it would be days before she came out of it, spoke to anyone.

Rolf had pushed his plate aside and was getting to his feet, crossing to the sideboard, picking up the bottle of champagne. He can't mean it, Hester thought. We can't drink it, we have nothing to celebrate.

She felt ill. Her arms ached, her head, her teeth, everything ached.

Rolf was floating and the walls of the room were doing strange things, retreating and advancing in a concertina movement.

Hester tried to stand, and failed. She leaned towards Eva.

'Eva,' she said, 'Eva, I'm ill.' But there was no recognition in Eva's eyes.

Rolf was easing the cork from the champagne bottle. Hester tried to call to him, but her cry came out a mumble. She pressed on the arms of her chair, forced herself upright, and staggered towards the door. Outside in the corridor, she leaned against the wall. She was thinking of the medicine cabinet in her flat. Something there might help. And the telephone. She must call a doctor.

Slowly, very slowly, one hand on the wall, she edged along the corridor. Somehow she opened the door of her flat, and lurched forward into her living-room, crawled towards the phone. She heard the dogs, locked in the kitchen, break into a frenzy of barking.

She reached the phone, and punched in a number.

A voice spoke and she summoned up the last of her strength. 'Hester,' she mumbled. 'Coventry. Come quickly.'

The pain in her chest was unbearable. She fell to her knees, rolled on to her side and vomited.

The dogs had stopped barking and were crying. A black hole engulfed her, bottomless, cold.

Eva was screaming her head off.

Minette, emerging from the guests' cloakroom, almost collided with Thomas and a policeman, who were racing towards Hester's apartment. Eva in her wheelchair was hammering on Hester's door, screaming Hester's name. Thomas unlocked the door and the two men thrust past Eva and went through, closing the door in Eva's face. Her screams intensified.

Minette heard her name called. The housemaid Janet was running towards her, weeping.

The girl caught hold of Minette's arm. 'Madam, come quick, Mr Lenard's ill, he can't catch his breath. Thomas thinks it's something he ate.'

Minette straightened, shocked into cold sobriety. 'Go and help look after Mrs Lenard,' she said.

She ran to the dining-room. Rolf was lying on the floor near the kitchen door, and Arnold was kneeling beside him attempting artificial respiration. She knelt beside him.

'You breathe, I'll pump,' she said, and placed her hands over Rolf's heart, counting, monitoring Arnold's efforts.

The cook, the second housemaid, and the gardener René stood in the doorway to the kitchen. René pointed to the champagne bottle lying on its side near the sideboard. 'We should wipe that up,' he began, but the cook cut him short.

'No, we don't touch anything, the policeman said so. We keep out of that room, and we don't touch anything, until the police say we can.'

In Hester's room, the policeman felt for Hester's pulse.

'She's alive,' he said. He took the pager from his belt and spoke to the driver of the police car parked in the yard.

'Get hold of the nick,' he said, 'tell the Inspector we've got two down here, looks like heart attack. We need a doctor or paramedics, and an ambulance fast, the first hour is vital.' He looked up at Thomas. 'Do you know CPR? Good, then start it. Make sure her mouth's clear, she could inhale vomit.'

He got to his feet and moved away a space, returning to his pager.

'Tell the guv there're suspicious circs,' he said. 'I need back-up, and he should notify DCI Connor at Concorde Street, right away. Keep me in the loop.'

He turned to join Thomas in the battle to keep Hester Plum breathing.

XXIII

THE CALL CAME through to Concorde Street at 8.27 p.m. Thorneycroft, Connor and Abbot were in the incident room when DS Hogarth hurried in. He spoke to Abbot first.

'Set up the crime-scene squad, there's trouble at Coventry Hall.'

He turned to Connor. 'Healey from Richmond nick phoned from the Lenard house. Rolf Lenard and Miss Plum have been taken ill. The man Healey posted in the house has called for back-up, and a doctor and ambulance.'

'Are Lenard and Plum still alive?' Connor said.

'Alive but unconscious. The Richmond M.O., name of Sewparsad, examined them both, and diagnosed cardiac malfunction. He said that when two healthy people display similar symptoms, it suggests they've consumed the same toxic substance. Against the background of what's happened recently, he thinks we're looking at attempted murder. Healey concurs and so do I.

'Sewparsad packed both patients off to the Richmond Heart Clinic. I know the place, it's first-class. Sewparsad is waiting at the house, he wants to talk to you.'

'Good,' Connor said. 'How's Healey coping?'

'Well, I think. He's secured the dining-room and kitchen areas – Lenard collapsed in the dining-room – and also Miss Plum's apartment. She reached it before losing consciousness.'

'Did he say what was served at dinner?' Thorneycroft asked, and Hogarth smiled grimly. 'Home cooked food, and wines from the Goldmead warehouse.'

'Christ,' Connor exploded, 'what fool ordered that?'

'Mrs Eva Lenard, and it was supplied from the warehouse on the instructions of Jason Lenard. About five weeks ago, Healey says, according to the household staff. Looks as if Jason has some questions to answer. Get down there fast. I want a full report on what happened at tonight's birthday party.'

Thorneycroft and Connor travelled in the back seat of a speeding squad car. Abbot followed in the scene-of-crime van. Before they had gone a mile, the car's radio chattered. It was the sergeant on duty in the Concorde Street communications room.

'There's been a call for you, sir, from a Dr Silas Lenard. It came through at 8.40. He said he'd received a call from Miss Hester Plum. She was obviously ill. All she said was "Hester ... Coventry ... come quickly". Then the line went dead. Dr Lenard could hear dogs barking like crazy in the background, while the caller was speaking. He said Miss Plum owns two dogs.'

'Where's Dr Lenard now?' Connor said.

'He's on his way to Coventry Hall. He was at Great Ormond Street when Miss Plum phoned him. It took him a few minutes to leave the patient he was attending to.'

Connor at once made contact with Inspector Healey. 'There's a Dr Silas Lenard heading for Coventry Hall,' he said. 'He's Rolf Lenard's brother. He claims to have received a phone call from Miss Plum, evidently an appeal for help. When he arrives, corral him. Keep him separate from the rest. Don't let him communicate with anyone.'

'Understood,' Healey said. 'I've put the staff in the lounge of the house. Mrs Lenard senior is in her own bedroom; Dr Sewparsad insisted, he's sedated her, and a maid Janet is on call if she needs help. I put a WPC in her apartment. Mrs Minette Lenard, and Terry Arnold are with the staff in the lounge. She's been creating, wants to go to her husband in the Clinic. I told her we needed to talk to her first, and she wouldn't be allowed to see her husband because the doctors are still working on him, in the high dependency unit.'

'Good,' Connor approved. 'Keep her until I've been able to question her. No way does she get near to either of the patients.'

'I've sent the matter that Miss Plum vomited to Concorde Street forensics,' Healey said, 'because it looks to me that she was poisoned.'

'That's it, until we're proved wrong,' Connor agreed. 'Is it possible that an intruder could have entered the Coventry Hall property during the day?'

'I very much doubt it,' Healey said. 'The electric fence has been on since the troubles started. I've had a guard on the gate and a man inside the house since 5 p.m., and our patrol car has made circuits of the property three times between 6 and 9 this evening.'

'Good work. We'll talk soon,' Connor said.

Ending the call he muttered, "if Healey's right, and I think he is, either the poison ... if there was poison ... was introduced tonight by someone present in the house, or it's been brought in some time during the past weeks or even months.'

'Rolf Lenard's always been a target,' Thorneycroft said slowly, 'but why Hester Plum?'

Connor yawned, rubbing his eyes. 'The first three hits have all been on random victims. Maybe this perp doesn't care who goes down, as long as it strikes at Bonbouche.'

'No.' Thorneycroft was incisive. 'This attack is different. It took place inside the Lenard's home, on Eva Lenard's birthday. That's not random, that's specific and deliberate.'

'Yeah. Maybe.' Connor leaned his head back on the cushions and closed his eyes. Thorneycroft sat silent, trying to bring his thoughts into order. They seemed to be coming in disconnected flashbacks that formed no cohesive picture.

The first three attacks differed from these last two. They could be tied to Fishburn's warning that Bonbouche's structures and policies were under threat. His report was made on October 18th, the first attack on Jock Robins was on November 17th, the second on Ben Tifflin on November 18th, the third on Mrs Murugan on November 30th.

Then there'd been a break; no attacks until tonight's, for there could be no doubt that Lenard and Miss Plum had been poisoned.

What could have caused the break between November 30th and December 16th? Was it because the attacks had set the wrangling Bonbouche factions in Europe and the USA on the alert? Bonbouche was in trouble, and the call went out for unity?

But if the Bonbouche infighting was over, why were Rolf and Hester in hospital?

Minette Lenard was an enigma. What was it she'd said, at the first interview? 'I wish you could persuade Rolf to leave London. I'm afraid for him.'

Minette might enjoy a little on the side with Terry Arnold, but Rolf was her millionaire meal-ticket.

Could Arnold be planning to marry a wealthy widow? He was in a position to access Bonbouche premises without arousing comment. The staffs of the stores and warehouse must be used to seeing him around, Mr Lenard's driver, bodyguard, perhaps killer?

Why was Hester Plum a victim? Surely not by chance. She was part of the close Lenard circle. Ambitious by all accounts, hoping no doubt to inherit wealth from Eva Lenard, and perhaps even Coventry Hall itself. Hester might be seen by other members of the circle as a rival in the race for money and power.

And what of Eva Lenard, mentally unstable, prone to attacks of violent rage? Could she be involved in tonight's attacks? On her own son and her valued companion? It seemed impossible.

Connor spoke suddenly. 'When you and Abbot first met Silas Lenard, he called Plum a detestable woman, didn't he, so why did she phone him, rather than her own doctor?'

'Perhaps,' Thorneycroft answered, 'although they didn't get on, she knew two things about Silas: he's a doctor, and he's a Lenard. That lot doesn't tolerate interference from outsiders. Silas would provide medical attention, and he'd also watch out for the Lenard interests, which are in fact her own interests.'

'He broke that pattern this time. He phoned the police. He must have known we were bound to interfere.'

They passed through the centre of Richmond, and on its western margin, arrived at the gate of Coventry Hall.

Inspector Healey met them at the front door, a younger man than they had expected. He introduced them at once to Dr Sewparsad, who was anxious to be off.

'I've work to do,' he explained, 'I'm in court tomorrow morning, giving evidence in a case of culpable homicide. So if I can answer your questions without delay, I'd be grateful.'

He made an exact and lucid report: summoned to the house by Inspector Healey, he had examined Miss Plum first, as her condition was extremely serious. He had done what he could to stabilize her, and requested the ambulance men to convey her to the vehicle, set up the necessary respiratory machinery, and get her to the Heart Clinic, fast.

He had asked Inspector Healey to collect the matter vomited by

Miss Plum and have it sent at once for forensic examination. 'I read the papers,' he said. 'I had to expect this was a case of poisoning.'

He had then examined Mr Rolf Lenard. 'His condition is less serious than Miss Plum's,' the doctor said. 'He was unconscious, but his breathing was regular. He had a rapid pulse and his responses were erratic. The paramedics who came to the house conveyed him to the Heart Clinic. In cases of cardiac attack, it's important to hospitalize the patient within the hour.'

He gave Connor a half-smile. 'I'll put all the medical terms in my written report,' he said, 'but in simple English, I think Mr Lenard will recover consciousness in an hour or two. Miss Plum may or may not recover; she is very ill, but she will get the best possible care at the clinic.'

As Sewparsad took his leave, Connor turned to Healey, who was obviously torn between relief at being able to hand over responsibility to an old hand, and a longing to remain part of a major investigation. Connor let him down gently, praising the efficient way he had seen to the needs of the patients, and secured and protected the areas of a possible crime scene.

Healey then summoned Sgt. Griffiths, the man who had been in the house throughout the evening's events. Griffiths reported that he had been stationed in the hall and at 8.25 had heard Mrs Eva Lenard screaming. Running to the dining-room, he found that Mr Rolf Lenard was lying on the floor, near the sideboard. He had evidently collapsed while opening a bottle of champagne, which had spilled its contents on the carpet.

Mr Lenard was breathing but unconscious. His driver, Terence Arnold, was kneeling beside him, attempting CPR.

Mrs Eva Lenard was sitting in her wheelchair near the door, screaming, 'Hester, Hester'.

'That's Miss Plum, her companion,' Griffiths added. 'The cook Mrs Bonny was trying to calm Mrs Lenard. Everyone was yelling. Mrs Lenard and Mrs Bonny, the two housemaids and two gardeners were in the kitchen, and Arnold shouted at me to call Mrs Minette Lenard to her husband.

'I called on PC Collins, the second man in the squad car, to get the staff away from the dining-room and put them somewhere safe until we could talk to them. While I was speaking to Collins, Mrs Eva

Lenard went off in her chair, along the corridor. It's a motorized chair and she went fast.

'One of the gardeners, Thomas Jenkins, came to me and said we must go and find Miss Plum because she could have been taken ill as well as Mr Lenard. He grabbed my arm, and said it was urgent, and I believed him. I ran with him to Miss Plum's apartment. The door was not locked, and we went in, past Mrs Lenard. We found Miss Plum lying unconscious on the floor of the apartment. She had vomited, and her pulse was very weak, though she was still breathing.

'I paged the patrol car and told the driver to call for back-up, a doctor and an ambulance. Then I went to assist Mr Jenkins, who had started CPR on Miss Plum. Inspector Healey and the MO Dr Sewparsad arrived very quickly, and Miss Plum and Mr Lenard were taken to hospital in Richmond. Inspector Healey took over control of the situation in the house and grounds.'

Connor nodded. 'Thank you, Sergeant, good work, I'll talk to you again later.' He turned to Healey.

'Where have you put everyone?'

'Mrs Eva Lenard is in her own quarters,' Healey answered. 'She was hysterical; Dr Sewparsad sedated her.' He hesitated. 'She seemed more upset on Miss Plum's account, than her son's. The cook, Mrs Bonny, told me that the old lady and Mr Lenard had words during dinner. A maid, Janet Blount, is with Mrs Lenard. She's asleep. The doctor said not to try to question her until she wakes naturally.'

'Did you question the cook?'

Healey shook his head. 'No. I thought it best to leave all that to you, but she talked, they all talked non-stop. Nervous shock.'

'Umh. Where are they now?'

'Mrs Minette Lenard is lying down on a sofa in the lounge. Seems she drank most of a bottle of vodka tonight. She was under the influence at dinner. When she'd sobered up a little she was at me to let her go off to the hospital, but as you instructed I kept her here. She was crying a lot, shaking. Terence Arnold soothed her down.'

Thorneycroft said, 'did he dine with the family?'

'No, in the staff dining-room.'

'Are the staff also in the lounge?'

'Yes. It's a good big room, and there's a study right opposite which will do for interviews.' A woeful howling reached their ears, and Healey said, 'Thomas Jenkins has the dogs with him.' He looked at Connor. 'I had Griffiths and Collins do a quick search of the house. They found no intruders, no signs of a break-in. The place is very secure.'

At Connor's request, Healey and his team left the house to make a tour of the extensive grounds. Abbot and the scene-of-crime team were already at work in the dining-room, kitchen, and Hester Plum's apartment.

Thorneycroft stood for some time with Connor, in the doorway of the dining-room. A photographer was taking pictures of the dinner table, the food congealed on the cold plates, the chairs thrust back at odd angles. Rolf Lenard's wineglass was half-full Thorneycroft saw, but Hester Plum's was empty. The bottle of Shiraz stood near her place, a third full.

Men with gloved hands moved about the room, dusting surfaces for prints, scooping up material from the wine-stained carpet, lifting crumbs from under the table, vacuuming areas and placing the minutiae they recovered in sealed packets, for examination in the forensic laboratory. Beyond them, in the kitchen, a woman in a white overall was packing the remains of the meal into plastic containers, labelling each with care.

The plates and glasses and cutlery would also be packed and labelled, and sent with the contents of the rubbish boxes for forensic examination.

The experts would run their tests on the detritus of this birthday party, looking for poison, a quick-acting one. Or had there been drinks before dinner?

Connor turned away from the scene. 'I have to talk to Abbot. If Silas Lenard arrives, keep him apart from the others. Speak to him, not interrogation, just put him in the picture and see what he has to say.'

Thorneycroft headed for the hallway. As he passed the open door of the drawing-room, he saw the staff sitting stiffly on damask-covered chairs. Two dogs crouched at the feet of a burly man whom Thorneycroft recognized as one of the two gardeners he'd seen on his first visit to Coventry Hall. He remembered that Hester Plum had described them:

Thomas Jenkins, ex-sergeant of the Blues, who 'ran things'; and René Jones, was it, 'slow but clever with his hands'? Clever enough to load a sherbet toy with aspirin?

Next to the staff, leaning together on a sofa, were Minette Lenard and Terence Arnold.

Possible suspects, with the motive, means and opportunity to commit murder? It was no use speculating.

There was the sound of a car racing up the drive, stopping at the front door with a screech of brakes. Silas Lenard burst into the hall, saw Thorneycroft, and came forward at a run.

'Dr Thorneycroft,' he said abruptly. 'We met at my home.'

'Yes, Dr Lenard.' Thorneycroft extended his hand, but Silas didn't seem to notice it.

'Where's Hester Plum?' he demanded.

'In the Richmond Heart Clinic, in intensive care.'

Silas blew out a breath. 'She's alive, then.' His eyes narrowed, 'and Rolf, and my mother?'

'Mr Lenard is also at the Clinic. He's still unconscious. Your mother is in her apartment, she's been sedated, she's sleeping.'

Silas said nothing for a moment, gazing at the floor as if there was a decision to be made. He sighed, and his shoulders sagged.

'I saw the police cars outside. Were Rolf and Hester poisoned?'

'That's still to be determined.' Thorneycroft met Lenard's impatient stare, and said, 'it's probable they were.'

'God.' Silas was trembling, his lips moved but no sound came. Thorneycroft took him by the arm, led him into the study, and motioned him to a chair.

'It's a shocking thing,' he said. 'I'm sorry.'

Silas nodded. 'Yes. I tried to phone Inspector Connor.'

'He got your message. I understand you received a call from Miss Plum, before she collapsed?'

'Yes.' Silas leaned back in his chair. 'She spoke four words. She said "Hester. Coventry. Come quickly". I asked her what was wrong but she didn't answer. I heard the dogs barking, but nothing from her. I called her back, but there was no answer. It's my fault, my self-indulgence. I should have done something, long ago.'

'What could you have done?' said Thorneycroft quietly, and Silas met his eyes.

'I should have stayed. I shouldn't have run out on my family. I should have insisted that my mother receive proper treatment.'

'Would she have accepted it?'

'Perhaps not, but I should have tried. It's too late now. No use whining. Can I see my mother?'

'Not at the moment, I'm afraid.'

'Are we all suspects?'

'It's better if you let her sleep. Seeing her might, or might not, be the best thing for her.'

Silas nodded. 'Yes. Right. I'll be staying in Richmond overnight. The hospital told me I can't see Rolf until tomorrow.'

'I know Chief Inspector Connor wants to talk to you. He'll be here in a minute.'

'Of course. I'll wait.'

Silas sat slumped in his chair, eyes closed. Watching him, Thorneycroft reflected that it was strange that the first concern of Eva and Silas Lenard appeared to be for Hester Plum, rather than for son or brother Rolf.

XXIV

IN THORNEYCROFT'S PRESENCE, Silas Lenard told Connor of his telephone conversation with Hester Plum.

'Why do you think she asked *you* for help?' Connor asked.

'Well, obviously she needed urgent medical help.'

'Surely she knew of doctors closer at hand? Here in Richmond?'

'I can't explain why she called me,' Silas said impatiently. Then meeting Connor's impassive stare, he said, 'I think perhaps there was something she wanted to tell me, but she collapsed before she could say what it was. There was nausea, Thomas told me, she had an attack of vomiting. Maybe that's why she's still alive.'

Connor could get no more from him, and gave him permission to leave to find accommodation in Richmond.

Watching his retreating back, Thorneycroft said, 'he may be remorseful, but he's a typical Lenard. Doesn't actually lie, just doesn't tell the whole truth. Wants to control any situation that touches on the Lenard kingdom.'

The scene-of-crime squad was now working steadily, and their samples, with the cutlery, crockery and glassware used at the dinner were being rushed to Concorde Street's laboratory.

DS Hogarth sent a support team that included Ayusha Ramiah and Harry Davidson, Ayusha to be stationed in Eva Lenard's apartment, and Davidson to record interviews and maintain communication with Concorde Street.

At ten o'clock Connor phoned the heart clinic for news of the patients, and was told that Mr Lenard was in high dependency and out of danger, but Miss Plum was in intensive care and her condition was critical. Dr Hitchcock, the matron promised, would inform the Inspector if there was any change.

With Thorneycroft and Davidson, Connor settled in the study, to begin the preliminary interrogation of witnesses.

First to be interviewed was Minette Lenard. She made a poor witness, breaking into convulsive sobs whenever her husband was mentioned, and giving a garbled account of the dinner and its aftermath.

'It's all so horrible,' she wept, 'these dreadful weeks, the poisonings, the hatred, not knowing why. I can't handle it. I can't think straight. I'm frightened all the time. I want to go home.'

Connor treated her patiently, trying to piece together a story made incoherent by fear and alcohol.

Terence Arnold was next. He had little to contribute, having spent most of the evening in the staff living-room. He responded to questions with the phrases 'I don't know, I wasn't there, I forget.'

Thorneycroft decided that Arnold knew a good deal more than he was admitting to. He was plainly ambitious, and intent on pursuing his own plans. No doubt Minette was high on his agenda. He would lie to protect her, because that was in his own interest. And there was a tension in him that Thorneycroft had seen many times in men preparing to do a bolt.

Connor, clearly unimpressed by the duo, allowed them to leave, with the caution that they must remain in London, as there would be further questions to answer.

The cook, Maisie Bonny, was exact in her description of the meal, its ingredients, preparation and presentation.

'There's no poisons in my kitchen,' she declared. 'I taste everything I'm making, and if I put wine in a dish, I taste that too. Just a taste, mind. I'm not one for strong liquor.'

She had been too busy, she said, to take note of what went on in the dining-room. Asked if she had seen Rolf Lenard fall, or Miss Plum leave the room, she said she had not.

'That was during the meat course. I was busy preparing the dessert. Of course when Janet called to me that Mr Lenard was ill, I went to see how I could help. I didn't see Miss Plum. She must've left already.' Mrs Bonny clasped her hands against her bosom. 'This is Satan's work we're seeing. Satan's wicked work, and we must pray to the Lord to deliver us from his wicked wiles.'

The housemaid Janet Blount, called from her attendance on Eva

Lenard, was calm and practical. She described her own part in serving the dinner.

'Me and Dulcie Hawkins brought each course to the table, and cleared away after they'd finished,' she said. She admitted to having heard Rolf and Minette quarrelling, but denied knowing why they had quarrelled. 'We heard, but we didn't listen,' she said flatly. 'It's not our place to eavesdrop. We were busy fetching and carrying and putting things in the dishwasher, for after dinner was done.'

Connor asked her if, at the start of the party, the two bottles of Shiraz and the bottle of champagne were on the sideboard, and she nodded emphatically.

'Yes sir, Thomas brought them up from the cellar at five o'clock, and I put the champagne in the big ice bucket, and the other two bottles on the sideboard, with the bottle opener and cloth, as Mr Lenard liked.'

'When did Mr Lenard open the first bottle of Shiraz?'

'Soon as he came into the room. That was at half-past-seven. He said the wine must be let breathe.'

'After he opened the bottle, did he carry it to the table?'

'No. He just laid the cork aside, and left the bottle on the sideboard, until after the soup and fish dishes were cleared.'

'Did anyone else touch the bottle?'

'That I can't say. I wasn't in the dining-room all the time.'

The second housemaid, Dulcie Hawkins, was on the verge of hysteria, and too nervous to do more than repeat that she just fetched in the food and took away the dirty dishes.

The second gardener, René Jones, generally categorized as 'slow' was surprisingly lucid in his answers, and ended by saying 'it can't be the wine that upset people. Us staff finished a bottle of it, and we never turned a hair.'

Last of the staff members to appear was Thomas Jenkins, the senior gardener and evidently a power in the household. He stated that when Cook called to him that Mr Lenard was ill, he came from the staff living-room, and found Mr Lenard lying on the floor.

'I straightway told everyone not to touch anything. Mr Lenard was breathing, and his man Arnold was trying to bring him round, but what worried me was that Mrs Lenard and Miss Plum weren't in the room. I could hear Mrs Lenard screaming down the corridor and I told Sergeant Griffiths we must go to her and Miss Plum, because they might also be ill.

'Griffiths and me ran to Miss Plum's apartment. Mrs Lenard was at the door, in her wheelchair, and she was screaming for Hester. I banged on the door, but there was no answer, so Griffiths and I went in. The door wasn't locked. We left Mrs Lenard outside the door. I don't think she knew where she was.

'Miss Plum was lying on the floor, out cold, and breathing funny. We worked on her till the doctor came, and the ambulance.'

'Who called for them?'

'Griffiths did. He talked to his radio car. I heard him say it was suspicious circumstances and he had to have a doctor and ambulance, and back-up.'

'Did you think the circumstances were suspicious, Mr Jenkins?'

'Course I did. I was shocked, like everyone, but I wasn't surprised. I've thought from the beginning that it's the family this sod's after. If you want to cripple a company of men, you take out the man in charge, don't you. To my mind, Mr Rolf was always in danger.'

'And Miss Plum? Was she a target?'

Thomas shrugged. 'Reckon she got hers by chance. She likes her drop of wine. Maybe she drank more than Mr Rolf did. She threw up in her room.' Thomas paused. 'She's been worried, these past few days. Usually when she met me in the garden, she'd stop for a chat, but not lately. Something on her mind, I'd say.'

Thorneycroft, listening to each witness in turn, watching their body language and noting their hesitations, was struck by a peculiarity. All of them expressed, for the general situation, a proper concern, but not one of them displayed grief for the plight of Rolf Lenard or Hester Plum.

If they died, Rolf and Hester would become the late unlamented.

The questioning ended soon after midnight, and the staff retired to their quarters, the women to bedrooms in the house, and the two gardeners to a cottage behind the garages.

'We'll re-examine tomorrow,' Connor said, 'when we have the lab reports.'

Abbot appeared in the doorway of the study. 'Finney says the team will need another hour,' he said. 'They're done in the dining-room and kitchen area, for the moment, but they're still busy in Miss Plum's rooms. There's a glass-fronted medicine cabinet in her sitting-room, Finney's had the outside printed, but he hasn't unlocked it. He wants to seal it and leave it for a pharmacist to check it tomorrow.'

'Yes. I'll talk to him about that, but right now I want to hear your version of what was drunk at the dinner, tonight.'

Abbot perched on the arm of a chair. 'When I went into the dining-room, I took a good look at the glasses on the table, which had been used and which not. Mrs Eva Lenard, Mr Lenard, and Miss Plum all drank sherry. Mrs Lenard's glass was clean. It seems she stuck to vodka all night. She also refused the Shiraz.

'Mr Lenard and Miss Plum both drank Shiraz, regardless of the fact that it was supplied by the Bonbouche warehouse, at Goldmead. According to the label on the bottle, the Shiraz was imported in bulk, and transferred into Bonbouche bottles at the warehouse. I thought they'd stopped selling their products.'

'Not bottled or canned goods,' Connor said. 'Still, you'd think the family would steer clear of any Bonbouche stuff.'

'Those bottles could have been in the Coventry cellar for months,' Thorneycroft said.

'Not them,' Abbot said. 'There was a message written on each bottle, in a felt tip pen. The bottle the guests drank said "Happy days, favourite Gran. Jason". The bottle Minette took to the staff said "see you soon, love you lots, Jason". The champers bottle just said, "pop goes the weasel, love Jason".'

'God!' muttered Connor.

'Champagne is called "pop",' Thorneycroft suggested. 'It could be a family joke.'

'Killing!' Connor said. 'You could die laughing.'

Davidson looked up from his laptop. 'Sir? The warehouse will have their records on computer. They'll be able to tell us who ordered the wines, and when. We can get print-outs.'

'First thing tomorrow,' Connor approved. 'Your job Harry. Get as much detail as you can, the estate, the year of production, name of producer and shipper, method of payment used by the warehouse and the buyer. Take it back over six months when it comes to the sales made. Take Malherbe with you. He knows wines.'

He stood up, stretching cramped limbs. 'I don't fancy the Coventry menu,' he said. 'I'll ask Healey to have pizzas and coffee sent in for us. We'll take a break.'

The scratch meal over, they returned to the study. Connor cast his eye over the notes Davidson had taken, and summarized them.

'We have the basics in place,' he said. 'Scene of crime's been identified, secured and protected. Search for evidence is being conducted. Victims are hospitalized and under guard. The house and grounds will be searched thoroughly tomorrow. We need to review what we know, or think we know, at this point.

'We know that at six p.m. yesterday, Eva Lenard, Rolf and Minette Lenard, and Hester Plum, assembled at this house to celebrate Eva's birthday. They had drinks in Eva's apartment. The glasses there indicate that Rolf drank whisky, Minette vodka, Miss Plum sherry, and Eva soda-pink. They sat talking until seven-thirty when they moved to the dining-room.

'The dinner consisted of thin soup with savoury pancakes, *Sole Veronique*, roast mutton and vegetables. All the guests shared in the first two courses, and with the exception of Minette, who stuck to vodka, they all drank sherry. When the main course was served, Minette quarrelled violently with Rolf, and left the table to take the second bottle of Shiraz to the staff dining-room. She was, on her own admission, drunk. That bottle of wine was consumed by Minette, Terence Arnold and the two gardeners. They suffered no ill effects.

'The first bottle of Shiraz was still on the table when our team searched the dining-room. As Abbot has said, Eva and Minette did not drink any wine from that bottle. It's estimated that Rolf took less than half a glass of it, but Hester Plum must have drunk at least two glasses, leaving the bottle about a third full. That bottle, its remaining contents and its cork are now being examined by forensics.

'So we have the guests drinking – or refusing to drink – wine supplied by the Bonbouche warehouse, the labels of the bottles signed by Jason Lenard with messages relating to Eva Lenard's birthday.

'Forensics have already notified me that the contents of the first bottle include an adulterant – a poison – and they will identify its exact nature and quantity very shortly.

'It seems likely that it was conveyed here before Eva's birthday, in fact weeks before. Davidson will check the warehouse records for the bottle's provenance, and the date it was delivered to this house.'

Abbot looked doubtful. 'Computer records can be wiped by a good operator, and other facts substituted.'

'And fiddling can be detected by a better operator,' Connor answered. 'Davidson will get us the true facts. What's clear is that the wines were sent to Eva Lenard by Jason Lenard, who wrote messages to his grandmother on the bottles. Jason's his granny's darling. He stands to inherit a very large fortune when she dies.'

'Eva Lenard doesn't touch red wine,' Thorneycroft said. 'It gives her gout.'

Connor nodded. 'So if Jason aimed to top someone in Coventry Hall, it wasn't Eva. Possibly the poisoner didn't much care who else he killed. Sometime, someone at this house was going to crack open the bottle. Even if the results weren't fatal, they'd be dramatic enough to focus public attention on the attack. Agreed?'

Abbot nodded. Thorneycroft was silent, his mind on other possibilities.

'The poisoner knew,' continued Connor, 'that with Eva's birthday and Christmas coming up in the next fortnight, the wine-drinking was likely to take place around this time.'

'Does Jason know what's happened?' Thorneycroft asked.

'Yes,' Connor answered. 'He's booked to return tomorrow from Italy. We'll have him met at the airport.'

There was a short silence, then Connor said, 'Jason Lenard has two reasons for wanting his father out of the way: one, Rolf is blocking Jason's way to the chairmanship, and two, Rolf is a stick-in-the-mud who refuses to allow modernization of the company.'

Thorneycroft shook his head. 'Why would Jason organize poison attacks that wrecked Bonbouche sales and sent its share-prices through the floor? What's more, the publicity that's resulted from the attacks has united the company's factions, and put a stop to any plans of immediate change.'

Connor looked mulish. 'Jason had the knowledge, the means and the opportunity to access all the Bonbouche outlets and ware-houses. He could have doctored the mushroom package, the sherbet engine, and the curry carton. In previous interviews he's come across as a cold, callous bastard who feels no concern for the victims or their families. We know he has support in the USA. He probably has backing in Europe that Rolf and the old guard know nothing about. His pals right here on the Goldmead Estate may have been buying Bonbouche shares, getting ready to vote Rolf out at the next AGM.'

'It's possible to make out a circumstantial case against Jason,' Thorneycroft said, 'but do you honestly believe that a man as canny as Jason would put his signature on a bottle of poisoned wine?'

Connor sighed. 'No I don't. This perp may be mad, but he's not stupid. I think you were right when you said the killer belongs to the Lenard's inner circle. He knows this house and he's had access to it fairly recently. That brings us to Jason, Eva, Silas and Minette Lenard; Minette's toyboy Arnold; the household staff; and Fenella Batista and Peter Noble as possible outsiders.'

Thorneycroft still shook his head slowly. 'The whole case has changed,' he said. 'Its first phase lasted from the Fishburn warning on October 18th, to the Murugan attack on November 30th. That phase was driven by the attempts being made to change the structures and policies of Bonbouche. It ended when the rebel factions within the company saw the necessity for unity, and shelved their plans.

'In other words, the poisoner had achieved his aim. He felt he had succeeded, and the attacks stopped.

'The second phase, which we're now in, is different. Last night's attacks were different. The poisoner struck at two people last night, both of them members of the inner ring of the Lenard family. The victims were not, as in the earlier attacks, random choices. I believe they were attacked because they had become privy to information that poses a threat to the poisoner.

'If they recover, they will have to be protected from further attacks. Miss Plum is in particular danger.'

'Why?' demanded Connor.

'Because of what she knows. She tried to tell Silas Lenard about it. If she recovers, she will tell us. Her life's at risk as long as the poisoner's at liberty.'

'Can you name him?' Connor's smile was mocking.

'No I can't,' Thorneycroft answered, 'but I'd say you need to keep an eye on Minette Lenard and the chauffeur. They know more than they're saying, and they're ready to do a flit.'

'Yeah. They have the look. I've already got a man keeping an eye on them.'

At this point the telephone at Connor's elbow rang. He answered it, at the same time pulling a notebook towards him. He listened, and wrote, thanked the caller and replaced the receiver with delicate precision.

'That was Dr Hitchcock from the Clinic,' he said. 'He says Miss Plum is suffering from a violent allergic reaction. It's caused her throat to swell, affected her breathing and her heart function, and affected her kidneys. In other words, she's been given what could be a lethal dose of poison.

'Hitchcock's fetched her own GP from his bed, and they're treating Miss Plum with antihistamine, and what Hitchcock calls support and symptomatic treatment. He will keep us informed of her progress. She is still critically ill.

'Lenard is lapsing in and out of consciousness, but his vital signs are strengthening.' Connor was already dialling a number. 'We have to open a docket of attempted murder, and I want forensics analysis of what was in that bottle of Shiraz.'

He spoke for some time to DS Hogarth, and then to Dr Prout. When he ended the call, he said, 'The wine was poisoned with a heavy dose of something called Quintol. It's a preservative manufactured in several parts of the world, harmless to most people, but known to cause allergic reactions in a few subjects. Miss Plum is one of the few. So you see what this means?'

'Hester Plum was the intended victim,' Thorneycroft said, 'and the poisoner knows of her allergy. But what motive did he have for attempting to kill her?'

The question was to be answered sooner than he expected.

Head of the search team Finney appeared in the doorway of the study and addressed Connor.

'Something you need to see in Miss Plum's room, guv,' he said.

Thorneycroft, Connor and Abbot stood with Finney in the bedroom of Hester Plum's apartment, contemplating a painting of an eccentric highly-coloured house.

'There's a safe behind it,' Finney said with conviction. 'Look at the dabs. A hand each side of the frame, thumbs pointing upwards. See?'

He lifted his own gloved hands towards the picture, and Connor said sharply, 'watch it! That looks like a good painting.'

'Not as good as the original, and that's in America,' Finney said with a grin. He rubbed his nose. 'There's a ring of keys in her desk, might fit.'

Connor nodded. 'Get them.'

Finney fetched the keys and handed them to Connor. Stepping close to the wall, he took hold of the picture's frame, pressed gently and lifted firmly. He moved back, holding the frame. The safe in the wall was a simple one, operated not by a combination but by a slender steel key. Connor found the key and unlocked the door, swung it open.

The safe contained a folder of documents, and a number of jewellers' boxes; but the object that focussed their attention was a brown paper bag, sealed with several bands of sticky tape.

Across the bag was written 'recovered from Coventry Woods, by Hester Plum, December 12th'.

Connor tore the tape off the mouth of the bag and reached in a tentative finger and thumb. He lifted out a couple of brown leathery objects, that released a powdering of soil and mast.

'Mushrooms,' he said. 'We have to talk to Thomas Jenkins.'

XXV

WHEN CONNOR AND Thorneycroft approached the door of the
gardeners cottage, they saw that the lights were still on. Thomas
Jenkins answered their knock at once. He was fully dressed.

'Couldn't sleep,' he explained. 'Thought I might be needed.'

'We need you to take us to the woods,' Connor said. 'I understand
the gate's kept locked. Have you got a key?'

'Yes. I let in the woodsmen when they come, once a month.'

'Are there other keys?'

'Yes, all the family has one, same as in Mr Vincent's time.' He
squinted at the black night sky. 'We'll need lights. I've got battery
lamps.'

'Bring them,' Connor said.

They followed a paved path for several hundred yards, to the gate
of the woods. As they reached it, Thomas rolled his shoulders.

'Tell you straight, I don't like this place, never have. Always feel
there's something watching, you know?' He unlocked the gate and
pushed it open. 'It's all right in spring, there's bluebells.'

They passed through the gate, and Thomas closed it after them.
'Where'd you want to go?' he asked. 'It's a big place.'

Before Connor could speak, Thorneycroft said, 'to the covin tree.
The big tree.'

They took an overgrown path to their left, and came in a few minutes
to the great oak. It stood in a broad dell, the ground deep in mast.
Shining the lamps around, they picked out a mound on the far side of
the basin, and saw the incision that exposed a rectangle of bare soil.

They crossed to the mound and scanned it. Next to the recently
eroded strip was a second cutting, where nature had already begun to
claim control. There the coat of mast was thin, and dirty white domes
were pushing through it.

Connor knelt, took the trowel offered by Jenkins, and cut a third section, about six inches square. He slid it into a specimen bag, saying to Thorneycroft, 'you're my witness.'

Standing up, he turned to Thomas. 'Did Miss Plum come to these woods last Wednesday?'

'Yes, with me and René. We came to cut the Christmas tree. Miss Plum went walkabout.'

'Did she come to this tree?'

'Well, I dunno, she never said.'

Connor's flat stare rested on Thomas. 'I hope we get a chance to ask her. Meanwhile, you don't say anything about this to anyone. Is that understood?'

'Understood,' Thomas answered. Thorneycroft saw in him the readiness of an old soldier to accept an order without question and obey it without hesitation.

Back at Coventry Hall, Connor handed the two packets taken from the woods to Finney, to be properly packed and labelled and given to Dr Prout for examination.

'Tell him to get them identified by a botanist,' he said. 'And don't handle them without gloves. They're probably poisonous.'

When the scene-of-crime squad had packed their paraphernalia into the van, and left for Concorde Street, Connor said to Thorneycroft, 'what made you go straight for the covin tree?'

'I don't know,' said Thorneycroft frankly. 'It dominates the scene, it seemed the right place to begin.'

Connor sniffed. 'What else does your yappy gut tell you?'

'Hester Plum knew there were mushrooms in the Coventry woods. She took a sample of the ones at the covin tree. She saw that someone had already taken a sample, not long before. If those two samples, and the one we took tonight, turn out to be Gyromitra esculenta, then it's possible that the mushrooms that poisoned Jock Robins came from these woods.

'It follows that everyone who has a key to the woods had access to the mushrooms; Hester herself, all the Lenard family and the staff. Hester knew she was holding material that might identify the killer.'

'So why didn't she tell us at once?'

'I think because of her past history. She was once accused of having poisoned a patient, she was afraid she might be suspected of staging the Bonbouche attacks. So maybe she decided to tell someone she trusted, and ask him or her to inform the police. Only she chose the wrong person to confide in. She spoke to the killer, who decided she must be got rid of fast. Last night's party provided the opportunity.'

'And Rolf? Why was he poisoned?'

'We know this perp makes random hits. Perhaps Rolf was just in the wrong place at the wrong time, or perhaps Hester also told him about her find, making him a danger to the killer.'

'And perhaps,' said Connor glumly, 'Rolf told Jason, or Silas, or Minette. If Miss Plum regains consciousness, she'll tell what happened. If she doesn't, we'll never know.' He rubbed red-rimmed eyes. 'I need to get back to the nick, and I want to call in at the Heart Clinic on the way, talk to the doctors. Abbot, Davidson and the rest can stay on till morning. I'll drop you off at your place, you can get some sleep.'

'I'm past sleep,' Thorneycroft said. 'I'll go with you. I need to hear Prout's report.'

The Richmond Heart Clinic was modern, well-appointed, and staffed by people who looked confident of success. 'Place to die in style,' said Connor waspishly, but in Dr Hitchcock's consulting room he assumed his smoothest manner.

'Miss Plum has not regained consciousness yet,' Hitchcock said, 'but she's holding her own. The medication is reducing the swelling of the neck, and her breathing is stabilizing.' He went on to give details of the treatments being applied to her, ending with harsh words about firms that marketed preservatives with harmful effects.

'When your Superintendent called me to tell me that Miss Plum had ingested Quintol, I told him he should arrest that entire company, and charge them with culpapable homicide. The modern markets all sell allergens, I know, but Quintol affects more people, more adversely, than most. People buy it over the counter, to put in home-made jams and squashes. Luckily Miss Plum's own doctor was able to tell me what antihistamine is best for her.' He fixed Connor with a beady stare. 'How did Miss Plum come to swallow so much of the stuff? Was it by accident?'

Connor said smoothly, 'that's what we're trying to discover, sir. Until we're sure, my officer will remain on duty at Miss Plum's door, and no unauthorized person must enter her room or attempt to administer food, drink or medication to her.'

'I understand.' Hitchcock smiled. 'We've had considerable practice in protecting our patients from uninvited visitors. I am not allowing Mr Lenard visitors, as yet. He's conscious, but he's weak and disoriented. We'll keep him here for a few days yet. No doubt the strains put on him by the past few weeks' events have taken their toll of him too.'

'Thank you for all you're doing,' Connor said. 'If anyone asks after Miss Plum, please say that her condition is still critical, but stable. And if she regains consciousness, let me know at once.'

Connor made two stops on the way out of the hospital: the first was to talk to the constable on duty at Hester Plum's door; the second was to ask the ward sister in charge of high care to list the contents of Rolf Lenard's pockets when he was brought into the clinic.

'Wallet with cards, loose change, key-ring with car and house keys, mobile phone,' Connor said. 'He was wearing gold cufflinks and watch. Clean handkerchief in his pocket. No surprises there. Let's get going. The night's a-wasting.'

They arrived at Concorde Street at 1.30 a.m. Dr Prout greeted them with cheerful smiles and fresh coffee.

'The preliminary reports are ready for you,' he said, 'and my detailed analyses are being printed. We sent the mushrooms to Mr Lindhurst at Kew. We'll know by midday if they're Gyromitra esculenta.'

He handed both men pages covered with cabalistic writing. 'You can study those when you've had some sleep,' he said. 'In the meantime I'll give you the broad outline. First, the bottle of Shiraz from which Rolf Lenard and Hester Plum were served, contained a percentage of Quintol that's way above legal limits. The amount was certain to make a normal person ill, and could well be life-threatening to an allergic subject.

'Quintol is colourless, virtually tasteless in a strong-flavoured medium like red wine, and is rapidly absorbed into the body. It can be purchased in shops selling the ingredients of jam, cakes, fruit drinks and sweets, etc. It does not leave a visible residue.

'Persons including Quintol in their products are required by law to announce the fact on the label. Obviously there was no such warning on the Shiraz label. Miss Plum was fed a lethal dose, without knowing what she was drinking. Whoever put the Quintol into that bottle acted with deliberate intent. It's surprising she's still alive.'

'She's holding her own, Hitchcock says.' Connor folded Prout's detailed notes into his pocket. 'You can take us through the technicalities tomorrow. Right now, I want to know how long the Quintol would have to be in the wine before it was fully dissolved.'

'A few minutes,' Prout answered. 'I'll run a test for you. Of course, it might lie in the bottle for weeks or even months before it was consumed.'

'Would a long delay affect the wine in a perceptible way?'

'A connoisseur would probably pick it up right away, but ordinary mortals like you and me probably wouldn't notice a thing. What's more, I'm told that at the time the wine was served, Minette and Rolf Lenard were having a blazing row. In those circumstances, guests don't sip their wine and nose the bouquet, they close their eyes and slurp it down.'

'How would the Quintol be put in the bottle?'

'It would have to be added before the bottle was corked and sealed. The Quintol must have been in the bottle for some weeks. Under examination, the cork showed traces of the preservative.'

'The Quintol stained the cork?'

'Yes, and the staining is typical of a bottle that's lain on its side in a wine rack, and also been moved occasionally. That bottle was sent to Coventry Hall by Jason Lenard, was it not?'

'Yes.'

'Then one must suppose the Quintol was added at the time of the bottling at the Bonbouche warehouse.' Prout steepled his fingers. 'There's one thing that surprises me, and that's that a snooty lot like Bonbouche should use phoney corks instead of the real thing.'

'Cheaper,' Connor said, but Thorneycroft sat up straight in his chair.

'You mean they used composite stoppers instead of corks?'

'Only on the bottle of Shiraz that went to the staff room with Minette. The bottle in the main dining-room had a genuine cork.'

Thorneycroft frowned, trying to make his tired mind connect the scattering of facts.

'You're saying the wine was poisoned before it was sent to Coventry Hall. The bottle couldn't be switched later, could it, because Jason's messages to his grandmother were on the labels. Could someone have forged his writing?'

'The experts say not. He has a very distinctive hand.' Prout dropped his casual air. 'The Quintol was in the bottle long enough to stain the cork. Whether it was added some weeks or only a few days before Eva Lenard's dinner party, the adding was premeditated, it was intended to affect a person notoriously allergic to Quintol. Miss Plum was the victim of a murder attempt, and Rolf Lenard has also suffered from a murderous attack.'

Thorneycroft persisted. 'The original cork couldn't have been drawn and replaced, because the bottle was sealed as well as corked.'

'Yes,' Connor said, 'the seal was retrieved from the sideboard. Rolf Lenard was seen by several people to strip the seal and draw the cork. I assume the corks could be different because the bottling was done at different times. But the seals are identical, they're the Bonbouche seal, and we have them both here.'

'If only one bottle was poisoned,' Thorneycroft said, 'how could the poisoner be sure that Hester Plum would drink from that bottle, and no-one else?'

'The Shiraz was a present to Eva, not the staff. Eva wouldn't hand it on to them. She wouldn't drink red wine herself but Hester Plum would. Sooner or later, she'd drink it.'

'It's an odd circumstance that Minette removed one of the birthday bottles, isn't it?'

'She was drunk.'

'She's a Lenard. She could have accessed the warehouse, slipped the Quintol into a bottle, given it to a handler for Jason to sign.'

'In which case,' said Connor acidly, 'Jason or the handler will remember her actions. No John, if the bottle was poisoned in the warehouse, then Jason has to be the chief suspect.' He got to his feet. 'His plane gets in at three. I'll have him picked up for questioning. In the meantime I have to get after the Quintol, see if we can find who bought it when and where. Another needle in our haystack.' He jabbed a finger at Thorneycroft's chest. 'You go home and get some sleep.'

'What about you?' Thorneycroft asked.

'I'll kip here,' Connor answered. 'I'll join you at Coventry Hall tomorrow eight o'clock, we'll have a chemist check Miss Plum's medicine cupboard, chat to Mrs Lenard and the staff. We need to tie up some loose ends.'

Tired though he was, Thorneycroft found it hard to fall asleep. Facts nagged at him, refusing to fall into order. When at last he slept, he dreamed not of Coventry Hall or poisoned wine, but of a chubby prefect from his primary school days, who leered and yelled at him, 'you're talking crap, Thorneycroft. Put a cork in it.'

XXVI

BY MORNING THE sky had cleared, and sun struck rainbows from the spray of passing motorcars. Thorneycroft, restored by sleep, a hot bath and breakfast arrived early at Coventry Hall.

He walked slowly along the main corridor. Abbot had already left, and a fresh team was engaged in searching the house and grounds; a chemist and his assistant were assessing the contents of Hester Plum's medicine cabinet.

The chemist pointed to a row of antihistamines. 'If the lady's so allergic,' he said, 'why didn't she take one of those before she phoned Dr Lenard?'

'She knew she'd been poisoned,' Thorneycroft said, 'but she didn't know with what. She was on the point of collapse. She knew she wouldn't make it without help.'

'And will she make it?'

'The doctor says she's holding her own.'

The chemist grimaced. 'Poisoners kill people who love them. They smile and offer them poison. That's anathema to me.'

Connor and Sam Koch were in the study, sorting through a clutch of typed statements. Connor handed them to Koch.

'Go over them with the staff, and get them signed,' he said. He turned to Thorneycroft. 'I want to talk to Eva Lenard, see what she can tell us. I'll have to warn her that her blue-eyed boy is going to be questioned about the wine he supplied for her birthday party.'

'I don't think he poisoned it,' Thorneycroft said.

'I've said before, Jason Lenard had the means and the opportunity to commit the first three attacks, and this one.'

'But what motive did he have?'

'He hates his father and wants to replace him as the kingpin of the company.'

'So he poisoned Hester Plum and Rolf, and so we'd be sure to appreciate his efforts, he put his name on the poison bottle. And if Rolf was his intended victim, why did he use Quintol?'

'If Rolf hadn't been distracted by his fight with Minette, he'd have drunk a lot more Shiraz, it's his favourite wine. As it was, a few mouthfuls made him very sick.'

'Liam, I want to suggest to you that far from being the killer, Jason could well be the killer's ultimate target. We've had five victims. Robins, Tifflin, Murugan, Rolf and Hester. Rolf and Hester are countdown victims 2 and 1. But the lift-off number is 0, and that could be Jason. He's the one who'll be held responsible because he supplied the wine. It's possible he's been set up to carry the blame for all five attacks.'

Connor stared. 'There's not a scrap of evidence to support that statement—'

'... and it's possible that what we consider to be evidence has been carefully manufactured by the poisoner,' Thorneycroft agreed. 'I believe Hester Plum was the target of this last attack. She had suspicions, she found the mushrooms and drew conclusions. She didn't phone the police because of her past record, but I'll lay odds she spoke to someone in the Lenard circle, who very likely told others about her find. Jason was away in Italy at that time, so she spoke to someone nearer at hand. One way or another the murderer learned that she'd found something that linked him – or her – to the death of Jock Robins. Hester became a danger that had to be eliminated at once.'

'And if Minette hadn't set up a rumpus, Rolf and Hester would have polished off the whole bottle of Shiraz, and they'd both be dead. John, I'm not jumping to conclusions, but we have to know the exact circumstances in which Jason supplied the bottle of Shiraz that put two people on the critical list. We'll talk to him this afternoon. In the meantime I'm going to visit old Mrs Lenard. Are you coming?'

Thorneycroft rose without speaking and walked with Connor to Eva Lenard's apartment. Ayusha Ramiah admitted them and told them that Eva was awake and dressed.

They found her reclining on the *chaise-longue* in her living-room, with Hester Plum's dogs at her side. She turned her head to glare at them.

'Where's Hester?' she demanded. 'I want Hester, now.'

Thorneycroft stepped forward and took her hand. It was very cold, the fingers stiff in his clasp. She was in denial, body and mind. He said gently:

'Hester can't come to you right now, Mrs Lenard. She's ill, in hospital, something she drank last night. When she's better she'll come home.'

She rolled her head from side to side. 'Talk, talk, talk. Where's Jason, then? Where's he?'

'On his way back from Italy. He'll be here this afternoon.'

Connor came towards her, smiling. 'I'm sorry to intrude on you at such a time, ma'am. I need to ask you a few questions.'

She sat up so suddenly that one of the dogs yelped and fell off the chair.

'Go away,' she said, her voice soaring, 'go away, I have nothing to say to you, do you hear? Get out of my sight.' She began to cry, rocking her body to and fro. 'I want Hester.'

The two men retreated to the door. Ayusha followed them.

'Her own doctor's coming,' she said. 'They say he's good with her.'

'We'll come back later,' Thorneycroft said. Out in the corridor, he told Connor he'd not get much out of the old lady for some days. 'She's had a huge shock and if you push her, she'll close up like a clam. Best let her own doctor talk to her. That's Serge Joliffe, he's a snob but he's a good psychiatrist.'

They turned to the routine work of police investigation, checking reports and piecing together statements to try to reach a true picture of events.

At 9.30 the botanist entrusted by Prout with the task of identifying the mushrooms taken from the Coventry woods, arrived and handed over written confirmation that the mushrooms were indeed Gyromitra esculenta. Taken to the dell where they grew, he gave his firm opinion that the first lot had been dug from the soil a month ago, and the second and third lots a few days ago.

He showed great interest in the covin tree. 'Fine old monarch,' he said. 'Pity the mushrooms had to give his kingdom a bad name. They started a lot of trouble. Someone ate them and died, and the locals blamed old women for black magic. The witches were in the fire, so to speak.' He laughed, showing yellow teeth. He would have liked to explore the woods further, but Connor bundled him off the property without ceremony.

Heading back to the house, Connor said, 'so we know the mushrooms grow here, and that some were harvested round about the time Jock Robins was poisoned, but if we made the connection in court, defence counsel would cut us to pieces. We have no solid proof, John, nothing but a lot of reasonable suppositions, and you don't get a conviction on those. We'll concentrate the search on these woods. The perp may have left traces, a cigarette, footprint, anything that'll tie him to the mushrooms.'

Davidson and Malherbe, returning from the Goldmead warehouse at 10.15, had more positive news to deliver. They brought print-outs of the liquor delivered to the members of the Lenard circle over the past six months. All came from the warehouse.

'Rolf and Minette had a regular monthly order,' Davidson said. 'It always included whisky, vodka, brandy, sherry, several wines – white and red and mixers. There was always Shiraz, Rolf's favourite, and usually there were some more exotic drinks. The Lenards entertain a lot. Their booze bills are heavy.

'Eva Lenard doesn't place orders herself, but Hester Plum keeps the Coventry cellar well stocked. Not much red wine, though, because Eva doesn't drink it. The order includes beer and soft drinks for the staff.

'Silas Lenard apparently places his regular order with a merchant in his suburb, but he makes occasional orders at Goldmead when he wants high-priced vintage wines. His last order was in November, all French or German wines, including six bottles of Shiraz.

'The print-outs detail all the items purchased, with their provenance, price, etcetera.' Davidson handed over the papers to Connor. 'But the interesting thing, sir, is Jason Lenard's order that he sent as a gift to his grandmother, back in October. I spoke to the supervisor of the wine store at the warehouse. He dealt with the order himself. He told me that Jason came into the wine store and asked for two Shiraz and one Dom Perignon. The supervisor gave him two different bottles of Shiraz, one vintage, one new, for comparison. He handed them to Jason, who wrote messages on the labels. Jason handed them straight back to the supervisor, and they were packed and despatched at once. Jason had no opportunity to put poison in a bottle that was already corked and sealed.'

Connor sighed heavily. 'And you trust the supervisor as you would your own mum?'

Davidson looked him in the eye. 'More. My mum lies about her age, sometimes.'

'Right. Well, we'll have Jason here in a few hours, and hear the story from his own lips.'

In the event, they received a call at twelve o'clock, from the man detailed to meet Jason and conduct him to Concorde Street. 'He's here at the airport, sir. He got a cancellation on an earlier plane, and he says he's not going to any police station until he's seen his grand-mother.'

'Bring him here,' Connor said. 'The old lady's been asking for him. Maybe she'll be more co-operative if he's with her.'

Jason Lenard stalked into the hall of the house like a man looking for a fight. He marched over to where Connor, Thorneycroft and Abbot stood waiting, and said:

'I couldn't get any sense out of your goons who brought me from the airport. What happened? Are my father and Hester alive?'

'Yes,' Connor said. 'Your father's mending, but Miss Plum is still on the critical list.'

'God!' Jason stared from face to face, disbelieving. 'And my grand-mother? Is she all right, can I see her?'

'She's in shock,' Connor said. 'You can see her later, but first I want to ask you some questions.'

Jason nodded. 'Sure. The TV room's private.'

He led the way to the room, flung himself down in an easy chair, and said, 'tell me exactly what happened.'

Connor gave him a careful account of the night's events. Jason listened, eyes watchful.

At the conclusion, he said, 'are you saying I'm suspected of attempted murder?'

'No. I'm telling you that your father and Miss Plum were poisoned by Shiraz laced with Quintol, poured from a bottle with your signa-ture on it. The bottle was one of three sent by you to your grandmother in October last. You recall that, sir?'

'Yes, of course I do.'

'The bottle was opened last night by your father, in the presence of several witnesses, at the start of the family dinner. Your father and Miss Plum drank some of the wine, and were ... almost immediately taken ill. They were conveyed to hospital unconscious. Miss Plum is still unconscious.'

'If there was Quintol in the bottle, I certainly don't know how it got there. I signed a bottle handed me by our wine store supervisor, at Goldmead. It was sealed. I gave it straight back to him.' Jason was clearly incredulous. 'There is no way I could have tampered with the bottle.'

Connor nodded. 'So the supervisor says.' He paused, seeming to reflect, then said, 'Over the past three weeks, we have been making exhaustive enquiries into the business methods and structures of the Bonbouche shops and warehouses. You are in a position to handle the goods stored, and sold by Bonbouche. The fresh fruit and vegetables, the sweets, the take-away dishes. Isn't that so?'

'Yes, it's so.' Jason spoke with quiet deliberation. 'I have access to things like mushrooms, sherbet toys and curry cartons, but I am not a poisoner. For Christ's sake, why would I want to poison anyone?'

Connor leaned forward. 'What are your feelings for your father, Mr Lenard?'

Jason went scarlet. 'We don't get on. That's common knowledge. I want to bring Bonbouche into the 21st century. He wants it to remain in the past.'

'I understand there is a move to bring about change at the next AGM.'

'There was. But when the attacks began, the idea was abandoned, our need was for unity in the Bonbouche company. We had to stop the panic, end the divisions, and get Bonbouche back on an even keel. We were succeeding until this ... this abomination. Now we will have to start again.' He looked towards the television set. 'Have the media got hold of it yet?'

'Not yet,' Connor said. 'But it's only a matter of hours, I'd say. The press won't get to the hospital. They have very good security. But to the family and staff outside I can only say that it will be open season on all of you. I'm sorry, but the paparazzi have no respect for the feelings of others.'

'I'll talk to everyone, tell them how to respond,' Jason said. 'Silas and I will make a plan.'

Connor considered him, head tilted. 'Why did you write on the bottles, sir?'

'I always do. I just put a love message on each bottle I send Gran. It cheers her up. And on champagne, I always write "pop goes the weasel". It's a family joke. Was. Not any more.' He stood up abruptly. 'I must go and see my grandmother. If you don't trust me, come with me.'

They did as he suggested. Eva Lenard was asleep as they stepped into her living-room, but she woke and seeing Jason gave a cry and flung her arms wide. He went and knelt beside her, wrapping his arms round her, and she leaned against him, murmuring and stroking his head.

He stayed for some minutes, talking to her in a low voice, and she grew visibly calmer. At last he settled her on her pillows, saying, 'you rest, now. I'll come and see you tomorrow. Do what your doctor tells you.'

Outside her door, he turned to Connor. 'Am I free to go now? I have a lot to do, for the family and staff, and for the company.'

'Where will you stay?' Connor asked.

'With Silas, my uncle. He's waiting at the hospital, in case they let him see my father. I'll go back to his home for the night, and we'll make plans. You can reach me on my mobile any time. You have the number.'

He left by taxi, watched by Connor and Koch. But Thorneycroft returned to Eva's room. She was not asleep, and made a vague gesture of welcome as he stood by the door.

'Come closer,' she said.

He did as he was bid, and she put a hand on his sleeve. 'You can trust Jason,' she said. 'Not the others.'

Thorneycroft kept off that Tom Tiddler's ground. He said quietly, 'you've had a very bad experience. Do you want to talk about it?'

Her lips moved, as if she wanted to speak but was uncertain what to say.

Thorneycroft persisted. 'Did you see something last night, Mrs Lenard? Something that troubled you?'

She shook her head dumbly, and her face twisted, as if she looked down into an abyss. A picture rose to Thorneycroft's mind, and he said, 'apart from Minette, did anyone leave the dining-room?'

Her old eyes narrowed. 'Only the servants,' she said. 'In and out with the trays and dishes.' She drew a long breath. 'Perhaps Rolf saw something. He went to the windows to call the gardeners in, because of the storm. He says that dry storms are more dangerous than wet ones. Perhaps he saw someone, down there in the dark.'

She covered her eyes with her hands. 'I'm so tired. So tired.'

'Then sleep,' Thorneycroft said. He beckoned to Ayusha, sitting quietly in a corner. 'Stay with her. See that no-one disturbs her. Her doctor will be here soon.'

Connor and Koch spent the rest of the morning on what Connor called damage control. He cautioned the staff against talking to the inevitable media-hounds, reminded Hitchcock and his assistants of the need to keep Rolf and Hester secluded, and set Koch to arranging surveillance on Jason and Silas Lenard, Minette Lenard and Terry Arnold.

'There'll be squeals about expense, but it's cheaper than allowing the perp to have another go,' he said.

Thorneycroft stepped out into the garden and used his mobile to phone Claudia.

She greeted him with relief. 'I've been worried, not hearing since Friday. I know you've been busy.'

'Yes, very.' He told her in broad outline of the events at Coventry Hall. Her immediate response was to ask after Rolf and Hester, and he gave her what reassurance he could.

'You sound very tired,' she said. 'Do they allow you to eat and sleep?'

'I'm OK. We're close to answers, but not quite there. That's stressful.'

'Let your mind settle,' Claudia said, and he smiled. Letting her mind settle was Clo's way of solving what seemed insoluble. She would go off by herself, sit quietly, pray perhaps, and relax to the point of trance. Usually when she reappeared, she had come to a decision.

'I'll try,' Thorneycroft said.

He found a bench under a beech tree, and sat there, thinking about the case, from his point of entry at the Chelsea Bonbouche, until the present time. He received no burning inspiration, but he found himself discarding certain theories and evolving others. His thoughts centred not so much on facts and figures as on the Lenard family, the power they wielded, and the quicksands of character that made their power so uncertain.

Dr Serge Joliffe came to visit Eva Lenard. He saw Thorneycroft on his bench, and raised a cursory hand, but did not stop to speak. He was, Thorneycroft understood, not the solution to Eva's problems, but a part of them – a doctor who preferred to humour a wealthy patient rather than heal her.

He closed his eyes and breathed deeply. Slowly his mind emptied of the carefully docketed facts of the past few weeks. My job, he thought, is not to build a case and lay a charge. I'm here to describe the sort of person who can commit these crimes, to describe his mind and motives, and I have to do that by drawing on my own skills, experience and instinct.

He sat quietly, and reached first calm, and then certainty. He knew what he believed, what he must do, and why. He returned to the house and sought out Connor.

'There's a fourth cork.' he said. 'I know where to look for it. I need you as a witness. Bring gloves and a sterile bag with you.'

Connor sat without moving, a look of concern on his face. Thorneycroft smiled at him. 'It's all right Liam, I haven't lost the plot. We find the cork, we send it to Prout, and then we talk to two people who've been withholding information. Trust me, I'll make you famous.'

'I'd prefer rich,' Connor said, but he found the gloves and bag, and followed Thorneycroft out into the garden.

They found the cork within minutes. Connor slid it into the bag, which was sealed and labelled and sent in the charge of Sam Koch to Concorde Street. Connor phoned Prout and told him exactly what tests must be run on the bag's contents.

'Minette Lenard and Terry Arnold,' Thorneycroft said, 'are they still at Ennisdale Square?'

'They are.' Connor looked smug. 'I've had them watched since last night. I think we'll go and pay them a visit, explain the facts of life to Minette, and ask Arnold what are his intentions.'

Repeated ringing of the bell at number 12 brought Minette to the door. Terence Arnold hovered close behind her.

'What do you want?' she demanded.

Connor stepped forward. 'To speak to you and Mr Arnold, on a matter of urgency.'

'I've told you everything I know!' She seemed about to slam the door in his face, but Arnold put a hand on her shoulder.

'Let them come in,' he said. 'It's better.'

She flounced before them to the living-room and perched on the edge of a sofa. 'I don't know why you're harassing me, when my husband is so ill.'

Connor seated himself facing her. 'I understand from Dr Hitchcock that Mr Lenard is making a good recovery, and you can expect him home soon.'

Minette's lips tightened and she cast a glance at Arnold, who came to stand beside her.

'We're leaving,' he said, 'me and Mrs Lenard. The staff's already quit. I know you said last night we must stay around, but we haven't done anything wrong, we don't have to stay. We know our rights.'

Connor's eyebrows rose. 'The right to remain silent? You can do so, of course, but it might be a foolish choice. Concealing facts could put you both in grave danger, and you could be in trouble for obstructing the course of justice.'

Minette's face puckered and her face glistened with tears. 'I'm already in danger,' she said. 'I can't stay here. I hate them all. Terry and I are getting out.'

Thorneycroft, who had settled out of her line of vision, intervened. 'Mrs Lenard, the first time we met, you told me that you were afraid for your husband.'

She jerked round to face him. 'I was. I am. I don't want to be here when it happens.'

'When what happens, Mrs Lenard?'

She was silent, staring at him, and he said gently, 'do you make jam? Do you use Quintol in your kitchen?'

'No, never. I wouldn't touch the stuff.'

'Does your cook use it, perhaps?'

'No, no, no.' She clutched at Arnold's sleeve. 'I want to go away from here. I want a better life.'

'You'll be able to do that, but for the moment you must co-operate with the police,' Thorneycroft said. 'You can be free of all of them, the Lenards and their lifestyle. But don't you see, as long as you conceal the truth, they'll have a hold over you. You can't beat them at their game of Russian roulette. As the bible says, only the truth can set you free.'

She gazed at him, her tears flowing. 'If I tell you, will we be free to go? Will they let us go abroad, where no-one knows us?'

'That will be for Inspector Connor to decide. If you give him important information, that may count in your favour.'

'All right.' She hesitated, chewing her lip. Arnold came to sit beside her and clasped her thin fingers. Shakily, looking often to him for support, she began to speak.

Connor listened without interrupting, making an occasional note. When she made an end, he said, 'you've done right to tell us this, Mrs Lenard. I want you and Mr Arnold to accompany me to Concorde Street police station, and make formal, signed statements. I assure you that doing so will be in your best interests.'

'Then can we leave?'

'I can't promise that. It may be necessary for you to testify in a court of law. Again that will be in your best interests.'

Minette turned to Arnold. 'I'm scared. What must we do?'

Arnold got to his feet, drawing her after him. 'We do like he says. Let's get this over, the sooner the better.'

Their statements duly made, recorded and signed, Minette Lenard and Arnold departed in search of a hotel, cautioned by Connor to keep a low profile, make no phone calls and avoid communicating in any way with the Lenard family.

Connor, Thorneycroft, Prout and Abbot then met in Hogarth's office to assess the case. Hogarth was not encouraging in his opinion.

'You have a theory,' he said. 'It's just that. It's not a solid body of evidence that will convince a jury. Prout says the cork in the shrubbery was stained with Shiraz but free of Quintol. So what? You can't prove it was thrown from the window on December 15th.

'The statements made by Minette Lenard and Arnold could be a fabrication. They could be seeking to conceal their own guilt, or merely acting to spite Rolf Lenard. And the fact that Jason Lenard supplied the bottle of Shiraz, signed with his name, may well suggest to reasonable people that he's the poisoner.

'You don't have enough. So get back to work, flesh out your theory. Make a case that can't be broken by the best legal team money can buy, because that's what we'll be facing.'

Back in the incident room, Connor said explosively, 'the Super's right, we don't have enough, and the perp will try again.'

'We have Hester Plum,' Thorneycroft said.

'Yeah, unconscious, stiff as a board in a hospital bed, and the quacks won't let us near her.'

'She's an escaped victim,' Thorneycroft said. 'That's always a cop's best hope. If she recovers she'll want to talk to us. I can speak to Hitchcock, see if she's conscious. Tell him we need to be in the clinic so that we're available when she does come round.'

Connor spread his hands. 'Try then.'

Thorneycroft put through the call. Dr Hitchcock, summoned from a consultation, was terse. 'I told you, Dr Thorneycroft, that I would inform you as soon as Miss Plum is well enough to be questioned.'

'Yes, that's so. But tell me, is she conscious?'

Hitchcock hesitated. 'She is. That doesn't mean she's in a fit state to receive visitors, let alone the police.'

'She may need to receive us. Someone tried to kill her. She will need to talk about that.'

'I don't think …

'Has Miss Plum asked to see us?'

Again Hitchcock paused. 'Well, yes, in a rambling way. She is still very ill. Very distressed. I cannot risk causing her further distress.'

'I understand. You must of course act in your patient's best interest. But we need to speak to Miss Plum. Doing so may save other lives. We will come to the clinic, and trust that you will allow us to see her as soon as possible. Are you comfortable with that?'

'Yes. I am.'

'And Mr Lenard? How is he?'

'He's in a highly nervous state. Understandable, after what he's been through. He's on medication to calm him.'

'Good. Thank you, Doctor. See you shortly.'

They travelled fast to Richmond, Connor and Thorneycroft in a police car with driver, Abbot and Malherbe in a second unmarked car. Abbot's job, Connor said, was to take the place of the man currently on duty at Rolf Lenard's hospital room.

'When he learns that his wife and chauffeur have run off together, he'll want out,' Connor said. 'He won't go home to an empty house. He'll make for one of the family. I need to check where they are.'

He set about making calls on his mobile phone, talking to the men and women appointed to maintain surveillance on the Lenards and their associates, checking with controllers at Concorde Street and the Richmond police station. Concluding the task, he said:

'Healey has Coventry Hall sewn up. Silas Lenard is assisting at an operation at Great Ormond Street. Minette and Arnold are holed up in The Grove Hotel, Holborn. Jason's at a conference in Birmingham, but there's a problem. He took the Bonbouche chopper, and he'll be returning that way.'

'Back to Goldmead?'

'I don't know. He could land in a number of places. Our people will check the flight plan and let us know. We'll have to play that fish from Concorde Street. The Super will keep us informed.'

The Richmond Heart Clinic was settling for the night. The lights burning in its windows were subdued, and only the emergency sector was brilliantly lit. Opposite the main doors, three taxis were drawn up, their drivers relaxed at their wheels.

Connor led the way into the reception foyer, despatching Malherbe to check the back entrance to the building, and Abbot to the high care ward where Rolf Lenard was accommodated.

He then asked the reception clerk to inform Dr Hitchcock of his arrival, but before she could do so, Hitchcock himself appeared. His first words were addressed to Thorneycroft.

'You were right,' he said. 'She wants to speak to the police.' He turned to Connor. 'Understand, Chief Inspector, she must not be taxed in any way. I'm letting you see her for her sake, not yours. She's still very ill, but she needs to get something off her mind. You may have a few minutes. I will be present, and if I say "out", you leave at once.'

He led the way to the intensive care unit. Hester Plum lay quiet in the high hospital bed, attached to the tubes and trappings of survival. Her eyes were closed, but they opened as Connor approached her bedside.

He smiled down at her. 'Take it easy, Miss Plum, take your time. Is there something you want to say to me?'

'The mushrooms,' she said, her voice feather-light.

'Yes. We found them in the packet in your safe. We had them tested. They are poisonous.'

Her lips trembled. 'I meant you to know at once. I phoned Rolf. Asked him to tell you. He said, trouble for Coventry. He'd talk to Silas and Minette, ask their advice.'

'And did he talk to them?'

'I don't know.'

'Did he speak to Jason?'

'I don't know.' She stretched a hand to clutch at Connor's sleeve. 'They're at war. You have to stop them. You must.'

Her breathing had become uneven, and Dr Hitchcock stepped forward, motioning to Connor to leave. A nurse appeared, soothing and assertive, and the men left the sickroom.

As they stepped into the corridor, the sister from the high care ward blocked Hitchcock's path.

'I'm sorry sir, but Mr Lenard's demanding to see you. He wants you to sign him out. He's determined to leave.'

'He's not ready to leave.'

'I told him so, but he's made up his mind. I've persuaded him at least to let you examine him, and prescribe the proper medication.'

Hitchcock glanced at Connor. 'I can't force him to stay, you know.'

Connor nodded. 'Delay him as long as you can. Is there a back exit from the property?'

'Only for ambulances. There's an electronic gate, and the ambulance drivers have remotes to operate it. The rest of us, medical staff, nurses and patients, use the front exit from the parking lot.' Hitchcock met Connor's eyes. 'He shouldn't be on his own. He's a sick man.'

'I'll be in touch with his relations,' Connor said. 'We'll take care of him.'

XXVII

CONNOR AND THORNEYCROFT left the clinic at once. Connor walked to where the police vehicles were parked fifty yards short of the clinic. He meant to communicate with Hogarth, give and receive information, and decide on a course of action.

Thorneycroft stood in the shade of a plane tree and watched the front of the building. Visiting hours were evidently over. Three cars left the parking area; a Rolls delivered a wheelchair patient to the main entrance; a middle-aged couple climbed into one of the taxis and were driven away. The space in the rank was filled almost at once by another cab. No doubt the clinic was a lucrative pickup point.

Where would Rolf Lenard head for? For wherever Jason was? Hester Plum said the two were at war. She was probably right. They were natural aggressors, in conflict with the world and with each other.

Malherbe emerged from the building, spotted Thorneycroft and came to join him. 'Lenard will leave this way,' he said. 'The back gate's only for ambulances, and the parking's boom-controlled. You get a ticket coming in, and use it to get out.'

Connor had returned, and was speaking to the driver of the leading taxi. The man listened, nodded, and reached to raise his 'engaged' flag. Connor regained the pavement and beckoned Thorneycroft and Malherbe to him.

'Abbot will bring Lenard to the taxi rank,' he said. 'Lenard has been trying to reach Arnold, without success. He'll have to take a cab. Abbot will explain to him that for his own safety, he will have an escort following him to his destination. That will be Abbot and Malherbe with Grogan driving.

'We don't know where he plans to go, but the cabbie will inform his office controller of the destination as normal. We'll get it from there. Thorneycroft and I will be following you at a discreet distance.'

'Where do you think he's headed, sir?' Malherbe asked.

'I think he plans to meet Jason,' Connor answered. 'The Super has confirmed that Jason's at a conference in Birmingham. He arrived by chopper from the Goldmead estate, and the likelihood is he'll return there. There's a helipad attached to the conference venue. Hogarth's arranged that Jason's flight plan, once confirmed, will be sent to him at Concorde Street. He's also spoken to the flight controller at Goldmead. If Jason lands there, he'll be warned not to attempt to enter the Bonbouche warehouse, or his own apartment.'

'Will he listen to warnings?' Malherbe asked. 'By all accounts he likes his own way.'

'Which is why, if it is Goldmead, you and Abbot will be at the helipad to meet him. If he doesn't listen to warnings, take him in charge.'

'Rolf Lenard has a mobile phone,' Malherbe said. 'He could contact Jason and fix another meeting place. We could lose him.'

'Lose him,' said Connor silkily, 'and you will be food for the crows. Go and tell Grogan to bring your car up behind the taxis. Tell him there's no need for secrecy, you'll be acting as an escort, not a tracker.'

Thorneycroft and Connor retreated to the back seat of the darkened police car further down the road. It was fifteen minutes before Rolf Lenard appeared, sitting in a wheelchair propelled by an orderly, with Abbot in attendance. Rolf looked neither to left nor right, but climbed into the leading taxi, spoke to the driver, and settled back in his corner. The taxi pulled away from the kerb, followed by the car carrying Abbot and Malherbe, and behind them at a discreet distance, Connor and Thorneycroft's car.

They travelled fast on the trunk roads south of the River. Every so often, Connor spoke to Hogarth. The answer was always the same: Jason was still in Birmingham. This seemed to relieve Connor.

He needs to be at the warehouse before Jason, Thorneycroft thought. Aloud he said, 'you could prevent their meeting, you know. You could take Rolf in for questioning.'

'I could, couldn't I?' Connor's voice was mocking. 'I could do things by the book, ease the pressures on them, give them time to cool off and agree on a story. I could throw away the one chance I have of getting the truth out of them because by tomorrow they'll be in control of their nerves, they'll be in control, ready to lie themselves to freedom.'

Thorneycroft nodded. Connor was taking a calculated risk, and it seemed that Hogarth was happy to let him do so.

Connor looked at him sideways. 'I could take Abbot with me,' he said. 'You could go with Malherbe to the helipad.'

Thorneycroft smiled. 'I think, in these circumstances I may be more useful to you than Abbot.' Connor said no more.

They crossed the River at last, skirted the City and reached the dockland area. They were circling the boundary of the Goldmead estate when Hogarth's call came through.

'Jason Lenard's airborne,' he said, 'bound for the Goldmead warehouse. He's in a dangerous mood. I've asked the local nick to be ready with back-up if you need it.' There followed names and contact numbers and a gruff 'watch yourselves'.

At the entrance gate the guard waved them through, and they drove to the Bonbouche site. Rolf Lenard's departing taxi passed them on the way, and Abbot and Malherbe were waiting by their car on the parking apron.

Thorneycroft scanned the surroundings. The arc lights of the warehouse were on, and security guards stood at various points. A lamp burned over the door of the administration block, and the whole of the top storey of the wing was brilliantly lit.

Abbot came to meet them as they stepped out of their car. 'Lenard never spoke one word to us,' he said. 'He paid off the cabby, went straight through that door, and up to Jason's apartment. The lights went on then. He must have a key.'

'He owns the place,' Connor said. 'Jason's on his way here. You and Malherbe get down to the helipad. Let me know as soon as he lands. And don't let him near this property.'

The reception desk in the foyer was unattended, but behind it an operator sat at a bank of video screens. He greeted Connor with relief.

'I don't know what's going on,' he said. 'Mr Lenard didn't give notice he was coming. He went up to Mr Jason's flat. He doesn't look good. I should keep an eye on him, but he's switched off the mechanism up there.' He pointed to a blank screen. 'Mr Jason fixed it so's he could switch it on or off. He likes his privacy, doesn't like being watched.'

Remembering the photographs on Jason's walls, Thorneycroft wasn't surprised.

'Do you have a key to the apartment?' Connor asked.

The operator looked nervous. 'Yes, but I can't lend it to anyone, not even the police.'

'You're right about Mr Lenard,' Connor said, 'he's ill, he shouldn't be alone. You can take us up and unlock the door. We'll do the rest.'

'I s'pose that'd be OK,' the man said. 'If he's ill.'

He rode up with them in the lift, unlocked the door of the apartment, and took his hurried leave.

There was no sound of movement within the flat. Connor pressed the doorbell. Silence. He rang again. A faint footstep sounded in the hall.

'Mr Lenard,' Connor said loudly, 'it's Chief Inspector Connor, and Dr Thorneycroft. May we come in please?'

No sound, no answer. Connor pressed the handle of the door and opened it smoothly.

Three paces from them Rolf Lenard stood. He still wore his heavy overcoat and muffler. His hands clasped an automatic pistol, pointed at Thorneycroft's chest. Thorneycroft raised his hands to shoulder level and the gun's muzzle shifted towards Connor.

'What do you want?' Rolf's voice was high and scratchy.

'To talk to you,' Connor answered.

'Talk? I'm in no state to talk. I've been ill. Poisoned.' Between puffy lids, Rolf's eyes glittered like coal. 'This is private property. Do you have a warrant to be on my property?'

'I don't need a warrant, Mr Lenard. I'm here in the course of my duty. And put the gun away. You don't need it. We're not armed. We just want to ask you a few questions.'

Rolf chewed his lip, then shrugged. 'All right. Come in.'

They followed him through the living-room to the bar area. Rolf sat on a sofa, the automatic resting on his thigh. Connor settled facing him, and Thorneycroft took the chair nearest to Rolf. The safety catch of the automatic was in the 'on' position but it might be necessary to prevent Rolf switching it to 'off'.

Rolf fixed Connor with a basilisk stare. 'Well, Inspector, why are you here? Do you know who tried to kill me, or are you still floundering in the bog of police ineptitude?'

Connor said evenly, 'the attack on you and Miss Plum is linked to the three former attacks, Mr Lenard. Over the past weeks we've sought to discover who had the means and opportunity to put poisonous material into a pack of mushrooms, a sherbet toy, and a carton of curry. A large number of people, including members of your family and staff, fit that profile.

'It is a fact that all the victims were poisoned by food bought at a Bonbouche sales point. That led us to believe that the poisoner's aim was to damage your company, that the attacks were the work of someone wanting revenge for some past grievance.'

Rolf waved an impatient hand. 'Yes, yes, that's ancient history. I've said from the start that this was the work of a serial criminal, a madman. The target was, and is, my company, the company I've established at the top of the trade, respected by all, enjoyed by people of taste and distinction. Leave off stating the obvious, Inspector, and explain why you and your sidekick are here.'

'I'm endeavouring to do so,' Connor answered. 'It seemed to us that Bonbouche was the poisoner's target, but we didn't know why. We could find no motive. But in the course of our enquiries we learned that there was dissension in your company, over the future of Bonbouche. The issue of whether or not to change, that was the root of the trouble. You were opposed to change. You told me so.'

'Certainly. I make no secret of my views. Why change something that is perfect, beautiful?'

'Your son doesn't see it that way. He wants to modernize things, doesn't he?'

Rolf's face darkened. 'Corrupt and destroy are better words for it. Jason and his cronies wish to set up a string of second-rate steak houses, diners where the hoi polloi buy frozen fish and week-old vegetables. They will organize parties where the wine comes out of cardboard boxes and strippers come out of plastic cakes. Such shoddy stuff is not for Bonbouche.'

'We have learned,' continued Connor, 'that on October 18th you were informed by Mr Eli Fishburn of New York that a plan was afoot to modernize the company, that at the forthcoming AGM of Bonbouche, the Berlin branch would submit a resolution to that end.

It would receive the support of many American members, and of a body of European delegates. It was rumoured that your son Jason would support the resolution. Is that true?'

'Yes it is.' Rolf pressed a hand to a tic in his cheek.

'What was your response to Mr Fishburn's message, sir?'

'I at once informed all levels of the company of the proposed resolution. I left it to the individual formations of the company to deal with it as required by the company rules ... by democratic discussion and action.'

'Did you discuss the matter with Mr Jason Lenard?'

Rolf leaned forward and struck his clenched fist on the arm of his chair. 'I did. I told him he must not support a move that would tear Bonbouche apart.'

'What was his response?'

The fist pounded more forcibly. 'He refused to accept my ruling. He said he would make up his own mind.'

'What was his decision?'

'He wanted to enrich himself and his lickspittle friends!' Rolf's voice rose to a shout. 'Jason has never had a proper feeling for Bonbouche. To him it is just a way to make money, with no thought whatever for an honoured tradition.'

'Did you quarrel, Mr Lenard?'

'We disagreed sharply. In the end, Jason said he would do what he could to abort the resolution, but I knew it was an empty promise. Worthless.' Rolf drew a long breath, and said more quietly. 'I don't see what Fishburn's interventions have to do with the crimes you are investigating, Inspector. Nor do I see why you are questioning me in this way.'

Connor paused. 'Then I will be more specific. I have said that the members of your close circle, including your family members, have the means and the opportunity to place poison in Bonbouche goods.'

Rolf straightened in his seat. 'So have hundreds of other people. I very much resent the suggestion that one of my family could be guilty of these dreadful crimes, and of poisoning me.'

'Mr Jason Lenard has mentioned a fact that Dr Thorneycroft and I have also become aware of. The first attack, that on Mr Robins, took place on November 17th. That on Ben Tifflin was on November

18th, and that on Mrs Murugan on November 30th. Since that date there have been no further attacks, until this last one on you and Miss Plum. No more countdown cards have been sent. Your son believes that the poison attacks stopped because the poisoner felt there was no more need for them. The resolution had been withdrawn, the factions had closed ranks, and the threat of change that you so strongly oppose no longer exists.'

'How can you say it no longer exists? A few hours ago an attempt was made to kill Miss Plum and me.'

Connor regarded Rolf steadily. 'We have spoken to Miss Plum,' he said. 'She has given us certain information. She says that on December 12th, while in the Coventry Hall woods to supervise the selection of a Christmas tree, she found a stretch of mushrooms. She took a sample of them, and locked it in her safe. She made a phone call to you and asked you to inform the police of her find. You replied that you would consult your wife and brother about what you should do. Did you consult them?'

'Miss Plum is obviously confused, after her recent ordeal. She made no such call to me.'

'The mushrooms she collected have been examined by experts, Mr Lenard. They belong to the species Gyromitra esculenta, a poisonous species that was responsible for the death of Mr Robins.'

Rolf shook his head violently. 'What's your point? Poisonous mushrooms grow all over England.'

'We have examined the place where the mushrooms grow. It's clear some were harvested several weeks ago. Any member of your family or household could have gained access to the woods, could have collected some of the mushrooms, could have placed them in a Bonbouche pack, in a Bonbouche store.'

'This is all rubbish, rubbish. You should be trying to discover who poisoned me, instead of insulting me with these idiotic suggestions. I was poisoned by wine, not mushrooms, wine supplied by my son Jason, he sent it, he signed the bottles with stupid messages for my mother. It was Jason's wine that was meant to kill me and Hester. Jason wants me dead. Surely you have enough intelligence to grasp that simple fact.'

'Mr Lenard, the supervisor of your wine store at this warehouse confirms that your son did order the wines for your mother, and that he did sign the bottles. The supervisor selected sealed and corked bottles and handed them to your son, who signed them on the spot and handed them back. They were despatched at once to Mrs Eva Lenard, and have been locked in her cellar for the past three months.'

Rolf made a contemptuous sound. 'Jason visits my mother frequently. He could have substituted another bottle, suitably signed, at any time.'

'Did you invite your son to meet you here tonight, Mr Lenard? Did you intend to threaten him with his own gun? It must be his. You had no access to firearms at the hospital.'

'It's his, yes, he keeps it in his bedside cupboard. I armed myself for my protection. He's tried to kill me once, he'll try again.'

Connor ignored the statement. His eyes glinted, a cat watching a mousehole. 'You place a regular order for wine with the Goldmead store,' he said. 'In September last your order included a dozen bottles of Shiraz, did it not?'

'Very probably.'

'Vintage Shiraz, from Australia?'

'Yes, what of it?'

'That same month, Jason sent his two bottles of Australian Shiraz to your mother. He signed the bottles. On Saturday 15th, the night of her birthday party, those two bottles were to be served at dinner. A bottle of Shiraz was partly consumed by you and Miss Plum. That wine contained a dangerous amount of Quintol.

'A second bottle of Shiraz was taken by your wife to the staff dining-room, and consumed there. No-one suffered any ill effects from that bottle, and forensic testing of the dregs found it free of any poison.'

Connor paused, and in the momentary silence Thorneycroft heard the distant drone of an approaching aircraft. Rolf appeared not to notice it, his gaze riveted on Connor.

'We examined the corks,' Connor said. 'The cork taken by my team from the sideboard in the Coventry Hall dining-room bore strong traces of Quintol. The cork from the servants' hall was free of such traces. What is more, the two corks thought to have come from the bottles sent by Jason, and believed to be of the same origin and age, in fact differ markedly.

'The cork alleged to be from the poisoned bottle was a genuine cork, the bark of a tree, and a year old at least. The cork from the servants' room was synthetic, of a type commonly used when bulk wine is bottled in a warehouse. The conclusion must be that the two corks came from different job lots; one vintage wine, the other young wine.'

Rolf shrugged. 'Obviously the steward at the warehouse selected the bottles from different lots.'

'The differences caused us to search the Coventry Hall premises very thoroughly,' Connor said. 'In the shrubbery under the dining-room window a third cork was found, a synthetic one that matched the cork from the staff dining-room. It has been tested by our forensic experts. It is stained by wine but bears no trace of Quintol. Your fingerprints are on it.'

As Rolf started to speak, Connor held up his hand. 'I must warn you that your mother has stated that before you brought the bottle of Shiraz to the table, you walked to the window of the dining-room and called to the gardeners to come into the house, as a storm was brewing. Did you drop a cork into the shrubbery below the window, Mr Lenard?'

'No I did not! If you and your flatfoots had made a proper search of the shrubbery, you would very likely have found a dozen or more corks. We have parties at the house, I dare say corks are thrown from the window. I may have been guilty of the offence myself, on occasion.'

'We did make a thorough search. The shrubbery was remarkably clean. Your gardener Thomas Jenkins told us that on your instructions it was cleaned on the afternoon of your mother's party, and the rubbish burned on bonfires in the park. We found only the one cork.'

Rolf shifted restlessly in his seat. 'I fail to see where this is leading.'

Connor regarded him coldly. 'This afternoon,' he said, 'I visited your home in Ennisdale Square with Dr Thorneycroft, and in his presence questioned your wife and Mr Terence Arnold. They made statements concerning your actions on the evening of December 13th.'

'What statements? What did they say?'

'Mrs Lenard stated that on that evening, she and Mr Arnold visited the wine cellar of your home. They were in the recess at the end of the room, as Mrs Lenard wished to collect two bottles of vodka for the living-room bar. They heard footsteps on the cellar stairs, and saw you come down them, cross to the wine racks, and take out a bottle of Shiraz.

'Mrs Lenard was about to make her presence known, when you did something she considered strange. You went to the sink, opened the bottle, and poured the contents down the drain, saving just enough to fill a shallow dish. You dropped a number of tablets into the dish, and stirred the contents with a dipstick. You laid the cork in the dish. You disposed of the seal and the empty bottle in the trash can, washed the dipstick and laid it in its place, and left the cellar carrying the dish containing the cork.

'The bottle of wine you selected that evening was a mature Shiraz, and its cork came from a cork tree, not from a factory belt. This afternoon your wife gave me a bottle of the same wine. Its cork matches the one found on the sideboard in the dining-room of Coventry Hall after the party on December 15th.

'Your wife assures me that the corkscrew you use in your cellar is identical to the one used at Coventry Hall on the night of the party.

'So, sir, we have in all four corks. One without Quintol traces from the champagne bottle. One without Quintol from the staff dining-room. One without Quintol but bearing your fingerprints from the shrubbery. And one from the sideboard in the dining-room, stained by Shiraz and Quintol, and bearing your fingerprints.'

Before Connor could continue, Rolf heaved himself to his feet. The automatic slid from his knee to the ground but he made no attempt to recover it. He took a step towards Connor, swaying, and Thorneycroft put out a hand to steady him. Rolf struck the hand aside.

'Lies,' he screamed, 'this is a pack of lies! My wife is a bitch on heat. She and her lout of a chauffeur have concocted this rigmarole. No doubt they plan to blackmail me, but they won't succeed. I'll expose them, do you hear? I'll show them up for what they are, pigs in their wallow.'

Thorneycroft saw in Rolf's stiffening body and strident voice the onset of paranoid rage. He stepped between Rolf and Connor and said quietly, 'don't try to talk, Mr Lenard. You're ill. You'll be given a chance to respond to your wife's statement. Your rights will be respected.'

Rolf turned his head slowly. His eyes seemed to focus not on Thorneycroft but on some point far beyond him.

'What do you know of my rights?' he said. 'It is my right to protect what I love. I have fought to save Bonbouche from the hyenas who try to feed on its flesh. I have done nothing I regret.'

Connor was on his feet. 'Jock Robins died.'

Rolf scowled like a cross child. 'He was already sick. I didn't mean him to die. That was an accident.' He shook his head, smiling. 'I meant Hester to die. Hester's a traitor. She's fed off me all these years, and now she's ready to sell me out to Yankee riffraff. She's Jason's toady.' He collapsed suddenly, falling back on to the sofa, wrapping his arms about his chest. 'Hester should be dead, and Jason should be blamed for it. Traitors, both of them. All my work destroyed. Come to nothing. Nothing left but dust.'

Connor was speaking, reciting warning words, the right to silence and legal advice, but Rolf wasn't listening. His head dropped sideways and he crooned to himself making unintelligible sounds. Riding down in the lift between Connor and Thorneycroft he sagged with eyes closed, body limp and heavy as a dead man's.

Outside, on the parking apron, Jason Lenard stood between Abbot and Malherbe. He took a step forward, then halted. Under the amber lights his face glistened with tears. Thorneycroft halted, forcing Connor to follow suit.

'I want to speak to him,' Thorneycroft said. He met Connor's flat gaze. 'I'm a doctor, not a policeman.'

'Right.' Connor crooked a finger and Abbot came to take Thorneycroft's place at Rolf's left side. Thorneycroft walked across to Jason.

'Don't try to talk to your father,' he said. 'Right now, it would do more harm than good.'

Jason rubbed a palm across his face. 'I told him time and again he could trust me,' he said. 'When Fishburn's message came, I told him I'd stop the resolution, and I did, but he still treated me like an enemy.'

'He's mentally ill,' Thorneycroft said.

'I know. He's always been determined to do things his way, but I never thought he'd do ... these things. I just didn't believe it.' His gaze roved to scan the vast complex of buildings, the warehouses and administration blocks, the visible signs of immense wealth and power.

'What will happen now?' he said.

'He'll be taken in for further questioning, but I think he'll be put into hospital under guard. If he's charged, he'll be sent for psychiatric assessment. He's probably unfit to plead.'

'I spoke to Silas,' Jason said. 'He's appointing lawyers. I must go to my grandmother. Be with her. And I must phone to tell Fenella. Can I leave?'

'Certainly you can.' Thorneycroft remembered the police guard at Coventry Hall. 'Malherbe and I will see you safe home.'

The three cars left within minutes, two of them heading for Richmond, the third bound for Concorde Street.

There followed the weary process of building a case against Rolf Lenard.

A team of some of the best legal brains in Britain worked to prove that the attacks on Jock Robins, Ben Tifflin and Mrs Murugan could have been committed by a large number of people, and that the evidence relating to the poisoning of Hester Plum was either false, or so ephemeral as to be inadmissible in a court of law.

Connor had no doubt that Rolf Lenard was guilty of all the attacks, but he conceded that only the one on Hester Plum was likely to be proven.

'Rolf had to plant the Quintol in a bottle signed by Jason,' he said. 'He opened the first bottle of Shiraz as soon as they entered the dining-room, dropped in the Quintol, pitched the clean cork into the shrubbery, and left the cork he'd doctored on the dining-room side-board. He tried to avert suspicion by drinking a little of the poisoned wine. A bad mistake. It seems to have tipped him over the edge.

'Amateur stuff, all that. The fancy perps always make mistakes. Chucking the cork out of the window was a mistake, because on his orders the shrubbery had been swept clean that very afternoon. He should have remembered that. There was only one cork to find, and it had his sticky prints on it.

'Using mushrooms from Coventry Hall was another mistake. He forgot that Hester Plum keeps an eagle eye on everything that goes on there. She found the mushrooms and phoned Rolf. If he'd had any sense he'd have come straight to us. We couldn't have proved that he'd used the mushrooms in his Bonbouche package. Instead he decided to get rid of Hester and put the blame on Jason.'

'Yes,' Thorneycroft said, 'Jason was always his ultimate target. The lift-off victim.'

Rolf himself made no attempt to refute the accusations made against him by Minette Lenard, Terence Arnold and Hester Plum. Sometimes he responded by describing his actions as righteous efforts to preserve the sanctity of Bonbouche et Cie. At other times he seemed not to hear what was said to him.

Rolf Lenard was a small boat drifting on a vast sea of unreason, and no tide would ever bring him back to shore.

Connor and his team had perforce to continue work on the case, badgered by the media and harangued by authorities to provide instant answers to all questions. Thorneycroft's task was more easily completed, and on December 20th he drove across England to Appledore.

For the first part of the journey he thought about the case. He brooded over the fact that Eva Lenard's borderline personality disorder, her refusal to accept treatment, and her family's failure to insist on her having treatment, had led inexorably to alienation, estrangement, and a family in nothing but name. And that the final outcome had been madness, murder, and public panic.

He thought about Jock and Helen Robins, the Tifflins and the Murugan family, the Lenards laden with their share of guilt, and Hester Plum, struggling to regain health and belief in human goodness. He thought about Eva Lenard, old, ill, and mourning her lost son.

But by the time he reached Dorset, he was shaking off the effects of working in that miasma of hate and fear, and thanking God for the blessing of a happy upbringing and a family of his own.

He thought about Claudia and Luke and the grandparents. He made plans for them, and at last, near evening, he saw Appledore in the valley, the smoke rising from its chimneys, the last tractor chugging into its barn, and Claudia and Luke hanging over the gate, waiting for him.